MW00614054

Printed in the United States of America
Second Chapter Publishing
First Printing, 2017

ISBN : 978-0-9976677-2-1

This is a work of fiction. All incidents and dialogue, and all
characters with the exception of some well-known historical and
public figures, are products of the author's imagination and are not
to be construed as real. Where real-life historical or public figures
appear, the situations, incidents, and dialogues concerning those
persons are entirely fictional and are not intended to depict actual
events or to change the entirely fictional nature of the work. In all
other respects, any resemblance to persons living or dead is entirely
coincidental.

For those whom I have loved.
Never forget…

Angelique's Peace

Table Of Contents

Chapter One

Summer, 1862

Angelique stifled a yawn. She was weary, a delayed reaction, no doubt, to the dramatic events of the day. Looking over at her twin girls, she tried to find the proper word to describe her joy at seeing them reunited, marveling at the fact that the English language provided none that was sufficient. Retrouvaille. Yes, the beautiful French word that describes the delight in rediscovering a loved one was indeed perfect. And certainly, she looked forward to getting to know Aimee again after their separation, to learn how she had grown, changed, and to help heal the emotional wounds from her kidnapping. Most of all, she wanted just to hold her precious daughter, to reassure her that she would be protected from this day forward. Angelique tried not to think about the months that had been stolen from them or the deceitful villain who had taken her beloved child. But it was difficult not to plot her revenge, to think of diabolical ways to find the evil one and make him suffer as she had. She whispered a prayer and took a long deep breath, exhaling slowly. Only God could remove the bitterness from her heart.

It had been a long day, but such a happy one. She was grateful and that was more important than anything else she might feel. The children were excited, their incessant chatter and spontaneous giggles drowning out the noise of the city. And while she was amused by their unbridled enthusiasm, she could only hope that once their tummies were full, they would settle down and rest. When they arrived at the hotel, Angelique was relieved. She gathered her energetic brood and bid her driver and friend Robert goodbye. The doorman had disappeared days earlier, a result of the war, with its inevitable reductions, but Angelique thought it strange, inexcusably discourteous, that with so many Yankee soldiers milling about, it hadn't occurred to any of them to open the door for a lady and her little family. Conflict, it seemed, brought out the worst in people. But as her mother had always been quick to point out, there was no excuse for poor manners, regardless of the circumstances, and she tilted her chin in defiance as she passed the men lined up on the sidewalk.

She entered the lobby, still in a huff and then came to an abrupt halt, unable to move, fearful that her eyes had deceived her. Her mind raced as her heart beat wildly in her chest. He moved to her.

"Andrew. I knew you'd come back to me," she whispered, unable to say anything more as she fell into his waiting arms.

"My darling wife," he said, kissing her forehead, her cheek, her neck.

Angelique cried, the tears of pure happiness and complete relief flowing freely. Aimee and Aida threw their tiny arms around their parents, jumping up and down as squeals of delight filled the air.

And all who witnessed their happy reunion were moved. The end of missing someone is a beautiful moment. Indeed, it is.

"Poppa," the twins shouted as they lifted their arms in the air. And in one graceful move, Andrew scooped them up, bearing one on each side as they hugged him tightly.

"We missed you, Poppa," Aida said.

"Oh, how I missed you girls."

"You have been away for so long. And sissy, too, since she has been gone just like you were." Aimee simply nodded, a somber look on her face.

"Did you know that we just found her today? Mister Robert has magical horses, and he took us from one place to another until we got to the right one so that we could rescue her."

Andrew gently placed the girls on the lobby sofa, its crimson velvet worn in spots. "Then I am indebted to Robert for assisting you all. And I look forward to hearing all about everything that happened in my absence."

"And Franklin helped. We would have never known where to look without him, of course," Aida said, hands on hips.

"Franklin?"

Aida pointed to the young boy who still stood near the door. Clutching his hat with both hands, he fidgeted as his eyes darted from place to place. "Him. You will meet him soon. He is Aimee's friend."

Aimee nodded, her mouth forming a sad smile.

Angelique moved forward and took Andrew's hand. "We have so much to discuss. Perhaps we should move to a quieter place? I think we are arousing the curiosity of the entire population of this hotel."

"Let them gawk. I am more than willing to shout my happiness to the rooftops."

"As long as we don't get evicted."

He winked. "And we should talk to Mr. Wilson about accommodations for the family."

Angelique tried not to blush. She had readily shared a room with Aida and Franklin, thankful that they had been given a place to stay. But obviously that wouldn't work, especially for a couple separated for more than a year, and the logistics would be tricky. "I hate to ask him for anything more. He has been so very kind, accommodating us under difficult circumstances."

"And he is well aware of our situation. I doubt that he will refuse to help us if he can. I will see what the possibilities are."

"There are five of us now. Jubilee has not been allowed to stay in the hotel proper. Unfortunately."

"So the boy is to be included, I assume? I guess we do have plenty to talk over in the days ahead."

Angelique nodded and Andrew began to make his way to the reception desk, but after a few steps, he returned. There was an urgency on his face, a clear need to be understood. He looked deep in to his wife's steel blue eyes. "I am so grateful to be home."

"This isn't exactly our home," she said, pointing to the lobby filled with Yankee soldiers.

"You are wrong. Home is where you are, where Aimee and Aida are. My family is my home. To miss someone is painful, but it is also a reminder of the love. And I do so love you." It was the greatest truth he could utter, the only fact in his life he knew with certainty.

She smiled. "And I love you as well. The days of our separation seemed endless, but I held steadfast to my faith that this moment would come. I do believe that I can begin to breathe again, to live again, to hope again. Whatever the future holds with this dreadful war and all that it implies, we will face it together with a firm resolve and an unbroken spirit. Welcome home, Andrew."

"That's the woman I married," he said, kissing her on the cheek. "Now, let me see what Mr. Wilson has to say about our sleeping arrangements for the night."

Chapter Two

Mr. Wilson was accustomed to the buzz, the tempo of the lobby at the St. Charles Hotel. He had, after all, spent the past ten years serving as its general manager. It was, at times, a formidable task, given the sheer number of guests who stayed there on any given night. And upholding the standard for stellar service, while overseeing a sizeable staff, required the utmost in diplomacy and skill. But the hotel was more than a building. No, it was a jewel in the crown that Lady New Orleans wore, the hub for activity and a place where business and political deals were arranged in hushed whispers over glasses of cognac and fat cigars. Now, it was far more common to see Yankee soldiers than ladies in fancy ball gowns. And although beyond his control, it gave him pause to think that war strategy was being discussed there instead of more pleasant negotiations.

He heard the muffled noise of high-pitched squeals and spontaneous laughter as he sat in his office preparing the monthly report. It was an unusual sound, given the current climate, but an agreeable one, and he closed his eyes for a moment just to listen before walking out into the lobby to investigate. He had reached the massive walnut reception desk just about the same time as Andrew Slater, who was smiling broadly.

"Mr. Wilson!" he said, extending his hand.

"I take it by your expression that you have been reunited with your family."

"Indeed, I have. What a glorious day this has been for us."

Mr. Wilson smiled as he looked over to see Angelique engaged with the children. She waved her arms as she spoke to them and they clapped in response. She stopped periodically to hug one of the twin girls, holding her close to her heart. "And they all certainly look happy."

"We have had a challenging year, sir. It has been difficult for all of us, but especially Angelique and my dear daughter, Aimee."

"And her return is an answer to prayer, most certainly."

"It is. I expect that there will be an adjustment period. She has been through so much for one so young."

"Fortunately, she has a remarkable mother to help her."

"Very true. Very true."

"May I be of service to you?"

"Ah, yes. I know that much of the hotel is occupied, but I was hoping that perhaps you had a larger room, one that would accommodate all five of us. I understand that there will be an additional cost involved, but I am prepared to cover that."

Mr. Wilson smiled as he opened the guestbook. "Let me see what is available."

Andrew gripped the cold marble counter as he waited.

"Ah yes, this will work out nicely." He turned to remove two brass keys from the wall. "406 and 408. I keep them for families such as yours. They are two separate rooms, but joined together by an internal door, so the children can have their own space while you and Angelique have yours. It is private, but affords you the chance to keep an eye on them as well."

"That's perfect, sir. I couldn't ask for anything better. Would you like payment in advance? I am not sure how long we will be here, of course."

"Angelique is on what I like to call 'the family plan,' and that comes with a significant discount," he said with a wink.

"I am ever so grateful to you, Mr. Wilson, a sentiment I know that I share with my wife. You have been incredibly kind. And it is my hope that the blessings you give to others will be returned to you one hundredfold."

"I am your humble servant," he said, bowing in his familiar way. He raised his hand. "John will show you to your new rooms and help with the moving from the previous one."

Andrew retrieved his satchel, which he handed to the bellman before making his way to his waiting family.

"We are all set," he said to Angelique. "But we need to quickly pack so that we can move your belongings to another room."

"That's good news. But first, let me alert Jubilee of our plans." Angelique moved to the door where Jubilee had stood, patiently waiting as she observed all that had transpired. "We are moving into a larger place, two rooms, I think. This day has been overwhelming, but so very happy."

"I am so pleased for you to all be together again, Miss Angelique, but especially to have Aimee home. I look forward to caring for my girls again and Franklin, of course, although I am sure he will insist that he is too old for a nanny."

"Staying at the hotel is less than ideal. Decisions will have to be made. Just not today."

Jubilee smiled. "I know. One step at a time. Now, you go on. And don't worry about me. I will be just fine."

Angelique nodded. "Stay safe," she whispered.

Within the hour, they had settled in, and as Angelique unpacked the bags, the children ran from one room to the other, amazed by what they called the secret door which connected the two spaces.

"You would think that they would be worn-out," Andrew said.

"I certainly am," Angelique said, sinking into the velvet chair near the window.

"My poor wife. You have had to be so strong for so long, bearing the weight of an extraordinary responsibility. I don't know many women who would have done as well, who would have bravely fought as you have."

"Well then, I am not surprised that I am tired."

Andrew laughed. "But you are no longer alone. I am here, and we will face whatever we must together."

"Well, the first thing we must face together is feeding these children some supper."

And as though she had somehow uttered the magic word, all three of them appeared, smiling.

"Aimee wants chicken," Aida said.

"Is that right?" Angelique asked, moving Aimee close. She placed her arms around the child, hugging her and kissing the top of her head. "Then, we shall have chicken." She examined her daughter's tiny hands. "But perhaps we should wash these first." Turning to Aida and Franklin, she added, "you two as well."

She rose to remove the pitcher from the washstand as she carefully poured the contents into the bowl. Handing the bar of soap first to Aimee, she gently guided her. And by the time Franklin was finished, the water was the color of a mud puddle after a rainy day.

Moments later, Angelique and Andrew proudly entered the restaurant, each holding the hand of one of the twins, while Franklin followed behind.

The menu was handwritten on a large chalk board tacked to the side wall. There were four items, carefully scribed with a flair, which only emphasized the meagerness of the offerings.

"War on," Angelique whispered.

Andrew nodded. He turned to the children. "I'm going to read what that big board says and you get to choose what you would like to have. Red or white beans, green gumbo, fried fish, or noodles."

"I want chicken and so does Aimee," Aida said, folding her arms.

"I'm afraid that they don't have that," Angelique said, "so you must choose something else."

Aida furrowed her brow, while Aimee remained silent. The waiter was approaching, and Angelique feared a public tantrum, born of fatigue more than anything else.

Franklin cleared his throat. "Aida, did you know that eating fish makes you a good swimmer? Plus, it makes you smart! My grandpa said so. When I was little, we used to catch them in the creek. We'd bring 'em home and grandma would fry 'em up. So good. Reminds me of some happy times. I sure do have a hankering for some fish, Mr. Slater."

Aida's eyes grew wide. "Really, Franklin? Eating it can make you smart?"

"Sure can."

Aida turned to Andrew. "I will have fish, Poppa. Even though I am already smart."

"Me, too," Aimee said.

Angelique breathed a sigh of relief.

When the waiter had taken their order and the girls sat back in their chairs, happily swinging their legs, Andrew leaned over to Franklin. "I can see that you are a very resourceful young man. I look forward to getting to know you better."

Franklin grinned.

"And thanks for the help." Andrew added. "It will be nice to have another man around to assist me with these women."

"I'll do what I can," he said.

An hour later, with the children properly fed, the weary parents breathed a sigh of relief as they tucked them into bed and tiptoed into their own room, quietly closing the secret door.

"Alone at last," Andrew whispered as he moved to kiss Angelique, his lips touching hers gently, yet with an urgency, as though she carried the key to unlock the pain he had carried in his heart for so long.

"Indeed," she said. "I have missed you so. But when the love is true it grows, in spite of the distance, the pain of separation."

"When I look into your eyes, I see the reflection of my own soul. Only you, Angelique. You are my once-in-a-lifetime miracle."

And as the lights of the city cast shadows on the walls, the pair whispered accounts of what each had missed during their separation as they clung tightly to each other. The world disappeared, and time stood still. Angelique and Andrew felt invincible, swept away by the magic of their pure, unbridled love.

Chapter Three

The children were up at sunrise, and soon discovered that the secret door opened easily, allowing them into their parent's room. Aida and Aimee stood by the canopied bed staring as Angelique and Andrew slept. Franklin hesitated, remaining in the doorway.

"Do you think that they are going to wake up soon?" Aida whispered, a little louder than necessary.

Aimee shrugged.

"Don't they know that it is daytime?" Aida asked.

Angelique stirred. "A few more minutes, girls," she mumbled. "Please?"

But Aimee and Aida stood riveted to the spot, watching and waiting. Although weary, her body begging for another hour or two of rest, Angelique sat upright, gathering the covers around her. She smiled. "Good morning, my precious girls."

"Good morning, Mommy," Aida said.

Angelique reached for her dressing gown and slipped out of bed. "Shhhhh…. Let's give Poppa a little more sleep."

The trio tiptoed into the adjoining room as Franklin stood wordlessly nearby. The girls sat on their bed, the covers rumpled and askew from the previous night. Angelique joined them, hugging Aimee first and then, Aida. "My goodness, this is our first morning together

13

as a family in a very long time. I have missed such moments."

"Me, too," Aida said.

Aimee nodded.

"What shall we do today?" Angelique asked.

"We should buy some cookies and then, we could go to the park and eat them," Aida announced.

Angelique chuckled. Her daughter did have an insatiable sweet tooth, which only seemed to grow stronger. The war, of course, had limited availability of such luxuries, but perhaps, she thought, they might find some sort of treat for the children to enjoy. It was, after all, a special occasion, the first day of their new life as a reunited family.

"What do you think of that idea, Frankliin?" Angelique asked, hoping that he would feel more included.

"Sounds fine to me, ma'am. I'm just happy to be here."

Angelique's heart softened. Aimee's kidnapping had been terrible, unimaginably painful, but it had brought Franklin into their lives, a boy to whom she would be forever grateful. And it had become obvious that he was meant to be a part of their family, the son they had always wanted. Chosen. She marveled at the wonder of it, the sheer miracle of falling in love with a child you don't really know. For indeed, she had. And she was certain that Andrew would, too.

"Poppa!" the girls said, slipping from the bed to greet Andrew, who had appeared, in the doorway.

"Good morning, girls."

Angelique smiled. "Good morning, my darling."

He moved to her, kissing the top of her head. "I trust that you slept well."

"I did indeed."

Andrew surveyed the room as though trying to capture the moment so that he could retrieve the memory at will. He closed his eyes and swallowed hard. "Together again...an answer to prayer, certainly."

Angelique nodded. "A new beginning."

The sun had moved higher in the sky, bathing the room with light. Andrew had had the good sense to dress, which made Angelique suddenly aware that she was still in her nightgown. "And the sooner we all get ready, the sooner we can start."

The girls jumped up and down as Angelique chose their outfits for the day. She was glad that she had optimistically packed clothes for Aimee. As she helped them dress, she instructed Franklin to change in the bathroom at the end of the hall.

By the time the family had left the hotel and walked out onto busy St. Charles Street, Angelique was exhausted. She was relieved when Jubilee joined them. "They are yours now," she said with a wink. And the family of six made its way to the market in search of breakfast cookies and a place to discuss their plans for the future.

Chapter Four

"We cannot stay here forever," Angelique said as they made their way through the crowded lobby. Yankee soldiers, sat in groups, some, studying maps, others, polishing pistols. One General sat with his feet propped up on a particularly beautiful carved tea table. It struck Angelique as rather unseemly for such a refined place as the opulent lobby of the St. Charles to be taken over by uncouth men with no respect for their surroundings.

Andrew adjusted the collar of his waist coat. He wondered about his status with this same army. Had he been reported as a prisoner-of-war after the surrender of The Congress, the ironclad to which he had been assigned. He doubted that the rebels had even bothered to make a record of whom they had captured, and so his perceived death on the march to the internment camp would go unreported as well. He was pretty certain that for all practical purposes, he no longer existed to the United States Navy, who would have bigger tasks than to search for their meteorologist, a man who had retained his civilian status anyway. He was glad that he wouldn't have to worry about being part of a manhunt. The war would present enough complications.

Jubilee had taken the children out into the hotel courtyard so that they could see the fountain. Aimee hoped to spy a blue butterfly, while Aida spoke softly to Sarah. Of course, the fact that the doll never answered wasn't a deterrent. Franklin wanted to feed the birds the small scrap of bread he had managed to find on the sidewalk. Andrew and Angelique followed, sitting on a small bench nearby.

"We have some decisions to make," Angelique said.

"I agree."

"The sooner, the better."

"Again, I agree. But we must also be cautious. I needn't remind you that there is a war on."

"That is only an obstacle. And I do believe that history has shown us that we are unafraid of obstacles."

He reached for her hand, lightly kissing her palm.

"And yes, I am reminded of the miserable war every time I enter the hotel, Andrew. But I needn't cite the reasons why we cannot stay."

"No, of course not. And it is unfair to continue to take advantage of Mr. Wilson's kindness. Besides, as we learned last night, feeding this brood is going to be a challenge. We are not going to be able to afford to dine in restaurants every day."

"I have a little of the money left I brought with me from Charleston. I have tried to be as frugal as possible. But as you have probably realized, my yearly stipend from the Countess has been suspended, held up by Mr. Davidson, her lawyer, until he can ascertain when I can safely receive it."

"He is a smart man, Angelique, and when the war ends, you will have a sizeable windfall to look forward to."

"Not if we all starve in the meantime."

"I don't think things will get that bad. But if it makes you rest easier, I also have some money."

"Really? And how did that happen. You didn't rob anybody on your way home, did you?" She laughed at the absurdity of her own joke.

"No, nothing quite so dramatic. It was a gift to us from your cousin Lilly."

"Lilly? I thought that she had lost everything in the fire except for that silly box of silver spoons that belonged to her grandmother. She almost died trying to save them."

"Well, it appears that your cousin was more clever than you might have imagined. That box also contained gold coins."

"And she never told me? All the time that she lived with me?"

"I think she saw it as a nest egg, something to save for a rainy day."

"Trust me, Andrew, it rained on plenty of the days that we shared."

"Well, I think it was kind and generous of her to make sure I had the funds to get here and take care of you all once I did."

"No, of course, I agree. My cousin became a very different woman than the one we met when we first arrived in Charleston."

"Tragedy does that to you."

"Indeed it does."

"But once that money is gone, we have no source of income, so we need a strategy for the course of our future. Do you wish to stay in New Orleans? I could get a job here. Would you prefer to return to Charleston?"

Angelique swallowed hard. "Charleston holds such painful memories for me. It is there that I lost you and Aimee on that horrible day when Ft. Sumter fell. Besides, it was never my home. Louisiana is where my heart is, and where I would like to remain if you are willing. But I don't believe that New Orleans is the place for us either. It is an occupied city with the potential to erupt into violence at any moment. Somehow, it doesn't feel safe here. And we have more than ourselves to consider."

"I don't disagree. I am more than willing to live wherever pleases you."

"Then, I hope you won't think I have gone mad, but I have an idea, one I began to think about when I found Aimee."

"I'm listening."

"My father always used to say that when you are in doubt about what to do, you should return to what you know, that which is comforting and familiar." She took a deep breath. "I would like to contact Monsieur Alphonse. He was my father's best friend from the time they were young boys. He is the kindest of gentlemen, and in fact, arranged my introduction to Mr. Wilson so many years ago, when I was alone and desperate."

"Really. And how did that come about? I don't believe you ever shared all of the details of how you two met."

"Mr. Wilson is a distant cousin of Monsieur Bourgeois' wife."

"Bourgeois? I thought you called him Alphonse."

"Indeed. I guess as a child, I always used his first name rather than his last. It is another one of those

Southern things that you Yankee boys couldn't possibly understand."

Andrew laughed. "So exactly how do you think Mr. Alphonse Bourgeois is going to fit into our future?"

"He lives on a huge plantation called Maison Blanche. Yes, I know you don't speak French. It means 'white house.' Would you like to guess the color of his home?"

Andrew shook his head. He had forgotten how charming his wife was. "Not pink, for sure."

"No, not pink. Anyway, my thought was to ask him to see if there are any smaller homes in the area that we could rent with the possibility of buying after the war when my funds are released. We could work the land, so we'd have food. I am sure that he would give us a chicken or two. Eventually, we could have a real farm."

Andrew turned to look Angelique squarely in the eye. "You are serious about this, aren't you?"

"I am."

"You do realize that I know nothing about crops or animals? He held up his thumb. I am reasonably sure that it is brown, not green. And I am not certain that I want to learn these things."

"Didn't you just say that you would live anywhere that pleases me?" And then, for effect, she lowered her eyes on him. "This does."

She had won handily. He shook his head, bewildered by how clever his wife was. "Are you sure? It will be a great deal of work."

"But it will make us self-sufficient, not obligated to anybody. Imagine how freeing that would be."

"That's true."

"And think about how wonderful it will be for the children, especially Franklin."

"Whom I gather is about to become our son."

"He already is, Andrew."

"Then, let's see if Mr. Wilson will loan us some ink and paper. We will pen our letter to Mr. Bourgeois and see what happens. If it is meant to be, then, it will all work out."

"Oh, it is meant to be. I feel it."

"And as I learned long ago, I do not question your special feelings."

Chapter Five

A cool breeze stirred the sheer white curtains, and Angelique opened her sleepy eyes as she watched what appeared to be ghostly forms dance at the windows. Reaching over to touch Andrew, she marveled at the miracle that his return represented. As she drifted off once more, a sound startled her. She paused to listen, curious, when she heard it again. There were shouts and whistles and laughter. Rising slowly, she walked to window and looked into the street below. Several drunken Yankee soldiers stumbled onto the sidewalk. One held onto the post of the gas lamp for support as he yelled obscenities to his comrades. Angelique sighed before returning to bed. She wondered what time it was. More importantly, she wondered when she would hear from her father's friend. It had been ten days since she had written her plea for his help, and she hoped it would be soon. Nights like these only served to remind her of the desperation of their plight.

The next morning, Angelique approached the front desk to inquire about any mail deliveries that might have come addressed her. Mr. Wilson happened to be behind the counter and she was about to approach him with her complaint about the soldiers, when she saw the somber expression on his face. Something far more serious than a few rowdy men was troubling him.

"Mr. Wilson? Are you alright?"

He nodded and swallowed hard.

"Are you certain? May I help?"

He cleared his throat. "There is nothing you can do, Angelique, but I do appreciate your concern for me."

"Well, the Bible says a burden shared is a burden halved."

He turned to her and smiled. "Come into my office."

Angelique thought it odd that as much time as she had spent at the St. Charles, she had never been in Mr. Wilson's office. His desk was mahogany, large, but simple by design. It was made for serious work rather than show, and there were papers strewn about over most of its surface. He pointed to the green slipper chair, its arms worn so much that the muslin under the velvet was showing through. She wondered if it had been repurposed from the lobby or if he had failed to notice its dire need of recovering.

"Can I get you something? Tea perhaps?" he offered.

"No, thank you."

"I got some rather unsettling news today, Angelique."

"Yes?"

"The St. Charles is about to undergo a change in primary ownership, and it is their desire to bring a new manager on board."

Angelique sat quietly. This was devastating news for the kind Mr. Wilson, but there would be implications for her family as well. "Why? Don't they understand that you are the heart of this hotel?"

"I doubt that even crossed their minds. The old must give way to the new, Angelique. It is how it has always been."

"But what will you do?"

"Whatever I want, assuming this war doesn't impede my ability to travel and my funds hold out."

"Will you find another hotel to manage? Stay in New Orleans?"

"The answer is no to both of your questions. I am far too old to begin again professionally, yet not quite ready to sit on a rocking chair and wait for death. I have a sister who lives on a ranch in Texas. Maybe after so many years in the city, the clean country air will do me some good. I never did learn to ride a horse very well."

Angelique detected a note of sadness in his voice, along with the attempt at humor, and she understood that feeling, a longing for what was a part of your life for so very long. "I'm sure that your sister will be happy to have your company. And when does this change take place?"

"Two weeks. The new staff will be arriving in the new few days. Many here will keep their jobs, of course, but there will be training to do during the transition. Ironically, I am expected to oversee things. It is my final duty."

"And I am happy that we have had this moment to share. My dear Mr. Wilson, you have no idea how grateful I am to you for all that you have done for me and my family. I hope you know how you have changed the course of my life with your kindness. Because of you, I have all that I do. And for the remainder of my days, I will pray for your health and happiness."

He rose and offering his arm, walked her to the door. "Mrs. Slater, the pleasure was all mine. And I wish for you and your family to find joy as well. You have all had more than your share of turmoil."

"Then we are both due our blessings." Angelique said, pausing to kiss him lightly on the cheek. He blushed.

Angelique entered their room to find Andrew engaged in a lively game of hide and seek with the children. "What's wrong?" he asked, seeing her concerned look.

"Our dear friend Mr. Wilson has lost his position here at the hotel. I do so wish it wasn't so. This is his life's work. And his sadness was palpable. It broke my heart, Andrew."

He reached under her chin, lifting it until her steel-blue eyes met his. He moved the wisp of raven hair that had fallen across her forehead. She was beautiful, a woman of quiet determination and unwavering strength. And even when she was sad, she thought of others. Always. Her beauty was rare because it went deep down into her very soul. Oh, how he loved her.

"And we will pray that he finds a new life. A pleasurable one."

"Indeed."

"But I do have to ask. How is this going to affect us and our stay here?"

"While you are praying for Mr. Wilson, ask God to place a sense of urgency on Monsieur Bourgeois' heart. We need his answer soon. Very soon."

Chapter Six

As was her morning routine, Angelique approached the front desk to see if she had received a letter. It had been hard to conceal her disappointment when none arrived, but she held steadfast to the hope that Mr. Bourgeois would write soon with some much anticipated good news. Before she was able to make her inquiry, she was approached by a tall wiry man, with horn-rimmed spectacles and a black cowlick that stood on the top of his head like the plume of an exotic bird.

"You are Mrs. Slater, are you not?" he asked.

Angelique noted that his accent was definitely Northern.

He out stretched his bony hand. "I am Edward Smithson, the new general manager here at the St. Charles Hotel."

She smiled sweetly and nodded, but refused to give her hand in return to this Yankee scoundrel who had come to take away Mr. Wilson's job. "Nice to meet you," she said, trying to sound polite.

"I was hoping we could have a word."

She raised an eyebrow, wondering what he had on his mind. "Should I go and get my husband, sir? He is upstairs with the children."

"That won't be necessary at this point. Perhaps, later."

"At this point? Is this to be an ongoing discussion? I am afraid that I am confused, so I hope you will clarify for me."

"Sorry, Mrs. Slater. It is a simple matter. You have been a guest of this hotel for five weeks now."

She nodded.

He opened the book he had been holding until he found the place. "Ah, yes, here we are. You stayed in a regular room for the first three weeks before moving to a two room suite for the last two weeks."

She swallowed hard. Suddenly, she knew where this was going.

"According to hotel records, you have not paid a penny toward a quite sizeable bill."

Angelique stood tall. She would not betray Mr. Wilson. Ever. The talk of money in a public space was ill-mannered in her mind, and she questioned this man's diplomacy among other things. Perhaps he was accustomed to negotiating with women, although it was a foreign concept in the Deep South, where financial matters were handled between gentlemen. But more than likely, he saw her as weak, one would give in easily out of fear, crumpling into tears at the sheer thought of his strong arm tactics. She cleared her throat. "I was under the impression that such matters were handled at check out."

"They can be. Are you leaving us?"

"We will be. Soon. Very soon."

"I see. And I may expect payment then?"

"Certainly. If you would be so kind as to give me the total amount, I will see to it."

"The total is $437.50."

Angelique thought that she was going to faint. After all that they had endured, could the universe be so cruel as to possibly send them to debtor's prison, leaving all three of their children as orphans? She pinched her hand to keep the tears from flowing. She might die trying, but she would not go down without a fight. "And does this include our concession, sir?"

"I beg your pardon? What concession?"

She pointed to the lobby filled with soldiers. "Why I assume that all of these fine soldiers of the Union Army are occupying most of the hotel and paying to stay here as well. Are they not?"

"Yes, of course."

"May I ask the daily rate that you are charging the United States Government for their rooms?"

"You may not. That is private information."

"I am reasonably certain that they are not bearing the full cost, which you have asked me to pay. Am I right, sir?"

"I am not going to discuss that with you ma'am."

"Well, I understand that I am just a women and a Southern one at that, but it seems to me that only a cold and heartless man would charge a poor distraught mother in search of her dear kidnapped child more than he would charge a soldier, especially one whose expenses are paid by Mr. Lincoln himself. Our family has been devastated by this awful war. My husband was lost, presumed dead, and we have just recently been reunited. I was hoping for compassion, a bit of Christian kindness. Why, I hope I haven't misjudged you when I took you to be benevolent and noble, a true gentleman."

Angelique leveled her steel-blue eyes on him and locked them like a gun fixed on its target. Tilting her head slightly, she smiled before finally lowering her lashes. "Now, would you please be a dear and write down the total we owe this fine hotel, but this time include my discount?"

He nodded but said nothing, having been duly captivated. He wrote a number on a pad and handed it to her.

She smiled. "Now would you sign your name to it and date it? That's just to help my poor memory, of course."

He did as requested.

The front desk clerk appeared with an envelope. "This just came for you, ma'am."

"Wonderful. I have been waiting for it," she said.

Angelique then extended the hand she had withheld only moments earlier. "I thank you, Mr. Smithson. It has been a pleasure to stay at the St. Charles."

"The premises has only been graced by your presence, I'm sure. Please, do come again."

And as she walked away, she heard Mr. Wilson greet him. "Ah. I see that you have met Mrs. Slater. She has been one of our favorite guests."

"I can understand why, sir. She is quite a woman. Quite a woman indeed."

Chapter Seven

Angelique was breathless as she greeted Andrew. "I have much to share."

She had his attention. "Then, please do."

Holding up the envelope, she said, "We have our response from Monsieur Alphonse."

"And?"

"He regrets that he has taken him so long to answer us, but he has been unable to secure a property for us to rent. He thinks that will take time. So much is affected by the war. But he has invited us to come and stay with him and his family at his plantation for as long as we need to. He insists that there is plenty of room and that we can search for a place from there."

"How do you feel about that?"

"It isn't ideal, but I don't see that we have a choice."

"There is always a choice."

"Not as of this morning when I received this."

Angelique handed him the piece of paper with $135 written on it signed by Edward Smithson.

"I don't understand."

"It is our hotel bill, Andrew. The new management has been going through the financial records and discovered that we have been staying here without paying."

"That's a lot of money, Angelique."

"Yes, of course it is. But it was over $400. I charmed the man into reducing it. And unfortunately, we are going to have to pay this or face some serious consequences."

Andrew sighed, and Angelique could tell that he was mentally calculating their total funds. He furrowed his brow. "I don't know if we have enough between us. And if this depletes our reserves, what will we do in the days to come?"

Angelique moved to the dresser and took out a velvet box. She carefully removed the sapphire and diamond earrings and held them out to him. "I have these to sell."

He swallowed hard. They had belonged to her mother. She had worn them on the night of the masquerade ball at the Oceanview, the night he had first made love to her. And it was only because she had forgotten to remove them that she had been wearing them when the terrible storm came. Miraculously, they had remained on her ears through the brutal assault of wind and rain. They were, he knew, her most prized material possession, all that she had left of a life she once had so long ago. He would not allow her to part with them.

"No. There is another way. I just need some time to come up with a solution."

"I'm afraid we have no time. Monsieur Bourgeois said that we could arrive at our earliest convenience. We should prepare to leave tomorrow."

"Then, you busy yourself with that. I'm going to stretch my legs a bit. The fresh air will do me some good, you know, help me think."

"And will you go by the park near the market? It is where Robert spends his time when he doesn't have a fare. Please ask him if he will take us to Maison Blanche tomorrow."

Andrew nodded. "That's a far carriage ride, Angelique. It will take most of his day for the round trip. We need to compensate him in some way."

Angelique wiped away a tear with the back of her hand. "Of course. How inconsiderate of me. Why is it that lack of money can make life so complicated?"

"I believe it has always been that way. It's why those who have it hold such power. Unfortunately."

He crossed the room to kiss her goodbye. "I won't be gone long. And I will discuss our situation with Robert, whom I am sure will happily take us wherever we need to go."

But she didn't respond as she removed the tapestry satchel from the armoire and began to place the contents of the dresser into it.

Once outside, Andrew headed toward Royal Street. If he was to fetch the best price for his grandfather's watch, he would need to visit the fanciest shops. It had been his most prized possession, the only remnant he had of the man who had impacted his life in such a profound way. When he left the pink house for his stint at Fort Sumter, he had left it with Angelique, nestled in a velvet pouch in her jewelry box. He would do nothing to risk losing it. And that proved to be serendipity. His rebel captors would have surely found it and confiscated it.

But their future was at stake, and there was no room for sentiment. He had not been able to be a hero, to protect his loved ones while off at war, but he hoped that this would make up for that. At the first three stops, he was given a low offer, less than half of the value. But finally, at the fourth one, the merchant carefully examined the timepiece, commenting on the craftsmanship.

"They don't make them like this anymore. Exceptional."

"Indeed. It has been in my family for generations. I have treasured it. And would you make an offer for purchase?"

Andrew was pleased when he left the shop with eighty-five additional dollars in his pocket, enough to make up the shortfall and give them a little cushion. Somehow, he knew that his grandfather, a devoted family man, would have approved.

Within the hour, he had located Robert in the market and made arrangements for them to meet him at eight the next morning. When he learned that the customary fare was eight dollars for such a trip, Andrew cheerfully handed over the bills. "Payment in advance," he said. And although Robert didn't want to take it, in the end, he looked relieved that he wasn't missing revenue he might have made around the city.

He stopped at the reception desk, recognizing Mr. Smithson by the description Angelique had given of him. "Andrew Slater," he said extending his hand.

"Mr. Slater. I had the pleasure of meeting your wife this morning."

"So I hear sir. And as a result, I would like to settle our bill."

"Are you leaving?"

"In the morning. And so, here is the balance owed."

Mr. Smithson cheerfully gave Andrew the receipt marked "paid in full."

By the time he returned to his family, he was in a jovial mood. She, however, was not.

"We are all set," he proudly announced.

"Hardly."

"Robert will be here at eight in the morning. And he has been paid in advance. The hotel has been taken care of as well," he said, handing her the receipt.

"How did you manage it?"

"You aren't the only clever member of the Slater family, my dear," he said. "Now, let me help you with those bags."

***

Over dinner that night, the children were told of the upcoming move, and Angelique was careful to make it sound like a grand adventure. She emphasized that there would be fields to explore with room to roam, along with lots of animals. And she said to Franklin, "There are even fishing holes for you."

His eyes grew wide. "Do you mean I am going along, too?"

"Well, of course. Why wouldn't you?"

He hung his head. "Well, I figured that my job was to help find Aimee and now that she is back, I would return to Richmond."

For a brief moment, Angelique imagined herself accompanying Franklin to Richmond. There, she would begin her quest to find Jean Paul. She saw him sitting alone on a park bench as she approached him from behind and in one quick move shot him in the head with the gun the Countess had given her. She watched with satisfaction as he slid to the ground, a pool of crimson blood forming at her feet.

"So. Mrs. Slater, can I ask what time my train will be leaving."

And Angelique, suddenly back from her reverie, simply mumbled, "What train? No train, dear."

Andrew reached for her hand. "Franklin. You are not taking a train tomorrow or any day after that. We would like for you to become a permanent part of our family, if you'll have us."

"Really? Do you mean it?"

"Certainly. Family isn't always blood, you know, it's the people who want you in their lives."

Franklin grinned. "Gee, Mr. Slater that would be swell. I can't think of anything I would like better."

"And Franklin?"

"Yes, sir?"

"If you so choose, if you ever feel ready, I mean, you may call us Momma and Poppa."

He looked away and nodded. "Thanks," he whispered.

***

And early the next morning, the Slater family of six, bid New Orleans goodbye as they headed toward the river and their new life.

Chapter Eight

The cards had been dealt. He methodically rubbed his neck before picking them up, slowly revealing his hand. It seemed utterly impossible that he held all four queens, but there they were, staring back at him as though they knew their role was to make him rich. He smiled. Passing on the discard round, he placed his bet and waited. As the men continued to wager, he watched the pot grow larger and larger. Beads of sweat formed across his forehead. One of the players called and the hands were revealed. He had won handily, but it came as no surprise to him. Gambling, after all, had not only become his life's work, at the very essence of who he was. He was reaching over to scoop up the money when suddenly, he woke. For a moment, he stared into the darkness, dazed and disoriented. He searched his brain for some clue as to where he was, taking deep breathes to control the panic. And then it came to him with an undeniable clarity: he was Jean Paul Latour, a man who had been saved by the grace of God, a man stumbling along the road to redemption. And cards no longer had a place in his life.

He lay on his cot, hopelessly awake, trying to remember all the words to the prayer that the priest had taught him earlier that day. It was a petition to St. Jude, a powerful novena for help in the most impossible of cases. If there was ever a man whose plight fell into that realm, it was he. The lines didn't come easily as he stumbled, struggling to pray. Talking to God felt foreign and new to him, but he hoped that The Almighty already knew what was in his misguided heart. It was a pain so deep that he wondered if it would ever go away. Not that he deserved relief. After all he had done, he had earned whatever punishment came his way, and if it was indeed possible to wash away his sins, it was going to take a very long time.

He rose and walked over to the tiny window in his room. It was actually more like a storage closet, pressed into service as a place for him to sleep. The kindly priest had insisted that a private area of solitude would be essential to Jean Paul's personal recovery. But he spent most of his time working in the kitchen or garden, and retreated there only in the quiet of the evening, when the church and rectory were still.

And he often believed that being alone with his thoughts was indeed the just retribution of an exacting God, the memoriesstabbing at him as though Satan, with his fiery hot pitchfork, were wielding it himself. He had chosen gambling over and over again, his love of cards trumping his love for Angelique, whose heart he had broken so many years ago. But even worse was the grim reality that his preoccupation with the game had kept him from caring for Aimee. Her sweet presence, her innocence, had brought such light and joy into this life. She had trusted him to keep her safe, and he had woefully failed. Indeed, losing her, having her disappear in broad daylight, brought him to his knees like nothing else could have, forcing him to face the reality of the kind of man he had become. Ruthless. Selfish. Unredeemable.

He returned to bed and tried to sleep. The priest said that God forgives all and that in time he could claim a new life. He certainly hoped that to be true.

Chapter Nine

The carriage ride from New Orleans to Maison Blanche Plantation had taken even longer than Angelique had anticipated and by the time the majestic white house came into view, she was certain that the children would have exploded from the sheer confinement had they traveled one more mile. While Robert and Andrew unloaded the luggage, she seized the opportunity to issue one last warning about expected behavior. Their presence was going to be enough of an imposition without having her brood misbehaving. And she certainly didn't want the Bourgeois family to regret having extended the invitation.

Angelique was a bit nervous as they walked up the wide steps onto the massive veranda, its second story gallery supported by fat white columns. She hadn't visited the home since she had left Chauvin Plantation as a new bride in what seemed like a lifetime ago. And while she had grown up surrounded by these people, time has a way of changing relationships, the distance often turning friends into strangers.

The front door opened wide and Alphonse Bourgeois laughed from deep inside his belly. It was the one distinguishing characteristic that Angelique remembered of him as a child, his jovial way of making everything seem like a celebration. She immediately felt at ease. "Angelique, my dear girl," he said, putting his arms around her in a bear hug. "I had no idea that you would get here so quickly."

"I regret, Mr. Alphonse, that I didn't have the opportunity to let you know of our arrival. I hope that it won't be too much of an inconvenience to you or your household."

"Nonsense," he said. "Your father was like a brother to me. That makes you my niece. We do what we can to help family."

"I can only hope that you understand the depth of my gratitude."

He was joined by Marie, his wife, who Angelique remembered as rather quiet and demure, but always kind. But she smiled and whispered, "welcome," which seemed like all she could manage to offer. Madame Bourgeois, like he, had aged considerably in the decade since she had last seen them. As we are often reminded, time stands still for no one. But except for the cane Monsieur Bourgeois used and the noticeable gray in his hair, he still had a youthful zest that belied his years. And although it was painful to think about, she wondered what her own parents might have been like in their golden years, if the cholera epidemic hadn't taken them both so quickly, their deaths too impossible to understand then and now.

"Please, come on in," he said, gesturing toward the door. Angelique followed, along with Andrew, Aida, Aimee, Franklin and Jubilee. She wondered if Mr. Bourgeois was already calculating how long they would stay.

"Monsieur Alphonse, this is my husband Andrew, our twin girls Aida and Aimee, our adopted son, Franklin, and our nanny, Jubilee. I did try to warn you in my letter that our family has grown over the years."

He moved to shake Andrew's hand. "Nonsense. It will be lovely to hear the laughter of children. Our son is married but hasn't provided us with grandchildren yet. We're waiting for that blessing."

"How is Henry?" Angelique asked.

"Here he is. Ask him yourself."

Angelique turned to embrace her childhood playmate, now grown. "Henry," she said, "I would have never recognized you. I do believe that you were a teenage boy the last time I saw you."

"I suppose I could say the same about you. So good to see you again, Angelique. It is hard for me to imagine that you are a mother now, although a beautiful one, I might add."

Angelique blushed before turning to introduce Andrew. The two exchanged pleasantries. And in the background a short woman with curly red hair cleared her throat.

"My wife, Justine," Henry said placing his arm gently around her shoulder.

"How lovely to meet the woman who has captured Henry's heart," Angelique said, offering her hand. "I do hope that we will have a chance to get each other better."

But the woman stood, stone cold, offering neither her hand in return nor a smile. She simply stared at Angelique, the expression on her face speaking volumes as to what was on her mind.

41

"You must be tired," Monsieur Bourgeois offered in an effort to break the mood, which had suddenly turned somber. "Let me get the servants to help you settle into your rooms. I hope the children won't mind sharing. And I do believe that there is an empty cottage in the slave village for your girl."

"Thank you kindly, monsieur. And no, they will happily stay together."

Angelique had methodically unpacked the bags for the children and was almost through with the satchel belonging to Andrew, when she realized that hers was missing. She quietly slipped down the stairs to search for it when she heard a woman's voice coming from the parlor.

"I don't understand why they have to move in here."

"I told you, Justine, her father would have done the same for us. Our parents were incredibly close."

"But doesn't she know that there is a war on?"

He laughed. "I do believe that it is that same war that gave them no choice, no other viable option of a place to go."

"But we are already struggling to feed this household. Your father pretends that he doesn't notice the scarcity of food. Now we are expected to provide for another five. How will we manage?"

"We will do what we must. You will soon learn that Angelique is no fragile Southern belle, expecting to be waited on hand and foot. She is rather resourceful, and she will do her part to help."

"Well, that may or may not be true, but I don't have to like her or the situation."

"I think you should reserve judgment until you come to know her. But regardless, I would ask for you to be civil and polite in my father's house."

"I will do what is expected of me, but that doesn't make it pleasant."

Angelique spotted her bag in the hall and quickly retrieved it. "Andrew, she whispered, when she had returned to their room. "It appears that not everybody in this house is happy to have us here."

"Well, I suppose that shouldn't come as a surprise. We can be quite a handful."

"Henry's wife Justine. I just overheard her talking about us."

"And?"

"It seems that food is the biggest issue. We will need to be mindful of that at mealtimes. And perhaps we can help to supplement. After all, Franklin does like to fish."

Andrew laughed. "There you go, trying to make everything nice for everyone. By its very nature, war creates difficult times. I can understand her concern. But you will charm her as you have all who have come to know you, and I have no doubt that you two will be fast friends."

"Do you?"

"Indeed." He moved to put his arms around her. "Now let's don't go looking for problems that don't exist."

"At least not yet."

Later that evening, the Slaters joined the Bourgeois family in the dining room. The table had been carefully set with the finest of china and silver which glistened in the candlelight. One obviously overworked slave hurried from the kitchen with the small platters of food as he made his way from seat to seat to serve them. And Angelique was proud of her children who smiled gratefully as they were given one small sliver of chicken and a spoonful of peas.

The conversation was rather subdued as Monsieur Bourgeois told of how the war had changed everything. He recounted how the many slaves had fled during the first month of the conflict and what a struggle it was to maintain such a large plantation without sufficient help.

"War is unkind," Andrew said. "All we can hope is that those in power see the futility, the hardship and bring about peace soon."

"I pray for it daily," Mr. Bourgeois said.

"In the meantime," Andrew said, "We will do what we can to earn our keep."

Henry laughed. "I'm counting on it."

But his wife Justine sat wordlessly, eyeing Angelique with suspicion.

Angelique looked over at Aimee, whose eyes were heavy. "If you will excuse me, I am going to put these children to bed."

Andrew, too, excused himself, thanking their hosts for a lovely meal all the while hoping that the growling of his stomach hadn't been loud enough for them to have heard it.

Chapter Ten

It was close to sundown when Jubilee pushed opened the door and entered the dusty shack. It was dismal, in complete disrepair, with a saggy cot in one corner and a small cracked table with one tiny chair in the other. She was grateful when she spied the oil lamp, praying that it worked, relieved when she discovered that it did. She chuckled at the idea that Mr. Bourgeois had called this a cottage. It had about as much in common with one as a fish had with a tiger. But if it was to be her home, at least for the time being, she had better become accustomed to it. She was happy that her mother wasn't able to see her settling into slave's quarters, as though that is where she was meant to be. The woman had fought so hard, given up so much in order for Jubilee to be born a free woman. But with that liberty came the ability to choose her own path in life, and in spite of the obstacles, the hardships, she was currently exactly where she wanted to be. Besides, it was temporary, she reminded herself, a mere chapter in the book of her life. Still it was a bit unsettling. Yes, she felt undeniably loyal to the Slaters, but this most certainly felt like a very big step backwards.

Jubilee was making a mental note of what she needed simply to survive in the miserable place when there was a knock on the door. She jumped. A tall and very handsome black man stood in her open doorway. For a moment, Jubilee wondered if he was an illusion, an angel from heaven sent to comfort her in her hour of need, but when he opened his mouth to speak, she realized he was flesh and blood. And the reality wasn't altogether unpleasant.

"Howdy, ma'am," he said. "You Jubilee, right? I'm Terence. Mista Bourgeois told me to check on you, just to make sure that you were settling in, this being your first night here, and all." He smiled.

She searched for words, as though language had somehow become a foreign concept. He radiated strength, a calm power behind his kind eyes. "Uh, thank you," she mumbled.

He looked around the room. "Don't look like there is much in here."

"No. It is rather sparse," she said, gathering her wits about her.

"I think the folks that left took what they wanted. I know that once a place becomes empty, everyone makes a pass through to see if there is anything worth having. Picked clean like a chicken. I'll see if I can get you a bucket for water, and a pillow and blanket, for sure. Anything else?"

Jubilee could have rattled off a list a mile long, but simply shook her head instead. "Thanks. That will help."

And just like that he was gone, leaving her to wonder if he had been a figment of her imagination all along.

As she opened her satchel, wondering where she was to put her clothes, he reappeared, carrying the bedding. "Here you go," he said. His muscles rippled through his thin shirt as he placed the bucket filled with water on the floor. "Tomorrow, we'll get you some help with the cleaning. Maybe a piece of furniture. I know that this can't seem like much of a place, given your situation."

"My situation?"

"Well, Mr. Bourgeois said that you a nanny and a free woman at that. I suppose it ain't easy to be treated like a slave."

"I've only been here for a few hours, so I have no idea how I am to be treated here. Mrs. Slater is my employer and yes, I have a job to do. But I understand that there are sacrifices to be made because of the war. I would experience those, even if I was at home in the North.

Times are challenging for everyone."

He grinned at her, and she wondered if she had said something funny. "You a different kind of woman, that's for sure."

"Really? In what way?"

"Hard to describe, ma'am, just different, that's all."

Jubilee shook her head as she set to work making up the cot that was to be her bed. When she turned her back to him, she could hear his footsteps as he left again. She was just about done when he entered with a plate of food and a mug of what smelled like coffee.

"I figured you might be hungry," he said, placing it on the table. "Come and eat while it still be warm."

She did as instructed, as though under some magical spell. But the first bite was comforting and delicious. Her mood lifted. "Did you make this? Or perhaps your wife?"

He laughed. "I ain't got no wife, ma'am, but the house cook can whip up some mighty tasty food. I caught that rabbit this afternoon. Lucky for me, she let us have it instead of fixing it for the master and his company."

Jubilee stopped short. She had only heard the reference to a master a few times in Charleston by house slaves in the market. But it was always disturbing, the idea of being owned by someone else so foreign to her, so awful.

"How long have you been here, Terence?" She had carefully worded the question.

"Since I was born. I am lucky, compared to most. I ain't never felt afraid, if you know what I mean. Mr. Bourgeois saw to it that I always remained here with the family. I worked this place every day of my life for as long as I can remember. I know this plantation better than he does. And now, with so many gone, I am pretty much in charge of running things."

"That is quite a responsibility."

"Yeah, I guess, although I never think of it like that. But I know things. I can count and sign my name, read some simple words, even. I can tell you if a crop is growing like it should from forty feet away. And I can tend to most animals when they get to ailing. Someday, when this here war is over, and I am free, I am going to work my own little parcel of land, build something for my own tomorrow."

Jubilee was struck by his ambition, his hope for a future, even though his life currently didn't even belong to him. She liked that, and she liked him. "Sounds like a noble plan. And I sure do hope you get all that you want."

"No hoping about it, Jubliee," he said, bending over the table to look deep in her eyes. "It is going to happen as sure as I am standing here. You mark my words."

She felt flushed, emotion stirring deep within her heart. "I don't doubt it for one minute, Terence. Not for one minute."

He bowed low before bidding her goodnight. And as she crawled into bed, trying to find a comfortable place on the lumpy cot, she thought of him, and she wondered if he thought of her as well.

Chapter Eleven

The sun shone brightly through the tall windows, and Angelique woke with a start. Her mouth was dry, her brain fuzzy. She wondered what time it was. Andrew was still asleep as she got out of bed and quickly dressed. What would Monsieur Bourgeois think of her and her family, sleeping in like pampered guests?

"Andrew," she whispered. "It is time to get up."

He turned over, mumbling something incoherent. She repeated the request. He opened his eyes and smiled. "Good morning, my beautiful wife."

She was duly charmed, but only for a moment. "We need to get the children up and ready. I would hate for our hosts to think us lazy. What time do you think it is?"

He reached for his trousers and his watch, primarily out of habit, when he suddenly remembered that he no longer had one. "There's a clock on the dresser, isn't there?"

"My word! It is after eight. Hurry and dress so that we can make an appearance, offer our help with whatever they might need. I want for us to earn our keep."

And half an hour later, the family made their way down the stairs. The house was quiet. Justine sat in the parlor, sewing on what appeared to be a tapestry. She looked up just in time to catch Angelique's eye.

"Looking for something?" she asked.

"No, just wondered where everyone was."

"Well, you would have seen them at breakfast an hour ago. The men have been up before sunrise. Work to be done, you know. My mother-in-law is currently indisposed."

"Of course. And my husband and son will gladly do what is needed. I can assist as well."

But Justine merely shrugged and returned to her needlework.

Angelique stood in the grand reception hall, feeling rather foolish. "Let's go out to the kitchen to see if cook has a piece of bread and a glass of milk for the children. I need to find Jubilee. Their studies have been interrupted for far too long, and Monsieur Bourgeois has a lovely library. I'll find a book that she can read to them. Surely, the menfolk will come in for lunch at which time you can offer to go with them to help with the afternoon chores. In the meantime, I guess it wouldn't hurt for you to just have a look around, get the lay of the land so to speak." She was speaking a mile a minute.

Andrew nodded. He could see the anxiety in her face. "I think I will walk a bit. This is less than ideal, Angelique. It is not our home, and it is abundantly clear that we are guests. But I am grateful to have a roof over our heads, a safe place for our family. It is transitory. Remember that."

Angelique smiled. "You are right, of course. I have to remember that just a few weeks ago, I would have

51

slept on a bed of nails just to have been near you. And Aimee. How I missed my sweet girl. Justine's inhospitable attitude is nothing, compared to all we have been through."

"Right. Now don't forget it."

She reached for his hand, squeezing it tight before taking the children out the back door in search of the kitchen.

By the time she had fed the children and located Jubilee, it was mid-morning. Angelique wondered if they would find their pace, settle into a routine that resembled normalcy. When they moved into their own place, she figured. And she vowed never to complain about such things again, determining that excitement was highly overrated, the foolish dreams of young girls who had no idea what kind of havoc such moments could wreak, turning a perfectly ordered life upside down. No, Angelique prayed for calm, mundane, and ordinary.

Jubilee was happy to see the children and reached for Aimee's hand as she led them to the shade of the big oak tree. "Your momma going to fetch us a storybook to read," she told them, pointing to the grassy area. "And I want you to pay close attention because there will be questions for you to answer."

"Are we back to learning?" Aida asked.

"We are indeed, missy. And I trust that you will help Aimee and Franklin catch up. I will do some of the lessons and your momma will do the others. We can't have you children growing up without the proper education."

"But what about a real school?" Aida asked.

"That will come. We just got here yesterday. I suspect that if there is a school nearby that you three can attend, then, you will. But in the meantime, we are in charge of your instruction."

That seemed to satisfy Aida, but Aimee wrinkled her brow. "I have been gone for so long, Jubilee. I don't know if I remember anything I learned before."

"You will, sugar," Jubilee said, moving in to hug the girl. "Don't you worry about that."

Franklin sat wordlessly nearby. He cleared his throat. "I went to school before my father and mother died. I can read a little and do some ciphering. I never did take to writing very well, though."

"Thank you, Franklin. And don't you worry. Besides, you know more than your little sisters, so you can help them."

He sat tall and straight. "My little sisters," he repeated, as though it was the most beautiful three words he had ever uttered.

Angelique joined them with books in tow. "I was excited to find these in the library, left over from when Henry was a child, no doubt. Here is The First Book of Arithmetic. It should get us through the basics. And Aesop's Fables! I loved hearing these as a child. And they are short, so they should be easy to read and talk about. In fact, Franklin might want to try reading one out loud."

"And the third book, Momma?" Aida asked.

"It is the best one of all, but I am keeping it as a surprise for later."

Aida hung a lip, but Aimee clapped her hands. "I like surprises." And Angelique reached over to kiss the girl on the forehead. "Then, you will truly love this one."

They spent the rest of the morning giggling over the talking animals in the fables and discussing the lesson that each imparted. They gathered pebbles to use for the arithmetic lesson, since ink and paper was far too precious to be used for such purposes. But as they soon discovered, it was much easier to count real objects anyway. And by the time the lunch bell sounded, Angelique was pleased with how the morning had transpired.

Jubilee seemed momentarily distracted as Angelique gathered the books. She followed her gaze just in time to see a rather imposing figure of a black man tip his hat at Jubilee, who smiled and waved.

"New friend?" Angelique whispered.

"Sort of. I met him last night."

"And?"

"And nothing, Miss Angelique. I don't know him."

"Well, he seems to want to know you."

Jubilee folded her arms. "I am not about to fall for a common farm slave. Goodness, my momma would have a fit. Besides, I would never make a good wife for a man who likes to plow the fields and pick the crops. I left my home to escape that, remember?"

"Well, Jubilee, all I can say is that if you are thinking about him as a potential husband, even one you are claiming to reject, then, I'd say that there is some mighty powerful interest there."

The lunch bell rang again.

"Nonsense, Miss Angelique, now you go have your lunch. I'll come in to put the girls down for their naps afterwards. And you forgot the surprise book. Aida isn't likely to forget."

"Don't change the subject. You can dismiss me all you want, but I know what I just saw. Strange things happen on the road to love." Angelique giggled.

"Well, it isn't a road I plan to travel."

"We shall see, Jubilee. We shall see."

Chapter Twelve

Lunch was a simple meal of root vegetables and biscuits. Angelique figured the cook must have worried all morning about stretching the meager food stores to feed an additional five people, and she wondered if that was on Monsieur Bourgeois' mind as well. Andrew, who as always sensed her thoughts, spoke up.

"After lunch, I thought that Franklin and I would accompany you out to the fields. Until we are able to find our own place, and must impose upon your gracious hospitality, we want to do our part to help."

Monsieur Bourgeois nodded. "We could use it. Several of our slaves fled when the war started. I have Terence, who has been with me since he was born. Knows this planation like no other, but even he has found it difficult to keep up without the extra hands. Cotton is our crop, Mr. Slater, along with a few acres of sugar cane. But bringing them to harvest is a battle against the forces of nature, weather, insects, disease. Nothing more beautiful than seeing it grow, but I'd be lying if I didn't say it was a struggle."

Andrew nodded.

"In between those challenges, Henry and I hunt some. A mature deer can feed this plantation for a few weeks. The war has made food a challenge. We used to have a fine herd of cattle, but the Yankee army has poached them, one by one, like common thieves. The few who remain are guarded like fine jewels, especially the milk cow. Tell me, Mr. Slater, do you know much about farming?"

Andrew could feel the color rising in his cheeks. His scientific knowledge seemed of little practical use in such a place, but he would offer what he could. "I am afraid not. I grew up in the city. My profession lies in meteorology, weather forecasting primarily. But I am not afraid to get my hands dirty, to work hard. And Franklin here will, too."

Franklin grinned broadly, having suddenly realized that he was being included in this male realm, viewed as an equal rather than a child.

"Then we will most certainly put you to work. Franklin, do you like animals?"

"I sure do, sir."

"Then, how about we begin by putting you in charge of the chickens. We have a few remaining in the pen by the kitchen. You can crack the corn for feed and gather the eggs each morning. Can you do that?"

"Yes sir. And I won't let you down."

"Mr. Slater, after lunch we will ride the fields, and I will show you around Maison Blanche."

"I'd be grateful, sir. And please call me Andrew."

"Of course, Andrew."

Angelique smiled. She was proud of her husband, so far out of the realm of what felt comfortable and familiar to him, yet willing to do what was necessary to be honorable.

"And Monsieur Alphonse?"

"Yes, Angelique?"

"It is not our intention to become permanent houseguests. We hope to be able to find a place of our own soon."

"I understand, dear girl. You want to be independent. But I need to remind you that there is a war on, a conflict which has changed everything. So many of the menfolk are off doing the fighting. People who do have a roof over their heads and are able to grow a little food for their bellies are staying put. I am not trying to be discouraging, but it won't be as easy as you might think."

"But I don't want for us to impose."

"Nonsense. We stick together and do the best we can. But you need to keep in mind that you and your family may very well be here for the duration."

Angelique smiled, so grateful for the kindness of her father's dearest friend. But she could see that which he hadn't said, the worry and concern. He suddenly looked old and tired, the lines in his face more pronounced. He carried a great responsibility on his shoulders, and their presence only added to it.

"My family and I are indebted to you, Monsieur. May God smile on you for your kindness."

"I consider having ya'll here a blessing, Angelique. We will work together. It will be just fine. You'll see."

Angelique rose to help clear the table. And out of the corner of her eye, she could see Justine, the frown on her face making it abundantly clear how she felt about their status as permanent houseguests.

Chapter Thirteen

Fall, 1862

Angelique offered her hand first to Aimee and then, to Aida. Franklin and Jubilee followed closely behind. "Where are we going, Momma?" Aida asked.

"You'll see. Part of the fun of a surprise is not knowing what it is, right?"

The twins shook their heads simultaneously, a habit that never failed to delight Angelique. They walked the shady tree-laden path from the front door to the road, and made their way to the adjacent field. There were tall stalks of sugar cane in proud, ordered rows. "This way," she said, pointing to a cleared area, obviously designed for loading the crop. "Here." She stopped and spread the blanket on the ground. "Sit." And the foursome did as they were instructed.

"Is this our surprise?" Aida asked, scratching her head.

"It is. And as you will soon see, it is a good one."

Angelique reached into her pocket and pulled out a folding knife. She carefully opened it, the blade shining in the mid-afternoon sun. Adjusting her straw hat, she took one step forward and bending low, cut a stalk of cane at the place where it met the earth. Slowly and methodically, she cut it into five equal pieces and then began to peel away the tough outer leaves.

She handed the first piece to Aimee. "Taste it. Put it in your mouth and chew."

Aimee tried it tentatively at first, and then smiled broadly. "It's so sweet!"

"This is nature's candy."

Aida raised her hands. "Me next. I want to try."

And in several swift moves, Angelique had completed the task. They all sat as if in a trance, mesmerized by the warm syrupiness. Juice ran down their chins.

"So yummy," Aida said wiping her mouth with the back of her hand.

"Does this feed your sweet tooth, my precious girl?"

Aida grinned. "Better than cookies, I think."

"I agree. Reminds me of when I was a girl. My daddy used to peel the cane for me just like this."

"Really?"

"He did. Why I grew up not very far from here, in a house much like Maison Blanche."

"Can we go and see it?" Franklin asked.

Angelique swallowed hard. She hadn't considered the possibility of returning to Chauvin plantation, even just to witness how it had changed over the years. The loss of her family home was just too painful to face, and she doubted that she would ever be strong enough to make that trip. "Oh, I don't know," she said. "Lots of memories there."

And Jubilee, sensing Angelique's discomfort, quickly changed the subject. "I think that if we lay on our backs, we can look up at the clouds. What kind of shapes do you think you can spot?"

The children were duly distracted, pointing to bunnies and horses and beautiful ladies they saw in the sky. Angelique breathed a sigh of relief. She knew that there were limits to her strength, which had certainly been tested over and over again. Her mind wandered.

Suddenly, all was quiet. Angelique looked over to see Aida and Franklin sleeping soundly. Even Jubilee seemed to be nodding off. Only Aimee lay there quietly, blinking in an uneven rhythm as she stared up at the sky.

"Looks like they have all decided to take a nap," Angelique whispered.

Aimee giggled.

"But this gives you and I a chance to talk." Angelique said, moving closer. She took Aimee's hand in hers. "I think we need to, don't you?"

Aimee nodded, but said nothing.

"I want you to know how sorry I am that I failed to protect you that day. I wish you would have never had to endure all that you did. Oh how I missed you with every breath that I took."

"I know. And it wasn't your fault. Aida and I shouldn't have gone out like that. I missed you, too, mommy." Her voice sounded far off, as though she was reliving the moment that she was taken from all that she had known.

Angelique swallowed hard. "Yes, you and Aida have learned how important it is to be careful. Something can happen in an instant." She paused. "Can you tell me about the man who took you?"

Aimee looked at her as though she failed to understand. "Uncle Gaston? He is your brother, so you should know all about him."

This was going to be more difficult that she imagined. How could she possible explain to the child that Uncle Gaston didn't exist, that the man she thought was out to care for her, take her to a dreamy land of castles and fairytales, was a fraud, a liar, a thief. Worst of all, he was her mother's first husband, a scoundrel, whose misdeeds knew no limits. Someday, perhaps, she would explain, but not now, not when the wounds were so fresh for both of them. Aimee was fragile, still so young, and adjusting to being with her family again. They needed time. "He was not your uncle, Aimee. I don't have a brother. He was just a man who took you along with him against your will."

"Really? So he lied? Why would he do that? And how did he know your name?"

She dodged the last question. "Who knows why people do things that make no sense? Perhaps he was lonely and wanted a little girl."

"He said that once."

"Well, unfortunately, you are my daughter, and I am not likely to give you away."

Aimee smiled.

Angelique took a deep breath. This was hard, but there were unanswered questions. She had to know. "He didn't hurt you, did he? Was he good to you? I mean, did he treat you well?"

"Yes. He tried to be nice. He braided my hair every morning and made sure that I ate breakfast before we went to the place where he played cards. And he got

Sarah for me, too. The days were long while I waited, but once I met Franklin, it got better."

"Franklin is our hero, isn't he?"

"Sure is. Now I really do have a big brother."

"Yes, you do."

"And one last thing, Aimee."

"What?"

"Would you recognize him if you ever saw him again? Uncle Gaston, I mean," Her stomach churned at the mention of his fake name. "What he did is against the law. And it would make me happy to see him in jail. It is what he deserves."

Aimee's eyes grew wide. "I can see his face in my mind. He had a big scar right here," she said, touching her own cheek. "But I don't know how easy it would be to find him, unless he is still at the place where Franklin worked and is still playing cards."

Angelique nodded, trying to hold back the anger that stirred deep inside. She would have happily sent him off to prison and helped them throw away the key. Or worse. Much worse. She kissed Aimee's hand. "You have been my brave, brave girl. And I am so happy that we were able to talk a little. I hope you know that I am always here when you need me."

"Of course. That's what mommas do."

"Indeed. And I am mighty proud to be yours." She hugged Aimee tightly. Aida woke just in time to see her mother and sister embrace before turning her head upwards to the now cloudless sky.

Chapter Fourteen

Justine was in the reception hall, pacing back and forth.

"I've been waiting for you," she yelled, pointing.

And Angelique, obviously confused, responded, "You seem upset. I am here."

"I want to know what you did with my garnet broach."

"I beg your pardon. I have no idea what you are talking about."

"I suspected that you would deny taking it."

"Taking it? I am many things, Justine, but a thief is not one of them."

"I don't believe you." Her agitation grew as her voice became louder.

Angelique turned to the children. "Please go upstairs and wash your hands for dinner."

Once they were out of earshot, she turned to Justine. "I am appalled at your false allegations, but even more so that you would lodge them in front my children. Have you no sense of decency?"

"Perhaps they should know the truth about their mother."

She had gone too far, and Angelique curled her fists into a ball. Had she been a man, she could have punched her accuser, knocked her out cold on the walnut floor. But as a proper Southern woman, she was expected to control her temper, a feat which was becoming more difficult with each passing moment. "You are despicable."

"And you are a pickpocket."

Angelique took a step toward her just as the front door opened, and the men entered.

"Henry," Justine wailed, falling into his arms like a hapless victim. "Angelique has stolen my garnet broach."

They all stood speechless as Justine continued with her show. She had a captive audience and intended to give a noteworthy performance. "She sobbed and moaned." It belonged to my grandmother. I cherished it above all of my possessions. And now, it is gone. Make her return it to me."

Henry looked down at his wife, raising her chin so that her eyes met his. "How do you know that Angelique has taken it? I have known her all of my life and never would have suspected such behavior."

Justine only cried louder. "Of course she took it. Or her girl did. Or maybe one of her bratty children. There's no other plausible explanation, Henry."

"Do you think that perhaps you misplaced it, my dear? It is rather uncharitable for you to accuse one who has given you no reason to cast doubt. And the children? Really, Justine, this is very unbecoming of you."

Angelique took several deep breaths as she tried to control her anger. Andrew sensed her agitation and moved to her side. It was a stand-off, and he was concerned what the repercussions might be.

The tension was broken by a voice from the other room as Madame Bourgeois slowly entered the hall, carrying a small basket. "Justine, dear. I was searching through your sewing bag. My needle broke, and I needed to borrow one of yours. Goodness, child, I found this in there." She outstretched her hand to reveal a glistening broach, one made of garnets. "You really should be more careful to protect your valuable jewels. Anything could happen to them."

Justine's face blushed a crimson red. She opened her mouth to speak, but was immediately silenced by Monsieur Bourgeois. "May I remind you that this is my home, young woman? I choose whom I invite to stay here, and I would expect that you would honor that by extending the same hospitality to Angelique and her family that I have extended to you and my son. I will not tolerate your dissension, nor will I allow you to create turmoil. Am I making myself clear?"

She nodded.

"There is a real war on, a conflict that could threaten our very existence at any moment. We just received the news that General Lee and his brave soldiers suffered a bloody defeat at Antietam. Thousands of our Southern brothers will not be returning home. You will not wage a petty battle here. And I expect that an apology will be forthcoming."

Again Justine nodded as she looked at Angelique with contempt. "I will be polite, but I don't have to like you."

"Nor I you, although I am at a loss as to why you would despise me so. I am glad that you got your broach back. The next time you plan to hide it and falsely accuse someone, choose a better place." And with that, Angelique turned on her heels and made her way up the stairs.

Once securely in their room, Angelique fell into Andrew's arms, shaking uncontrollably. "I am afraid that this is only the beginning of the tension that will inevitably follow. I don't know how long we will be able to stay here."

Andrew laughed. "You certainly aren't serious," he said. "Why, I saw you take on the grand dames of Last Island, handily putting them in their place. And you managed to leave the snooty women of Washington City speechless with your wit and charm, scarcely batting an eye in the process. So you are telling me that you are intimidated by Justine Bourgeois? Surely, you jest."

She smiled. "None of them accused me of stealing, but yes, I suppose that you are right."

"Of course I am," he said with a wink.

Only Andrew could calm her shattered spirit, help to put things in perspective. He was a man of many talents... strong, intelligent, brave. But mostly, he was her hero, especially at times like these when she needed one the most.

Chapter Fifteen

The days turned into weeks. Time has a way of passing quickly when the hours are occupied by responsibilities necessary for survival. Such is life. The extended family had fallen into a rhythm, with the men taking to the fields in the morning and the pastures in the afternoon. The Bourgeois women did needlework or read, sometimes, taking on chores like polishing the silver. And Angelique and Jubilee attended to the children, avoiding the house, and Justine, whenever possible.

There were happy moments, like the morning when Franklin led Aimee and Aida into the chicken coup to present his lesson on how chickens were born. Angelique watched with pride as he held up an egg, describing how the hens lay several a day in a nest they share.

"Those that aren't delivered to cook, end up resting in the nest as the momma keeps them warm with her body until they hatch into baby chicks."

He paused to reach into the nesting area and removed two, which he placed in the girls' hands. They squealed with delight at the tiny bundles of softness, cradling them gently as they whispered sweet words of affection. And after that, Aida cheerfully ate the vegetables offered at mealtime, firmly resolving that she would never eat chicken again. Aimee wholeheartedly agreed.

A few days later, Franklin escorted them into the barn to demonstrate how cows were milked, offering a ladle of the warm liquid, first to the girls and then Angelique and Jubilee. When he displayed the bucketful that he had collected, he breamed with pride, viewing himself as a contributor to the household.

"You enjoy the animals, don't you?" Angelique had said to him.

"Yes ma'am. I find them interesting. You can learn a lot about life just by watching."

"You are a smart boy, Franklin. I think that the girls and I can learn a lot about life just by watching you."

He had smiled broadly, obviously pleased.

Some days, they collected cotton bolls, then sat under the shade of the old oak tree, extracting the seeds which they carefully placed in an old jar. They sang songs, some real, some made up on the spot.

Angelique was pleased at the lessons she was able to construct for the children from life on the plantation with each teaching them to respect the land and life and each other. The circumstances weren't perfect, and she longed for a place that belonged to them alone, but she was grateful to be safe, secure and fed. It was a blessing that she didn't take for granted.

But life was not without its challenges. Aida had learned to curtail her jealousy over what she perceived to be the extra time and attention her mother paid to Aimee. She had hidden in the fields for most of one afternoon in protest, and Angelique was frantic until they found her.

"What on earth were you thinking, Aida?" she had asked.

"I thought maybe if I was kidnapped, you might love me the best."

And Angelique's heart softened. She had underestimated the way she had doted on Aimee in an effort to make up for their lost time. And more importantly, she had failed to see the impact it had on Aida. "I am so sorry that you feel that way, my precious girl. I love you girls the same, of course. You are both, most certainly, two halves of my heart. You do understand that, don't you?"

Aida had nodded and her spirits brightened when Angelique presented her with a stalk of peeled sugar cane. "Sweets for the sweet," she had said.

One day rolled into the next as the family settled into the routine of life on the plantation. It was on one of those lazy summer afternoons that Andrew suggested a horseback ride. "Getting away from things for a while will do you good," he had said.

Angelique readily agreed, mounting the mare like the experienced horsewoman she had once been. "Feels good to be back in the saddle," she said as she galloped through the fields, Andrew following closely behind.

An hour later they stopped to rest the horses. "This was fun," she said.

"Agreed. No reason why we can't ride on occasion. Mr. Bourgeois wouldn't mind."

"No, I don't think he would. Riding out here reminds me of my childhood, the scenery so familiar, like an old friend."

"I can imagine. Must have been nice to have grown up here."

"It was, although I hate to admit that I was rather spoiled."

"As well you should have been."

Angelique reached over to squeeze Andrew's hand. "What time is it?" she asked.

He felt for his watch, one he knew wasn't there. "Must have forgotten my watch. Probably two or so, why?"

She took a deep breath. "Then we have time."

"For what?"

"To ride to Chauvin Plantation. I didn't think I was ready or that I would ever be, but I can't ignore my past, any more than I can discount my present or the hope I hold for my future. I need to see it."

"Then we should go. Now. How far a ride is it?"

"About fifteen minutes. Not far at all."

Angelique led the way down the road. She was unusually quiet, deep in thought.

When they rounded the bend and the stately home was in sight, she gasped. Andrew simply stared in disbelief.

"What happened?" she whispered, the question obviously rhetorical.

She dismounted and stood on the road looking at her once grand home. There were tall weeds surrounding the property. Crooked shutters hung by the windows. And peeling paint marred the outside, giving it the appearance of a snake shedding its skin. There were thick vines climbing up the porch columns, wrapping around the fretwork. "Does anybody even live here?"

Before he could stop her, she walked through the weeds toward the front door. She knocked, tentatively at first, and then, with more urgency.

It seemed like a long time had passed before anyone answered, and then, the door was only opened a few inches as the shadow of a lone figure appeared. "Go away or I get my gun," the voice yelled.

"Don't mean any harm. Just felt the need to pay a visit." Angelique realized how foolish she sounded and quickly added. "I used to live here."

"Well, you don't anymore, so get going."

She turned to leave, and then reconsidered. "Just makes me sad to see the place looking so bad."

"Not that it is any of your business, but times are hard, in case you haven't noticed. Taxes are sky high, and I can't pay 'em. Now, get off my property."

She nodded, but when she rejoined Andrew, there was a twinkle in her eye.

"Well?" he asked.

"Interesting."

"In what way?"

"Just gave me an idea."

"I start to worry sometimes when you get ideas."

"But this is a good one. What would you think of buying it back? The plantation, I mean."

He scratched his head. "With what? We have no money, Angelique."

"Not now, we don't. But when this war ends, I will get the funds left to me by the Countess. It should be a considerable amount. After all, it has been safely in the bank for the duration, earning interest, I would hope."

Andrew took a deep breath. "But that might not be enough. It looks like a lot of work needs to be done. Can we handle that? And besides, you don't even know that it is up for sale."

She nodded. "True. But he owes the taxes. I will talk to Monsieur Bourgeois, but it means the bill will have to be settled some kind of way."

"Seems a little premature. And a big decision. Are you sure?"

"I have never been more certain of anything in my life. It will give us something to look forward to, a plan for our family's future."

"Perhaps. The children have taken to country life."

"Indeed they have. And it would mean so much to me. Oh, Andrew," she said, "I just want to go home."

"Then, you shall, my darling. How could I ever deny you anything?"

She blew him a kiss. "Good. Now race me back!" And with that, Angelique guided the horse as it galloped away, the sound of her laughter echoing in the wind.

Chapter Sixteen

Winter, 1862/1863

T erence knocked on the door of Jubilee's shack. She was, as always, happy to see him, especially since he was carrying an armful of wood. "Come on in," she said. "It's powerfully cold out there."

"Sure enough is," he said, offering the wood. He stacked it neatly by the fireplace, which leaned so far to the right, that he found himself tilting his head just to align the image in his mind.

"Mighty grateful, Terence."

"Of course, Jubilee. I couldn't have my best girl freezing to death."

"So am I?"

"Is you what?"

"Your best girl?"

"I think you already know the answer to that, Sugar," he said, moving to pull her close.

"That may be fine for you to imagine now, but I have made it clear how I feel about my future. I have no intention of becoming the wife of a slave, even a mighty handsome one."

He grinned. "Well, then we are in agreement about that."

"We are?"

"Sure enough. I drove Master Bourgeois into town yesterday, remember?"

"Yes, so?"

"Well, it turned out to be a pretty important day. I told you that I can read a little. While he was doing his business, and I waited, I spied a newspaper. From what I could make out, it looks like Mr. Lincoln done wrote some sort of law that says that all slaves be free, both in the North and the South."

He had her attention. "Are you sure?"

He nodded. "Heard some of the white men talking about it, too. They weren't happy one bit."

"No, I can imagine that they weren't. Anything else?"

"Don't think that they want us to know that we is free in the eyes of the United States of America. But now, this here war is all about what happens to us."

"My goodness. That's progress, Terence. Think of what that will mean for our people. For you."

"For us," he added.

She smiled.

"You might want to reconsider your thoughts about me in light of that piece of information," he said, "Could you become the wife of a free man?"

"I won't say yes and I won't say no. But I might consider it," Jubilee said. "But none of this has happened yet. And the war could go on for a very long time."

"Or it could be over by planting time."

"True. In the meantime, let's see how well you can build that fire. I have some dandelion root. I'll put the water to boil, and we can have some tea."

Terence laughed. "I sure do miss the smell of real coffee."

"I miss a lot of things that the war has taken away."

"That's cause you think like a free woman. I look at what this war is about to give me."

"I suppose that you are right."

"Like my momma always said, you can't put no price on love." He winked at her.

"You getting mighty sure of yourself now that you have a little taste of freedom."

"I sure is, Jubilee. For the first time in my life, I got a future. One I get to choose. And I sure do hope that you let me choose you."

She moved to him, handing him a cup. "May our tomorrows be better than today."

"I'll drink to that," he said, "I sure will."

Chapter Seventeen

It was the kind of day that chills to the bone, the howling wind making it even more uncomfortable. He lifted his collar, quickening his pace, limited only by his noticeable limp. As he reached the back door and stepped into the kitchen, the comforting smell of soup simmering, combined with the warmth of the fireplace immediately cheered him.

"Errands run?" the housekeeper asked.

"Yes. Everything on the list."

"Good. I do believe that Father would like to speak with you. He asked me to send you to him straight away when you returned."

Jean Paul nodded, taking a moment to remove his heavy coat and hang it on the hook in the adjacent hall. The priest had begun to send him out regularly a few months earlier. At first, it was simply to mail a letter or retrieve a package from a shopkeeper. But lately, the tasks had become more involved as he delivered personal messages to church benefactors or brought religious tokens to the sick and infirmed. He wondered if each was a test, a measurement of his progress. And if so, he was proud that he had passed them all, never wavering from the mission he had been given.

He lightly tapped on the office door. "Father? You wished to see me?"

"I did indeed, Jean Paul. Come in and have a seat." He motioned to the chair across from his desk. "Everything went as expected this morning?"

"The deliveries, you mean? Yes, all were accomplished in record time. I think the cold weather makes me move a little faster than usual."

The priest laughed. "Good. I have come to depend on you."

"And I am most grateful for the confidence that you have invested in me." He hoped that he sounded sincere.

"I am pleased with how well you have done in your time here. Those who may have known the man you were before you arrived, might be surprised at the transformation."

"I continue to gown in faith, Father. But this has become my home, a safe place for me to learn when I must do to change."

"I am reminded of a story, one I think is among the most powerful given to us by our Lord Himself. Shall I share it with you?"

Jean Paul nodded.

"The story is fairly brief. A father has two sons. When the younger son comes of age, he asks for his share of the family inheritance, unwilling to wait until he is to rightfully receive it. The father obliges the request, and this son quickly departs to another country, where he wastes his wealth with frivolous spending and extravagant living. After the young man's money is gone, he is hungry and penniless, barely surviving by taking a job feeding pigs. He is saddened and defeated, remembering the life he once had. And he knows he must return to his homeland. Filled with guilt and remorse, he throws himself at his father's feet apologizing for his foolish conduct. He hopes that he will be accepted him back as just one of his servants in the household, since he has no rights to anything more. To his surprise and his older brother's disdain, their father welcomes the younger son home with a great celebration, joyful to be reunited with his precious child."

"It is a nice story," Jean Paul said.

"It is an important one. Do you understand fully what it means?"

"I think so."

"We serve a God of the lost, one who welcomes us back into His presence regardless of our past deeds."

"And fortunately for me, I have found this place, which has been my sanctuary."

"The angels rejoiced over your repentance."

Jean Paul smiled. "Then, I will do what I can to serve you until my days on this earth are done."

The priest shook his head. "No, my son. Your days here are limited. You will rejoin the world soon. Perhaps not tomorrow or the next day, but soon."

And Jean Paul swallowed hard, trying to keep the panic at bay. The world held far too many temptations for him. And although his resolve was firm, the thought of leaving scared him. It was, in fact, the most terrifying thing he could imagine.

Chapter Eighteen

Angelique was in the field, harvesting the remainder of the mustard greens. She hummed a little tune, pleased that she was able to gather enough for dinner, her attention focused on the way the knife sliced into the leaves, leaving the stalks and roots in the ground. She hadn't noticed the approaching horses until they were almost upon her, taking her by surprise. Ten Yankee soldiers looked down on her as she squinted in the afternoon sun, trying to focus on their faces.

"You live here?" one asked. She wondered if he was in charge or simply chose to be the spokesman. The stars and stripes on his uniform meant nothing to her.

"I am a guest, related to the family by choice."

"My soldiers and I are marching through on the way to Vicksburg. We will be setting up camp on the front lawn within the hour."

"Is that an order, sir?" she asked, the anger stirring in her soul.

"Take it as you like, Miss, but it is what is going to happen."

"Without the consent of the owner?"

"Don't need consent from anybody. New Orleans is currently occupied by Union troops. Our navy controls the port at the mouth of the Mississippi. This land is in close proximity and currently needed for our use."

"For how long?" She asked, afraid of the answer.

"Our battalion will be here for a few nights, but there will be others in due time. Now, if you will excuse me, I will prepare my men."

"And I will warn my family."

"As you wish, miss. We intend no harm, just need a place to stay."

Angelique narrowed her eyes. Experience had taught her otherwise. She had not yet met a Yankee soldier who didn't wield his power like a sharpened sabre. What would transpire remained to be seen. She grabbed her basket and ran back to the house.

"Monsieur Alphonse," she yelled as she entered the reception hall. She ran from room to room until she located him in the library searching for a book.

"Problem, Angelique?"

"Yankee soldiers headed this way. They are going to camp on the front lawn."

He grabbed his pistol and headed for the veranda just as the mounted soldiers reached the steps. Several hundred on foot appeared in the distance.

Henry and Andrew joined them, while Angelique instructed Jubilee to keep the children inside.

The officer tipped his hat. "Afternoon." He motioned toward Angelique. "Guess the little lady told you our intentions."

Monsieur Bourgeois took one step forward. "How about you tell me yourself."

"These men are tired. I need a place for them to rest for a day or two before we continue our march. That's it."

"We are a family struggling during this time of war, sir. Our food stores are dangerously low, and we face hunger on a daily basis. We have none to share with the ten of you, much less your army."

"We have some provisions with us, having recently replenished in New Orleans. I assure you, we will be as unobtrusive as possible. There will be no demands other than perhaps water from your well to fill our canteens and refresh the horses. It is not our intent to destroy your property or do any ill will to your family."

"Do you give me your word as a gentleman?"

"I do. And I will shake your hand on it."

Alphonse Bourgeois, being a noble and honorable man, then moved to take the hand of his enemy.

But behind the house, Franklin was gathering eggs, preparing to turn the dresser drawer in his room into a hatchery. In his few short years on this earth, he had learned not to trust anybody, and most of all, to be prepared for the poorest of times that he hoped wouldn't come.

Chapter Nineteen

Fall, 1863

As the warm temperatures of summer gave way to fall, the family steeled itself for the months ahead. Maison Blanche had become a regular stopping point for Union troops, forced into service as a makeshift military camp. Once one regiment received orders to move out, another soon took its place. The lawn, once lush and green, had been trampled by the many heavy boots. Litter dotted the landscape. Everything looked tired and used, worn thin like the family's patience.

The men did what they could to keep the crops going, to prepare for the autumn cane harvest. Madame Bourgeois wandered from room to room, mumbling to herself, while Justine spent days on end in her bedchamber, refusing to come out, even for meals. Angelique did what she could to keep the children engaged as she and Jubilee looked for new ways to teach them, but even they seemed distracted, uneasy at times.

There was an implied rule to maintain a distance. A chance encounter with a soldier at the well was tension-filled, awkward, so the family avoided such instances at all cost. Angelique had not forgotten her experience with the Yankee scoundrel on the streets of New Orleans, the fear and anger rattling her to the core. And when she spied a soldier staring at her as she tended the kitchen garden, she vowed not put herself in a place of such vulnerability again, especially now. All she could hope and pray for was an end to this miserable war, which seemed like nothing more than wishful thinking.

But the conflict waged on. There were major battles and minor skirmishes, all with the same result, a disastrous loss of life. One afternoon, an overconfident Captain, who wanted to show his rank and position sauntered up to the front porch and knocked on the door under the pretext of having some news to share. The men listened, shaking their heads in sadness as the bloody details of Gettysburg and Vicksburg were related. And the Union officer simply pointed to the obvious: the Confederacy was losing badly, its Southern citizens punished for their ultimate disloyalty.

Occasionally, a rowdy group rolled in, much to everyone's dismay. It was easy to judge the commander by the behavior of his men, and while some seemed committed to maintaining order and discipline, others were completely lax and the subordinates knew it. During those days, Angelique kept a close eye on the children, and the doors remained locked at all times, the curtains tightly drawn as they simply waited for it to be over.

Monsieur Bourgeois despised being a prisoner in his own home, unable to control what happened around him. And Angelique was concerned for his health, the furrows on his brow growing deeper, the dark circles under his eyes indicative of the sleepless nights. He was a true Southern gentleman, a breed born of a different generation. There was an honor and grace that accompanied his heritage, a cultural way of life that he felt certain would soon be gone. For all intents and purposes, Monsieur Bourgeois was grieving, the impending loss incomprehensible.

Henry had stepped in to handle most of the responsibilities of the plantation, taking over the paperwork and overseeing the duties that his father had so easily managed for decades. He woke early to ride the fields, while Monsieur Bourgeois often stayed in bed until mid-morning or later. He checked in with Terence, who had thankfully remained with the family, even after Mr. Lincoln had proclaimed him and the rest of the slaves to be free. And he assumed the worry and anxiety, which was perhaps the greatest burden of all.

When the war indirectly came to Maison Blanche, it changed everybody and everything. And yet there was always that fear, the knowledge that the figurative cannonball was simply waiting to explode, along with the threat of a literal one, shattering what little peace remained. It was difficult. But as they were often reminded, it could get worse, especially as the days of fighting stretched on into years.

Chapter Twenty

Summer, 1864

Henry Bourgeois woke with a start. It was barely dawn, a noise from downstairs, shattering the silence. He paused to listen before going to investigate. Someone was in the house.

Slowly, he tiptoed down the stairs, heading toward the library, the place where the guns were kept. But as the sound grew louder, he followed it into the dining room instead. He moved to the doorway to see a soldier, the dark blue of his Yankee uniform in stark contrast to the lightly painted walls. As he paused to watch, an odd curiosity overtook him, and he almost chuckled, as the soldier brazenly rummaged through the walnut buffet until he located the box of silver flatware.

"Are you trying to steal my family's cutlery?" Henry asked matter-of-factly.

The soldier jumped, turning to face him, still holding the box. "Maybe."

Henry was surprised by the thief's boldness, but he slowly moved to the fireplace and reached for the poker. "I'm afraid that I can't let that happen."

The Yank felt for his gun and then registered the alarm on his face when he realized that he wasn't carrying it. He dropped the box and bolted for the front door.

Henry swiftly moved to intercept him, swinging the fireplace tool low and hard. The soldier screamed at the contact with his shin, blood immediately oozing from the wound. "Not sure about Yankee morals, but here, we don't take too kindly to people who try to take what doesn't belong to them. And we protect what's ours. You might want to relay that to your comrades, just in case any of them get a similar idea."

The soldier hobbled out the front door without uttering a word, and Henry smiled. He had managed to disarm a thief and defend his home before the rest of the family had even awakened. "Not bad for a morning's work," he said out loud.

He was sitting on the bench in the reception hall, pulling on his boots when there was a knock at the door. "What now?' he muttered to himself.

Henry was not totally surprised to see the commander. He wondered if the bandit soldier had gone to whine about his injuries, reported it as an assault, which seemed rather foolish given the circumstances, but over the long year that the Union troops had occupied the lawn of Maison Blanche, Henry had seen it all. And nothing was surprising.

"Major Roberts here on official business, sir."

Henry was taken by the formality, given the fact that the man had probably used a latrine in his front yard only moments earlier. It was a peculiar thought, and he tried not to laugh.

"State your business, Major." Henry had grown weary of the ongoing negotiations, the constant demands from each new officer who moved in for a day or two. He had no intention of accommodating this one or any others.

"Beginning today, we will be appropriating the downstairs rooms of your home for use by the Union Army. We have several sick soldiers, who cannot receive adequate care in tents. In addition, I will need a base of operations for the next two weeks." He said it as though it was the most normal request in the world, a simple appeal for the good of the nation.

"I'm afraid that I can't allow that to happen," Henry said. "There are nine of us here, including my elderly parents. There are children as well. We will not be confined to the second story of our own home. And more importantly, I will not permit you to bring disease into these premises."

"You have no choice in the matter. Federal law provides for the assumption of whatever an enemy can provide for the sustenance and safety of the army."

"But this is the Confederacy. Your federal law doesn't apply here." Henry tightened his grip on the tool he still held.

"It most certainly does. For all practical purposes, your land is occupied. I thought you realized that."

Henry would not be defeated. "Hardly. Can we defer this for a few days, just to prepare?"

The major shook his head. "I'm afraid not. The men need care now."

And almost by instinct, Henry raised the metal rod ever so slightly.

In an instant, the major had drawn his gun. Henry took two steps back just as the sound of the pistol firing echoed through the house. He stumbled, before falling, blood from his thigh flowing out of the wound and onto the Oriental rug.

The room was spinning as Henry fell. And within seconds, the members of the family were by his side just in time to hear the major loudly pronounce, "no boundaries, no rules, no exceptions, no mercy."

Chapter Twenty-one

Angelique heard the ungodly sound and sprang to her feet. With a growing sense of urgency, she bound down the stairs. The scene seemed surreal as though she was reliving some unsettling memory. And for a moment, she could see Jean Paul, a similar gunshot wound in his thigh, that same look of pain on his face. She pushed the image out of her thoughts, willing herself to be strong.

"Henry," Justine cried. "How did this happen?"

He reached for her and as she leaned in close, he shared the events of the previous hour, starting with the silverware thief.

Angelique curled her hands into tight fists, disappearing into the pantry in search of strips of muslin and a bottle of whiskey. Both would be useful

By the time Monsieur Bourgeois had shuffled into the room, there was a flurry of activity. He stood in silence, trying to make sense of what had happened, his addled mind unable to process it. "You alright, son?" he finally asked, staring at the soldiers still positioned in the open doorway.

"Will be, Father. Just a little accident." There was no point in relating the truth. Henry was grateful for the quick thinking of all present, since he appeared to no longer be hemorrhaging. But his leg was throbbing, and he was suddenly tired, a combination of the stress and blood loss, no doubt. He closed his eyes.

Andrew pointed to the major. "Instruct two of your men to help carry him upstairs."

But the commander stood stone silent the defiance in his eyes. Andrew took one step forward. "This is your doing. First, you tell a man that you are taking over his home, and then, to add insult to injury, you shoot him? You have superiors, sir, and I wonder how they would respond to news of your actions?"

Andrew was bluffing. He knew that the Union generals would view this as a non-incident, but his stint with the Navy had taught him that the chain of command was a strong tie that binds. The threat of having ones leadership questioned could potentially derail a military career.

"He threatened me. Threatened me," the major said and repeating it for emphasis. "Besides,
 I doubt that this would garner much interest."

"A fireplace tool is no match for a pistol, not now, not ever," Andrew said. "And you know it." He then pointed to the two men who stood with the major. "You and you. Help." And much to his surprise, they moved forward to carry Henry up the winding staircase into his bedroom.

The major turned on his heels. "We will be bringing the sick in within the hour."

By the time Henry was safely in his bed, and Justine had wiped the blood from his leg, his anger had returned. "How dare they assume that they have the right to invade our home in this way?" His eyes were frantic as he looked from his wife to Andrew and then to Angelique.

"How dare they assume they have the right to shoot you?" Andrew asked.

Henry winced, the pain evident. "Could be worse. He could have aimed a little higher."

"You must rest now," Justine warned.

He pushed her aside. "We must have a plan in place. We have to know how we will defend ourselves."

Andrew cleared his throat. "I'm not sure that we can, Henry. This major has an entire army at his disposal. We have three woman, an old man, me, and you, who, I might add, is currently injured. I say bide our time and pray that it will be over soon and that they will move on to bigger battles."

"And if we are to become a Yankee hospital?"

"Well, maybe their doctor will look at your leg, for starters. But other than that, it, too, becomes a situation out of our control."

Henry turned his head. "Will you go to the library and remove the guns. Bring them here for safekeeping. And Angelique?"

"Yes?"

"Will you make sure that the silverware is out of the dining room? Get Jubilee to help. Momma's tea set is in there, too. Damn Yankees will rob us blind if we aren't careful."

Both Andrew and Angelique set about the tasks, but neither was surprised to discover the soldiers were already moving furniture, dismantling many of the fine antiques to make way for the Union patients.

"They certainly waste no time," Angelique remarked.

"It is a hallmark of the North, my dear. Quiet efficiency. Unfortunately, for us."

Chapter Twenty-two

Within a week, life had changed for everyone at Masion Blanche. There was a frenzy of activity on the lower level, the incessant sound of moaning men, interrupted with occasional bouts of coughing. Angelique had heard of such makeshift hospital wards as a young woman, when various epidemics had ravaged New Orleans. She knew that efforts to contain the disease, usually made for a place where the sickness was concentrated and ultimately, more deadly.

She had tiptoed down the stairs one day on her way to the kitchen when she overheard the doctor giving his report to the major. "Measles."

And as the word struck fear in her heart, she rushed toward the fields, searching for the children, who were with Jubilee.

"You must stay away from the house," she announced, breathless from running.

They all looked at her with a quiet curiosity until Aida, always the spokesman for the group, asked the inevitable question. "Why?"

"There's measles among the soldiers. If you are there, you may get it. And it can be very serious."

Jubliee nodded. "I have seen it when I was a child. It can be mild for some people, but kill others."

Aimee's eyes grew wide. "What shall we do, Momma?"

Angelique turned to Jubilee. "Can you take them? I know that your cabin in small, but they can sleep on the floor. I will make sure that they have bedding and some books, of course. And I will advise cook that you will be getting food for them."

"Of course they can stay with me. It will be like a grand adventure won't it?"

Aida eyed her mother suspiciously. "I am not so sure how much fun it will be."

"Right now, my priority is keeping you safe," Angelique replied.

Franklin stepped forward. "We will do whatever we must do, Momma. Of course, we want to be protected."

Angelique smiled. She had come to depend on Franklin's calm presence, his ability to tame his sisters and make even the most bizarre requests seem like their idea.

"Thank you, Franklin."

She had just returned from moving clothes and bedding into Jubilee's tiny shack, and had even delivered the surprise book, *Children Studying Practical Astronomy*, for them to read. She was imagining a quiet moment in her favorite rocker, when Justine met her in the hall.

"Please. I need your help."

Angelique raised her eyebrows. "Mine?" she asked. There was an implied understanding between the two women, to avoid contact at all costs. The history between them continued to cloud the present, and no amount of time could heal the rift. But if her mother had taught her anything, it was that kindness matters, and so she put aside her feelings, her resentment over the petty differences and followed Justine into their bedroom.

Henry was moaning, the beads of sweat forming on his brow. He writhed in pain. "He's getting worse."

Angelique moved to his side. "Have you looked at the wound?"

Justine shook her head. "Then, let's do that."

Both women winced at the sight of Henry's leg, red and swollen, with a thick white liquid oozing from the side of the bandage.

"It looks like it isn't healing."

Justine nodded, and then swallowed hard. "But there is more."

"More?"

"Come with me."

They entered the adjacent bedroom where Monsieur Bourgeois and his wife lay side by side in the ornately carved canopied bed. The room was dark, light obscured by the curtains drawn tight. It was oppressively warm. Madame Bourgeois began to cough and seemed unable to stop until Justine offered her a sip of water. She opened her eyes for a moment before falling back upon the pillow. Monsieur Bourgeois sported a tiny rash on his left cheek.

"What is it?" Angelique asked.

Justine shrugged her shoulders. "I don't know."

Angelique took a deep breath. She feared that the sickness downstairs had made its way to them. "I am going to see if the Yankee doctor will examine them."

By the time she had reached the bottom step, Angelique had her speech already firmly in mind. She would march into the major's office and calmly, yet firmly, ask to speak with the doctor, at which point she would describe what she had observed and hope he would agree to have a look.

But the major was not in the mood to be accommodating, and after his third refusal, she simply turned on her heels and marched into what used to be the front parlor, searching for the doctor among the ailing soldiers.

"Sir," she said, taking care that her wide hoop skirt didn't brush up against any of the men.

He looked up at her, his eyes tired, his white shirt stained with the bodily fluids of so many infirmed men. "Yes?"

She used the only weapon at her disposal, her charm, as she smiled sweetly, batting her eyes in his direction. "I do hate to trouble you, knowing the responsibility that you hold here with the men, but I was wondering if I might impose upon you for just a brief moment. The son of the owner of this house is ill, unfortunately shot by your overzealous major. He seems to be getting worse, and I was hoping that you might look at the wound."

He listened, but said nothing. Angelique continued. "And his parents seem to be doing poorly today. Coughing. Monsieur has a rash. It would be ever so kind of you if you could peep in on them as well. I mean, we have no other recourse being as though we are, for all practical purposes occupied."

She tilted her head and looked at him with anticipation.

For a moment, she expected for him to laugh at her, but he nodded. "Take me to them, but it must be quick."

She led him to the stairs, passing the major's office. He was shuffling papers, but looked up just in time to see Angelique, doctor in tow, wave a greeting.

"Wound may or may not heal," the doctor pronounced. "The bullet should come out, but that might make it worse. I don't see gangrene, but keep an eye on it. You start to see a color change and the leg will have to come off or he will die."

"His parents have the measles, just like my men. At their age, it is likely that they will develop complications, pneumonia, in all probability. Keep them comfortable and hope it ends quickly."

Justine burst into tears, while Angelique stood silent, struck by the emotional detachment that the doctor had to have developed over so many years of witnessing the cruelties of war.

This terrible conflict will leave scars, Angelique thought, deep wounds on the nation and on us as individuals. Someday, we will pick up the pieces, resume the habits of daily living. And hopefully, we won't forget what it is to experience joy.

Chapter Twenty-three

Angelique stood at the window watching the sunrise. The night had been a long one, having spent part of it sitting with Henry, and the remainder with Monsieur and Madame Bourgeois. The morning had come, bringing with it the same worries and concerns that had left her exhausted the day before. But she still fought them because she had no choice, no option to surrender. In some ways, that's what real bravery, true courage, was all about, she thought. But she also knew that it was what changed a person as one day rolled into the next until time no longer had any real meaning. And she wondered if it still had the magical ability to fix things, the way it once did.

Andrew came in to kiss her goodbye before heading out to the fields with Franklin. She was proud of her husband and son, the way they had stepped up to take over the jobs that Henry was unable to do. Fortunately, the cotton and vegetables had been planted in the late spring, and much of what was required mostly involved overseeing. Disease and pests were the biggest threats, not counting the Yankees who spied the food crops like a coyote lying in wait for a fawn. Terence was vigilant, often catching problems that Andrew would have never noticed until it was too late. And Franklin did a good job of protecting the animals, moving them from place to place with such quiet regularity that the

Union soldiers simply grew tired of the game of hide and seek, settling on whatever fare the army provided.

She entered the bedroom where Henry lay, pale and feverish. Justine sat in a chair nearby, her eyes hollow from worry.

Two days earlier, Angelique had visited the doctor once more, asking to borrow medical tools. When he looked confused, she explained that if the bullet in Henry's leg needed to be removed, she and Justine would just have to do it. He had laughed at their foolhardiness, explaining the grave risk they were willing to take. But when he saw that she was serious, he simply surrendered, performing the surgery on a makeshift table that Franklin and Andrew had put together and placed near the bed. Justine had fed Henry the rest of the whiskey, a poor substitute for anesthesia, and his screams could be heard for miles. But in the end, both woman thanked the doctor kindly and remarked that not all Yankees were bad Yankees.

"Did you sleep?" Angelique whispered.

"No. Not possible with the sick ones to attend to. Did you?"

"No. For the same reason."

"Once we get Henry's dressing changed, you should go into the children's room and rest for a bit. I'll take care of things. Then, you can do the same for me. We are never going to survive if we don't work together."

Justine nodded.

Angelique went to work washing the wound with soap, carefully rinsing away the poison that oozed from where the bullet had entered his thigh. She smeared it with fresh honey, then sealed it with egg white, a trick she had learned from Jubilee when Aimee had burned her arm so long ago. She placed a pillow under his leg to elevate it. "Let's leave the bandage off for a few hours. I think the air might do some good."

Justine moved to the washstand. She poured water from the pitcher into a bowl and then dipped a rag into it before placing the cool compress on Henry's sweaty brow. "He's still pretty warm."

"Will be until the fever breaks. I'll keep an eye on him. Now you go rest."

Justine paused at the door. "Thank you. I don't know how I would have made it through these days without your help, Angelique. I am afraid that I misjudged you terribly."

"It won't be the first time. Sometimes people make you prove what is in your heart."

Justine smiled as though pondering that idea. "I suppose that you are right. But still, I am grateful to you. Wake me if you need me."

Angelique entered the room where the old couple lay, their breathing simultaneous, yet labored. There was a heavy rattling noise coming from Monsieur Bourgeois, deep within his chest. She wondered if this is what death sounded like, as though the bones themselves were signaling for St. Peter to open wide the gates of heaven. Moving to the edge of the bed, she took his hand in hers, trying to remember the prayers for the sick that the nuns had taught her during her days in the convent school. But in the end, she simply told God what she was feeling, and asked for His infinite mercy on the kind couple, who had saved her not once, but twice. She owed them a debt of gratitude that would never be repaid.

And so, she waited and watched. At times, she held Madame Bourgeois, bony hand, as she hummed a soft tune her mother often sung at bedtime. Within the hour, they had been called home, together in death as they had been in life, their pain and suffering ended.

Chapter Twenty-four

It took Terence, and the remaining field hands three days to dig a grave large enough to accommodate two. Andrew and Franklin assumed the task of building the caskets, which were nothing more than simple boxes, partially constructed from Madame Bourgeois' rosewood hope chest. It seemed befitting, Justine had said, when questioned about the scarcity of wood since it symbolized their union more than anything else on the plantation.

On the morning of the funeral, Jubilee and the girls gathered wild flowers. Henry had regained consciousness. It was a miracle, they all proclaimed. But he was faced with the task of laying his parents to rest, a monumental feat for even someone in good health. The men bore him down the stairs on a chair like an Egyptian Pharaoh. And he laughed as he commented that his father would have enjoyed calling him "Your Majesty" before bowing low.

Like so many such occasions in South Louisiana, steeped so heavily in the culture, this was different. There was a joy which punctuated the sadness, as it was a celebration of two lives well- lived as much as it was mourning a loss. And the most powerful force on earth, love, made it possible.

Andrew and Franklin, unaccustomed to the Southern ritual of death, followed along as best they could. Father Hebert arrived on horseback, incense and holy water in hand, to perform the Catholic Rite of Burial, a long litany of prayers that he recited loudly in Latin, with a sprinkling of French for good measure. And when it was over, they all joined hands to sing "Amazing Grace," most certainly a protestant prayer, but Monsieur Bourgeois' favorite.

Having lost the dining room and parlor to the Yankees, the family moved to the shade of the big oak tree, where they swapped stories, remembering the couple tenderly and conjuring up their presence so profoundly, that it was almost as though they had pulled up a chair to join in on the laughter. It was a final goodbye, a lifting of the veil that separates this place from the great beyond and a tender tribute to a devoted mother and father who possessed an indomitable spirit, a true partnership in life, close as though they truly shared one soul.

Cook brought them a pan of warm biscuits with a small dish of wild blackberries. "Been saving the last bit of flour," she said. "This seemed like a fitting use for it."

Henry thanked her and agreed. "Father sure did love your biscuits, Dolly. I think it is what he missed most about the war rations."

She nodded, obviously pleased. "I'm gonna miss them folks, Mista Henry. They was always so kind to me."

"You were important to them, Dolly. And they were always grateful for your care."

She wiped away a tear before returning to the kitchen.

Henry then suggested the singing, and everyone joined in, although mostly off key. They finished with a rousing version of "Dixie." While the others clapped to the rhythm, the twins jumped up to dance.

"You know," Henry said, "it is rumored that President Lincoln himself loves the tune and orders it played regularly."

"That is probably more of a victory cry where he is concerned than a real affinity for the song. But in any case, I think we should sing it once more in his honor," Justine said.

And again, the chorus of voices were lifted to the sky. The girls were joined by their mother as they stepped in time to the music. But as they started the second verse, Angelique felt dizzy, the world spinning around her. She was light-headed, unsteady. By the time they had reached the end of the song, she had fallen into a heap in the grass, having fainted straight away.

Chapter Twenty-five

She was dreaming.

The man walked a few feet in front of her, but it didn't take her long to recognize the rhythm of his gait, the way his shoulders moved ever so slightly, the cowlick which formed where his jet-black hair touched the base of his neck. It was Jean Paul. She could feel the anger bubbling below the surface, flowing through her heart like a tidal wave. He had done so much to her, unforgiveable things, but having taken her child was evil and contemptible, sealing his fate where she was concerned. She reached into her velvet bag and pulled out the pistol. The Countess had given it to her years ago, and although she carried it always, more out of habit than anything else, she had often wondered if she would ever feel the need to use it again. She laughed when she thought that the first and only time she had ever fired it was at her wicked husband, the one who had been dead in the eyes of the world for years. Quickening her pace, she narrowed the gap between them. She wanted to make certain that the shot would be straight and true to accomplish the task. There would be no room for misfires. He sensed her presence and turned. There was a look of recognition on his face, and he smiled. So did she, but for a different reason. She wanted for her eyes to be the last thing he saw, her words to be the last he heard. For indeed, she had appointed herself judge and jury. This was his sentence.

"I send you to the depths of hell, Jean Paul," she said before squeezing the trigger.

The first bullet struck him in the chest. He staggered, panic and confusion in his eyes. She aimed to the right and fired once more. He fell.

Had she been able to show mercy, she might have held his hand as he slipped from this existence into the next. But even though she had once cared deeply for him, compassion was impossible. Not now. And so, she simply watched and waited until he took his last breath. He was, in many ways, like a cat with nine lives, and this time she had to be sure that he was gone, to know that he would no longer revisit her life as he had so many times before. When he had departed this world, she exhaled, the relief washing over her with a force that made her shake uncontrollably, the power of the catharsis bringing tears to her eyes. But as she wiped them away, she stood straight and tall. "Done," she simply said, as she turned on her heels and walked away.

"Angelique," Andrew whispered. He patted her hand and caressed her cheek. "Wake up."

Her eyes fluttered, and she squinted in the bright light of the sun. "What happened?"

"You fainted, a result of exhaustion, no doubt."

She tried to get up, but he held her back. "You must rest now."

"Here?" she asked, suddenly aware that she lay in the yard.

"No, of course not. Let me help you." He scooped her up in his strong arms as he carried her into the house and up the stairs. Gently, he placed her on the bed.

"Andrew," she said. "I had the strangest dream."

"I am not surprised, given your state. Want to tell me about it?"

"I killed Jean Paul."

He kissed her cheek. "His actions weigh heavily on your mind, no doubt."

"I don't want to think of him, remember all that he has done to me, to our family, but I must."

"You must?"

"So much pain and heartache because of him."

"True. And I wouldn't mind taking a shot at him myself. But you are the ultimate victor. You weren't stuck in the burning pit of misery. No, you showed a strength that inspires me each time I think of it. My beautiful, resilient wife is like no other."

Angelique smiled. "Will there ever come a time when I am able to think of him without anger and revenge in my heart?"

"Forgiveness is a gift you are not ready to give. The rage must subside before you can even consider it. Who knows? Maybe someday you will be ready, maybe not. The choice is yours, of course. And time will show you the way. Now get some rest."

She nodded, her eyelids heavy. And as she drifted off to sleep, her thoughts were of the abundance of love and its limitless ability to multiply. The dragon had been slain, at least in her mind. For now.

Chapter Twenty-six

Fall, 1864

As the months faded away, the Union soldiers recovered and the troops moved out. Thankfully, there were no replacements as Maison Blanche was finally returned to the family, still in mourning.

With the aid of a cane, Henry was able to move around, although the pain still persisted. And as he stood on the front veranda surveying the destruction to the lawn, he shook his head. The house had been equally damaged, the once stately manor looking more like an old hag than a grand lady. And he wondered where he would ever get the funds to repair it. But worse than any physical loss, the fact that the Yankee take over had brought about the demise of his beloved parents was difficult to accept, impossible to understand. Henry was a Southerner, of course, but he had no real political ties or strong opinions about the conflict. He had gladly paid another to go in his place through conscription, and didn't regret that decision one bit. The war was simply an inconvenience until it came to roost in his home, bringing with it grave consequences. His ambivalence had turned into bitterness.

"It seems like the North is hell bent on doing away with us. They come in and take over our homes, starve us with the blockade, and show no mercy or compassion in the process," he said over dinner one night. "The South didn't wage war on the United States. It just wanted to remove itself from the union, collectively pursue its own way of life. I may be a simple man, but I don't understand why there was no peaceful recourse, no manner to part ways without so much hostility."

It was a fair and legitimate observation, and Andrew, aware of his status as a Northerner, one who had indirectly served in the Union Navy, had no logical answers. "War defies all reason, robs humanity of its sanity as emotions rule and the fight for control of what each side believes is right begins," he said.

Henry nodded. "And when it is over, all of the strife and bloodshed and pain has ended, when every family has paid the price exacted for this war, then what? Can we even hope to restore the nation, and by that I mean individually and collectively, to what it once was? Can we return to what it once meant to be an American? I don't know if we will ever be one nation again, regardless of the outcome. The Yankees may bring us to our knees, break us in the process, but they can't own our souls. We are very much a fractured country."

Angelique cleared her throat. She usually left the political discussions to the men, but she had something to say this time. "We are all changed, no doubt. It has been a difficult period, a hard time to be alive. And yes, we pray that it won't last forever. But we also have to know that when peace comes, we can heal. We are going to have to pick ourselves up and move on, believing that there are joys ahead. Otherwise, we have nothing."

"You always were an idealist, Angelique," Henry said, "even as child."

"Well, this idealist has big plans for after the war."

"Really? Want to share them?" Henry asked.

"Indeed. I am going to buy Chauvin Plantation. My family and I are moving home."

Henry chuckled. "We shall see, little lady, although who am I to doubt you? If anybody can figure out a way to do it, you can."

Angelique smiled. "I will. Just you wait and see."

***

The next morning, Angelique entered the library to discover Henry rummaging through his father's massive walnut desk. Some of the drawers had been removed and were on the floor. There were stacks of papers covering the surface, an attempt, no doubt at organizing the contents. "At least the Yankees didn't ransack this," he commented. "Guess there was nothing in here of interest to them. But I did find something that might be of interest to you."

Angelique moved forward. "What's that, Henry?"

He handed her a stack of letters and pointed to a nearby chair. "Sit. Read. See for yourself."

She took the bundle. The first letter came in an envelope marked with the return address of the St. Charles Hotel. Her curiosity was piqued. She opened it and began to read.

My dear Mr. Bourgeois,

I suppose that I should address you as Alphonse, given that Marie and I are cousins, but it is a familiarity that I would not presume to take. I do regret that distance has kept us from seeing each other over the years. I hope that perhaps someday soon, I can arrange for a weekend visit. I would love to see your plantation, and my dear relative, of course. But as you can well imagine, managing a hotel of this size takes most of my time and attention.

I was happy to receive your letter regarding Mrs. Latour. Based on what you have said, it seems that the poor woman has had more than her share of grief and disappointment. And I will take great pleasure in providing a place for her to stay here at the St. Charles. Of course, your generosity makes that possible. The amount which you provided is more than enough to cover her lodging for at least two weeks. And based upon how you would like to handle it, we can arrange regular payments at the end of a four-week period since we don't know what her future plans might be. Of course, I extend to you my professional discount, along with the utmost in discretion. I can assure you that Mrs. Latour will be none the wiser as to how her room was funded. And perhaps, she will take it more kindly to think that I simply honored a family request since she doesn't know me and therefore will not feel obligated.

I will write to you from time to time, apprising you of her status and well-being. It is wonderful for you to look out for her in this way in the absence of her father, and I am certain that the Good Lord above smiles on you for your benevolence.

Sincerely,

George Wilson

Angelique sat quietly, the letter resting in her lap. She swallowed hard, but was unable to hold back the dam of tears which flowed. "I can't believe that he did this for me," she said between sobs. "And I never knew so I could properly thank him."

"I don't think he wanted you to know Angelique. There is a certain nobility, an unfathomable kindness when something is done for someone out of true compassion, not for some desire for gratitude or indebtedness. The anonymity. That's real generosity."

She wiped her eyes with the back of her hand. "Indeed it is. And I will remember his thoughtfulness all the days of my life."

Angelique was struck by the fact that we don't truly understand the nature of death until it touches someone we love. And sometimes, we don't understand the person who lived until they die.

"Here it is," Henry announced, holding up a bulging envelope.

"Found what you were looking for?"

"I did. Father's will and the deed to the plantation. Our conversation last night got me to thinking. You are right. This war won't last forever. Why can't I begin to dream of a future for Justine and me? Let's face it, I will never love the fields like my father did. Planting was in his blood, just as I think it is in yours. I have no children to inherit the place. Besides, I want more than this. And selling the plantation will give me the capital to do it."

"You would sell Maison Blanche?"

"Indeed I would. Father might have grumbled, but Mother would be secretly happy. She had quite the adventurous spirit, although I think she kept it well concealed."

Henry moved to the bookcase. He removed a big fat volume of Shakespeare's plays. He placed it on the desk and opened it wide. There, in the hollowed out pages was a hidden flask. "Good," Henry proclaimed. "The Yankees didn't find it."

He removed two small glasses from the nearby table and poured them each a good measure of brandy. "Here's to our future, Angelique, and believing that when this war ends, anything is possible."

"Anything," she repeated, downing it in one gulp.

Chapter Twenty-seven

Spring, 1865

They could hear the sound of approaching horses from inside the house. A feeling of dread swept over Angelique. "You don't think the Yankees have returned, do you?"

Andrew walked out onto the veranda. Henry stuck a pistol in the waistband of his trousers and joined him. "Help you?" he asked, as the men got within earshot.

"Got some big news," one of them yelled. "Going from house to house."

"Then, let's hear it."

"War's over, sir. General Lee surrendered yesterday in Virginia. Details came in over the telegraph this morning."

"Are you sure?"

"Yup. This war is over."

"Thanks for telling us," Henry patted Andrew on the back before calling for Justine and Angelique.

"No problem, sir," the younger man said before tipping his hat. "Y'all have a good day now."

"It is over," he announced as the women joined them. And the foursome yelled with joy, dancing in circles around the veranda.

"I had forgotten what a powerful word peace is," Angelique said as they sat in the parlor, contemplating their future.

"I have forgotten what it is like to live it," Justine said. "This war has robbed us of moments free from strife and uncertainty for a very long time."

"But we survived," Henry said, "picked up the pieces and went about daily living as best we could."

"Agreed," Angelique said. "But survival isn't even close to being happy. Merely getting by brings no joy. And now we have the freedom to live again. We cannot sit and stare at our wounds forever, always looking back at where we have been. No, we must move forward and embrace what it to come."

"And I pray that good fortune awaits us. It is a happy day," Henry said, "a happy day indeed."

Chapter Twenty-eight

Angelique was sitting at the dining room table, a prized piece of paper before her, along with pen and ink. She carefully thought of how to word the letter since her family's future rested in the balance, but she had to make her urgency clear without sounding demanding. Mr. Davidson had been the Countess' lawyer for decades and as such was in charge of her estate. He had wisely suspended Angelique's yearly stipend immediately after war was declared, sending her a letter explaining that he would hold it for safekeeping for the duration. It took her almost six months to receive his message, but she was grateful for his foresight, especially after the southern banks starting converting all of the funds they held into worthless Confederate bills. If her calculations were correct, she had five thousand dollars coming to her at a time when most people, especially those in the South, were penniless. It was that buying power that would make it possible for her to obtain Chauvin Plantation, especially since the floundering parish government would be looking for those back taxes to be paid. If all went well, she hoped to pick it up for a song and have her family moved in before the end of summer.

She had just affixed the wax seal to the envelope when Andrew came into the room. "I've been looking for you."

"And now you've found me."

"What are you doing?"

She held up the letter. "Our future. It's my request for funds to Mr. Davidson."

"It may be a little premature. I think you might want to wait a month or so before you send that."

"Really? Why? Waiting only defers hearing from him in return. And what if Chauvin comes up for sale in the meantime?"

"It is a chance we take, of course, but I suspect that it will be some time before the financial cog in the wheel begins to turn the nation."

Angelique whistled low. "That was an impressive way to put it."

"Not meant to be. We had visitors again with news to share. And in light of it, I think that recovery will be slower than we might have thought."

"News? What news?"

"President Lincoln is dead. Shot in the head by an assassin. Vice-president Johnson has assumed office, but as you can imagine, and from what I am able to determine, the nation is at unrest."

Angelique buried her head in her hands. "Is peace so short lived that we are only able to get a glimpse of it, only to have it taken away once more?"

"I pray that isn't so, but I can't imagine that this would incite another war. The man responsible was a rebel sympathizer, but born and raised in the North. I can't see this being blamed on anything more than a crazed zealot with an opportunity to exact his revenge on the President."

"And until Lincoln is laid to rest, the country will be unsettled, which means the banks and the mail."

"Well, yes, and the people, of course."

"Of course. So we will wait."

"We will wait."

Aida and Aimee entered, breathless from running. "Come quickly. You have to see what Franklin did," they said, in unison.

Angelique and Andrew followed their daughters out the house and into the barn. There stood Franklin, his clothes bloodied, his shirt torn. He smiled broadly as he held the tiny calf.

"Look," he said. "Isn't he swell?"

Henry shook his head. "This boy of yours is a miracle worker."

"Milk cow here got herself in a bind with a breech birth. I tried everything and thought I was going to have to put her down until Franklin showed up. Got himself right in the thick of things and delivered that calf when I certainly couldn't."

"Well done, son," Andrew said, "I'm proud of you."

"He's got the healing gift, Angelique," Henry said. "I have seen him with the animals, fixing their hurts. Getting them to eat when they are sick. He is special."

Franklin moved the calf closer to its mother, carefully guiding it until it latched onto a teat and began to nurse. "There you go," he whispered, petting the cow on the back of the neck.

Henry walked over to Franklin and put his arm around the boy. "The calf is yours."

"Really?" Franklin asked.

"It is. And I only hope that someday he is able to father an entire herd at Chauvin."

"I will name him Francis."

Angelique smiled. "After the patron saint of the animals? To father a herd? Wouldn't that be lovely? And that makes today an important one for us, right? It's our beginning. The bad news often comes, but sometimes, it is followed by the good." She winked at Henry and Andrew before addressing the calf. "Welcome to our family, Francis."

Chapter Twenty-nine

Summer, 1865

Just because a truce is declared and peace is proclaimed doesn't make it so. War is a means to an end, but sometimes, it is just a beginning. Over the months that followed the Southern surrender, conditions only grew worse. The economy was shattered, supplies limited. And social upheaval, combined with political posturing only made the situation more difficult for a land devastated by battles fought so close to home.

Angelique tried to remember that patience was paramount, but she had never been much of a patient woman, even under conditions more favorable than these. She had mailed the letter to Mr. Davidson two months ago and had hoped for a reply within a few weeks. As time stretched on, she began to wonder if he had even received her plea, and with no way of knowing for sure, decided to give it another week before writing him again. So three days later, when Andrew returned from town, waving an envelope, she breathed a sigh of relief and prayed for good news.

She carefully read the letter and then, after pausing for good measure, read it again.

"Well?" Andrew asked. She passed it to him.

"Goodness, Angelique. This is amazing, even better than we had hoped for."

She nodded. "I think I am in a state of disbelief. Not only is my money from the Countess safe, but it has grown significantly thanks to Mr. Davidson's wise investment. And once he can locate a solvent bank, he will send the funds for transfer. In fact, he even offered to make the trip here himself to be certain that they were not lost or stolen by some unscrupulous banker."

"He was exceedingly loyal to the Countess, and a shrewd lawyer. He understands what could happen and is prepared to prevent that."

"And were you able to find out anything about Chauvin? I would assume properties to be auctioned would be listed in some public forum like the court house."

"I checked there, even asked the clerk. I was glad that I did because it seems that they store such records behind the counter. Rather secretive. It seems a little underhanded to me, a practice meant to keep folks away from the buying process."

"My smart husband. I am so grateful. And?"

"Chauvin Plantation is scheduled for auction three weeks from Tuesday."

Angelique clapped her hands. "It seems like a dream, Andrew. I am so happy."

He cleared his throat. "There is more."

"I'm listening."

"I wasn't the only one inquiring about property. It seems that there are several Northerners here hoping to profit from the misery of so many Southern land owners."

Angelique's eyes widened. "Really?"

"One of the men at the post office called them carpetbaggers. And while some are open to their presence because of the need for Northern capital, others, view them with suspicion."

"As well they should. So what you are telling me is that one or more of these Yankees might have their sights set on Chauvin."

"It is a possibility, one we must be prepared for."

She nodded. "Then, I think we should send Mr. Davidson a telegraph informing him of our plans. And we should probably visit a few banks with this letter to see if we can be given a line of credit on auction day."

"That sounds like a reasonable plan. We will do that tomorrow. But Angelique...."

"Yes?"

"I don't want for you to be upset if this doesn't work out the way you have imagined it in your mind. Lots of things can go wrong. And even if you are able to buy the place, you have a long road ahead to bring it back to what it once was. It isn't going to be easy."

She moved to hug Andrew. "I know. After so much that has happened to us, so many disappointments, I have to believe that this is what is meant to be. I want a place for our children to live and grow, a place that feels like home. Chauvin can provide us with that. I must have faith."

"And I only want to see you happy. I pray that you are right. Truly, I do."

Chapter Thirty

Jean Paul was hauling a load of wood into the shed when he heard the first cries. He thought perhaps he had imagined it until he heard it again, more urgent this time. It sounded like it came from the alley behind the rectory, a seldom-traveled path connecting two streets. Kids sometimes played there and once, a cat had a litter of kittens under a scraggily bush that had miraculously sprung between the cobblestones. Otherwise, it was a place of quiet and calm. He ran in the direction of the noise.

A group of teenage boys had an elderly man on the ground. One held his arms, while another rummaged through his pockets. When the boy withdrew a pocket watch, the gold chain sparkling in the sunlight, the others cheered. "What else?" one asked. But before he could answer, Jean Paul appeared, wielding the ax he had used moments earlier to chop wood into neat logs.

"What do you boys think you are doing?" he yelled.

And with fear in their eyes, they dispersed, running in different directions.

The boy with the watch, dropped it only a few feet from where the old man lay.

"Are you alright?" Jean Paul asked, bending near the man. "Do you need a doctor?"

The man shook his head. "No, no. I will be fine. Just a little shaken up, is all, although I can't imagine what might have happened had you not come along."

Jean Paul extended his hand, helping the man to a sitting position. He moved to retrieve the watch, "And I think this belongs to you."

The old man smiled. "I am mighty grateful. Sentimental attachment to the watch."

"Happy that I was in the right place at the right time. Now, can I get you home?"

"I'd be obliged. I only live around the corner. That won't be too far out of your way, will it?"

Jean Paul shook his head. "Not at all."

They had safely reached the old man's door. "Would you like to come in? I can make you a cup of tea. I think I might have a bit of hidden whiskey if you'd prefer that."

"No sir, thank you kindly. I'll just be on my way."

The man extended his hand. "I am Jonathan Fletcher. And you are?"

"Nobody, sir. Truly, I am nobody." And with that, Jean Paul tipped his hat and disappeared into the dim light of early evening, a smile of satisfaction on his face.

Chapter Thirty-one

Angelique was pacing the floor and becoming more and more anxious with each step.

"How much time?" she asked Andrew.

He had long since broken himself of the habit of reaching for his pocket watch and instead looked at the clock on the mantle. "We leave in about forty-five minutes."

She took a deep breath. "You are going to do the bidding."

He furrowed his brow. "Are you sure? This is your dream, your money. I think it should be your call."

"I know how these fine Southern gentlemen work, Andrew. They may claim to play fair, but the auctioneer would simply ignore my bids and move on to the men in the crowd. You must do it."

He nodded. "But we agree on a cap, the highest amount we will bid, right?"

"Yes."

"And if we win, the property is to be deeded to you."

"I would love that, of course, but you forget that we live in a state that isn't as progressive as we'd like it to be. I can only own and manage property if you are incapacitated, which clearly you are not."

Andrew scratched his head. "Seems unfair. I guess I hadn't even considered it to be any other way, having never been in this situation before."

"It is how Jean Paul was able to sell Chauvin to begin with, Andrew. Sometimes, it seems like the black folks aren't the only ones fighting for rights."

"I suppose so. And know I will do my best to make sure that it goes in our favor today."

"That's all I can ask for."

Angelique donned her best bonnet and extended her hand. "Let's go and buy ourselves a plantation."

When they arrived, they were surprised to see at least a dozen men milling around, the sound of their idle chatter filling the air. In the months since Angelique and Andrew had last visited Chauvin, it seemed to fall into even worse disrepair, a sad and neglected version of its former self. Seeing its deplorable state only strengthened Angelique's resolve. "Good luck," she whispered to Andrew as he took his place in the front of the pack.

The auctioneer raised his hand and cleared his throat. "By order of the court, State of Louisiana, St. Charles Parish, this property known as Chauvin Plantation is to be sold to the highest bidder. All contents therein will be deeded along with the house, land, outbuildings and equipment. Sale will be deemed as final at the conclusion of this absolute auction. Payment due in full in United States currency. Do you have questions before we proceed?"

There was a deafening silence. Angelique held her breath.

"Do I have an opening bid of fifty dollars?"

Several hands went up.

"Do I hear one hundred?"

Hands were raised.

"Who will make it two?"

"Now three?"

"One thousand," came a bid from a well-dressed man to Andrew's right. There was a low murmur among the crowd. A few of the men shook their heads.

Angelique struggled to keep her composure. Andrew had not yet bid.

"Do I hear eleven hundred?"

Andrew raised his hand.

The man smiled. "Twelve."

"Thirteen," Andrew said, staring straight ahead.

"Thirteen fifty," the man said.

"Fourteen," Andrew responded.

The crowd watched wordlessly as the two men battled it out, fifty dollar increments at a time. By the time the bidding reached eighteen hundred, Angelique thought that she was going to faint. They had agreed that they would not exceed two thousand, figuring nobody with deeper pockets would have any interest in her family home.

The man rubbed his brow. "Two thousand," he called.

Andrew was silent.

"I have a bid of two thousand. Going once, going twice..."

Two thousand one hundred," Andrew said.

The man threw his fancy hat on the ground and cursed under his breath.

"Two thousand one hundred going once, two thousand one hundred going twice. Sold for two thousand one hundred dollars."

Angelique ran to Andrew, throwing herself in his arms. "You did it. I can't believe it's ours."

"Yours, darling. It's yours. Congratulations. May this place bring you the peace that you seek as we make a new life for our family."

"It will. I just know it will," she said. "Thank you for once again being my hero."

"Always happy to oblige, ma'am," he said, tipping his hat and kissing her lightly on the cheek.

Chapter Thirty-two

There had been a steady stream of visitors to Maison Blanche once it officially was offered for sale. Some, Henry figured were simply curious, seizing the opportunity to get a look inside of the grand plantation home. Others, like the carpetbaggers, were hoping that they would be able to scoop it up for a bargain price, underestimating Henry's need to sell.

"It is a bad time to be doing this," he had remarked to Andrew as he joined him on the veranda. "I suppose if I was a patient man, I would wait until the economic recovery was complete. Might mean a big difference in the amount I am able to fetch for the place."

"Can't say that I disagree," Andrew said, "although I have come to believe that life is short and deferring a dream makes little to no sense. Besides, if you choose to buy somewhere else, in the city perhaps, that same bit of fiscal logic will work in your favor."

"That's true. And when are you and Angelique planning the move to Chauvin?"

"At the end of the week, we hope. It hasn't been easy to return the place to livable condition. The previous owners not only let it fall into disrepair, they managed to leave a trail of filth. I suppose they were angry at having lost the place and they exacted their revenge on whomever would assume ownership. But Angelique has been working tirelessly to get it ready."

"And are the children excited?"

"They are, especially Franklin, who will have a menagerie firmly in place before we know it. Starting with Francis."

"He has already begged a few eggs, keeping a watchful eye on the hatchlings. He is going to have a full coop by the end of the month."

Andrew laughed. "The boy is certainly resourceful."

"I can imagine that it will mean so much to Angelique to have the girls grow up in the same place that she did."

"Indeed. Aida and Aimee think the big house is much like a castle. Since they fancy themselves to be fairy princesses, it works out well."

Henry chuckled. "Well, if you will excuse me, I have some paperwork to do."

"And I will sit out here just a moment longer. Angelique will have a list of things for me to accomplish once she finds me."

Andrew, deep in thought, didn't notice the stranger as he walked up the worn path. It was only when he heard his footsteps on the stairs, did he look up. It took him a moment to determine why the man looked familiar and then he remembered. The auction. Like so many others, the Yankee carpetbagger had come to see if he could scavenge through the remaining pieces of property in the area and based on the desperation of the owners, make a good investment in the process.

"Good afternoon," Andrew said when the man had reached the veranda.

The man adjusted his fancy tie and Andrew wondered if his attire was meant to display his wealth or if it was simply an illusion. For all he knew, the man might have been an agent sent to buy on behalf of his employers with strict instructions to adhere to a prescribed budget.

"You," the man said.

"Me," Andrew acknowledged.

"Here to buy?"

"Perhaps. This is a fine home with profitable fields. It would be a good investment for me and my backers of course. You can never have too many plantations, you know." Andrew was having fun, toying with the man. This was one instance when his Northern accent could be used to his advantage.

"Where you from?" the man asked.

"Baltimore."

"What you going to do with the rundown place you bought last week?"

"Fix it up, live in it a bit. Sell it down the line. My wife is from the area and wanted a place. It will be a nice little project for her."

The man nodded. The explanation was plausible. "Put your bid in for this one yet?"

"Gave it to the owner just now."

"Want to share?"

"Wouldn't be very good business on my part now, would it?"

"Guess not."

"I will simply tell you that if this is the place you want, you need to go at least ten percent above the asking price. Otherwise, it is going to be mine."

The man furrowed his brow as though calculating the numbers in his mind.

Andrew rose and headed down the stairs. He went to the barn and fetched a horse, which he mounted. If he was to play a part, he just as soon, see it through to the end. Slowly, he rode away, waving to the man, who still stood on the veranda.

An hour later when he returned to Maison Blanche, Henry and Justine were in the parlor, toasting with the last bit of brandy hidden in the Shakespeare book.

"Come and join us," Henry called. "We are having a little celebration."

"And what are you celebrating?"

"We have sold the plantation, at a price well above what we hoped to get. For the first time, in a very long time, fortune has smiled on us."

"Congratulations," Andrew said, raising his glass. "Here's to new beginnings for all of us."

Chapter Thirty-three

"You wanted to see me, Miss Angelique?" Jubilee asked as she entered the library.

Angelique was going through the many books on the shelves, stopping to open one here and there before placing it in a stack on the floor. "Henry has allowed me to take whatever I want to Chauvin. The children will have a never-ending supply of reading material."

"Mighty generous of him. Did you need my help?"

"No, sorry, I got distracted. I have so much on my mind with the move, which is what I wanted to talk to you about."

Angelique reached for a fat envelope that rested on a nearby table and handed it to Jubilee.

"What's this?"

"Your back pay, of course. When I think of the years you stayed with us, your devotion to the children never wavering for a promissory note you only hoped would someday be good, I am overwhelmed and grateful."

"You took a chance on me when I desperately needed a job. And you protected me wherever the road took us. We weathered some mighty difficult times together, Miss Angelique. And I am proud to have been a part of your family."

"You still are, of course. But this money should give you the means to pursue whatever you choose in the future. Perhaps you might want to attend college? Open a school of your own someday? It has been a long time since you have seen your family. I am certain that they miss you, worry about you. With the war over, returning North should be much less difficult. Regardless, I wish you the very best in whatever path you take."

Jubilee sighed. "Does this mean that you are firing me?"

Angelique laughed. "No, of course not! I would never do that, but the girls are no longer babies in need of a nanny. I suspect that the school will reopen soon. Everything changes with time, including people and their situations. And I can imagine that you still have dreams of your own to chase."

Jubilee nodded. "Sometimes those dreams can change, Miss Angelique. Sometimes, everything you thought you didn't want turns out to be the very thing that makes you happy."

"I don't understand."

"I know that I said I never wanted a man, and I thought that was my truth, but then, I met Terence."

Angelique smiled. "I have watched you two in the quiet moments. It was just a matter of time."

"We are to be married. And for now, we may just have to jump the broomstick, as Terence calls it, but I want a real wedding, one that is recognized in the eyes of the law."

"And you should have that. I would be pleased for you to be married at Chauvin, although it isn't yet restored. But it is my home and as such, will always be open to you and Terence."

Jubilee's eyes filled with tears. "I'd be proud to say my vows there, Miss Angelique."

"Then, we will plan it. Any idea of where you will go afterwards? Terence is free. Maison Blanche is being sold, so even if he wanted to remain here, it might be difficult. You two now have a little money and a whole world of possibilities."

"We've talked about that, too. It sounds all well and good to talk about the future as though we can go off and become rich folks. But doors that were closed for us because of the color of our skin aren't going to suddenly open because the war has ended. Besides, Terence knows nothing of life outside the plantation."

Angelique sighed. "That makes me sad, but I suppose that you are right, of course. Then what do you want to do?"

"Something I never thought possible."

"Which is?"

"Farm the land. I swore I would never return to the life I left behind when I said goodbye to my momma. I saw no value in crop planting or taking care of the animals. Maybe it is Terence or maybe it is being here, but I want to do it, to have a little bit of earth that belongs to us that we can make our own."

Angelique smiled. "What if ya'll came with us to Chauvin? I am going to need so much help getting the fields back to being profitable. Nobody knows how to bring about a harvest like Terence does. I could hire him to be my overseer. There is the cottage that comes with the position that you two could fix up to your liking. And if all goes well, when the first cane crop goes to market, I will give you two acres for your homestead as a bonus."

"You would do that for us?"

"For you? Jubilee, it would be an answer to prayer for me."

"And I don't even have to ask Terence because I know that he will agree."

"Then, it's settled. Did you ever think that we would have been here two years ago?"

"No ma'am, I didn't. And I am mighty grateful for the blessings."

Chapter Thirty-four

Angelique hated goodbyes, the way they always felt so final.

"We'll only be down the road," she said to Henry and Justine. "I expect regular visits until you two move to Savannah."

Henry smiled, but Angelique could see the emotion in his eyes, the words he couldn't say. "Andrew, you have been like a brother to me. Don't know how I would have made it through some of those war days without you."

"You would have done just fine. We certainly wouldn't have survived without you. Goodness, your family gave us a home when we had none. There is no way to repay that or express our gratitude."

Henry shook his head, "No need." He turned to embrace Angelique, "My childhood friend. You certainly are grown up."

"Thank you for all that you have done for us, Henry."

Justine moved forward to take Angelique's hand. "I am sorry that we got off to such a bad start and that I was so pig-headed. Can you ever forgive me?"

"Nothing to forgive, Justine. We wiped that slate clean a long time ago."

The children were already in the wagon, anxious to be off on their new adventure. But Angelique lingered, remembering, for just a moment the lessons written upon her soul during her time at Maison Blanche. And she wondered if she would miss the person she had been while there because moving on meant that she would never be the same again.

As Andrew guided the horses down the driveway and they waved their farewells, Angelique cried. And for the life of her, she couldn't decide if they were tears of sadness or tears of joy, but she set her sights on the road ahead and the future that awaited.

The trip, which only took fifteen minutes by horseback was an hour in the wagon. The children were restless and Angelique rubbed her aching back. But when Chauvin Plantation came into sight, it took her breath away. "I'm home," she whispered to the wind.

Aida, Aimee, and Franklin were running through the yard, the sound of their giggles muffled by the thicket of trees. Andrew moved to help Angelique from the wagon. Arm-in-arm they slowly walked up the steps. He paused outside the front door. "Let's do this right," he said, gathering her in his arms to carry her over the threshold. The twins began to call, "Mommy, Mommy, look," and Angelique turned just in time to see a blue butterfly hovering nearby.

"We have not seen one in so long," she whispered to Andrew. "Surely, it is a sign, a mark of the peace that is to come, the calm and tranquility being restored to our family."

"There is something incredibly hopeful about this day, isn't there?"

And Angelique thought of all that had happened, all that they had endured. Perhaps like the butterfly, we crawl into a crysalis of sadness just to survive until time makes it possible to emerge and face the future. "Indeed," she said. "It is magical, a brand new start."

Chapter Thirty-five

The priest entered the kitchen, startling the staff. He rarely ventured into this part of the rectory, but judging by the look of urgency on his face, he had something important on his mind.

"Father? May I get you something?" the cook asked.

He shook his head. "No, I am trying to gather everyone. We will meet in my office in fifteen minutes."

When the group had assembled, he addressed them from behind his desk. "The war has had an impact on all facets of life, including, sadly, the service of our Lord. Our congregation has grown smaller with each passing year, and now, the decision has been made to merge St. Luke's with the larger and more viable St. Francis. At least for now."

No one spoke. The head housekeeper wrung her hands as she stared at the floor. She had worked at this church for close to thirty years. Priests had come and gone, but her presence had been constant. She wondered what was to become of her.

"Most of you will be offered employment at St. Francis. I understand that it will be an adjustment, but we go where God leads us, stepping out, as always, in faith."

The collective sigh of relief was audible. In a country ravaged by war, a lost job was an additional tragedy.

"And you, Father?" the cook asked. "Will you be going too?"

He cleared his throat and swallowed hard. "I am afraid not. My hour has come, and the decision has been made for me to retire. I will still serve, minister to the sick and infirm, for example, but I will no longer be at the helm of a church."

One of the maids began to cry, and the others whispered among themselves.

"I will let you get back to your duties," he said. "We have the next thirty days to prepare for the transition. There will be much to do. Remember, God's will, not ours, always."

Jean Paul stood in the back of the room, listening, trying to process all that he had heard. Mostly, he wondered what his fate might be. And the priest, sensing his concerns, called out to him.

"Stay for a while, my son," he said, pointing to a straight back chair.

And Jean Paul obeyed. "You have been with us for close to three years now, and I have witnessed your steadfast loyalty to the church, to me. Transformation is never easy, and redemption comes at a cost that few are prepared to pay. I had no idea how you would take to our quiet life here, how much of the world you would be willing to reject in order to save your soul. But you have proved yourself to be worthy of the grace bestowed upon you. These walls can provide a respite for a while but ultimately, you must learn to live a pious life on your own. We will all experience change in the days ahead. Including you. And when the doors to St. Luke's close, it will be time for you to begin your new life."

"New life?"

"Indeed." The priest opened the drawer of his massive desk and pulled out a plain rosary. "This was given to me when I was confirmed many years ago. I want you to have it."

Jean Paul shook his head. "I couldn't take it, Father, not when I know the sentimental value it must hold for you."

"Which is what makes it even more important for you to have it. You have been protected from the world as long as you have been here, but that isn't realistic. It is time for you to face whatever you must, test your strength and resolve. May these simple beads remind you that you are not alone. I will pray for you daily."

Jean Paul nodded, reverently outstretching his hand to receive the gift. "Thank you for this, for everything. I am so grateful," he whispered.

"And if you can remain in that place of gratitude, you will ultimately be successful."

"I will remember that."

"One more thing," the priest said, holding out an envelope. "You are going to need money. You have received no compensation during your time here, and yet, you have worked as hard as any member of my staff. It is a small amount, but enough to get you to a new destination and pay for a few nights of lodging. Use it wisely. And may our gracious Lord God protect you every step of the way."

The priest made the sign of the cross for good measure, before Jean Paul, whose eyes filled with tears, wordlessly left the room.

He stood in the empty hall like a stone statue. His mind raced, searching for answers. Where was he to go? What was he to do? And then, it came to him as though the voice of God Himself was whispering in his ear. A journey toward redemption must make a full circle, which meant facing the temptations that had robbed him of everything honorable and good. He must do battle with the demon: he must go home.

Chapter Thirty-six

Winter, 1865

Angelique spent the colder months exploring her childhood home. It was like reuniting with an old friend as she crawled through the tiny doors which led to the space in the attic. There, where the roof soared and timbers exposed the underbelly of the structure, where cobwebs hung from the rafters like delicate party streamers, she rediscovered herself, reclaimed her life. And indeed, she was delighted to find remnants of a time she once knew, items she figured were lost forever. She often shivered in the damp, the fog from her warm breath clouding the air, but it failed to deter her as she rummaged through trunks, looking for the precious memories that confirmed all that was important to her.

After lunch, she would sit with the twins and share what she had found, carefully explaining the cast of characters in the tintypes that her mother had tenderly placed in albums.

"These are your grandparents right after they married," she had explained, holding up a tiny, blurred image of two people who stood shoulder to shoulder, somberly looking into the lens of the camera.

Aida examined the frame and smiled. "I think you look like your momma, just as we look like you."

Angelique winked. "And you two girls remind me of her."

"Do we?" Aimee asked.

"Yes. It is the loveliest of thoughts that a part of them live on in you."

"Tell us about growing up here," Aida had said. And soon, it became an afternoon ritual as Angelique would relate the stories of her youth, the mischievous pranks that she and cousin Lilly had pulled on the unsuspecting house servants, the long rides in the pastures with lazy days spent napping under the trees, the weeks of harvest when the fields buzzed with activity.

"I am so glad that you are interested," she had said, pouring tea into a porcelain set that had belonged to her as a child. "Family history is perishable. It disappears with time as memories fade and loved ones move on. Preserving a record is the best gift to bestow on the future. And someday, I hope that you will share these accounts with your own children so that they, too, can know that they were a part of those who came before them."

The girls nodded in unison. "We won't forget."

Angelique sighed. She did not tell them of the reckless Jean Paul who had swept her off her feet one summer night, brazenly taking her in his arms as her dance partner stood helplessly by wondering what had happened. Nor did she mention how he had shown up the next day in the same library where they currently sat, asking for her father's permission to court her, his boldness leaving her breathless and filled with romantic notions of a happy future. She simply did not talk about how quickly they were wed and how he had deceived her, faking his death and stealing her inheritance to pay for his wicked gambling habit. And she didn't speak of their baby sister, Josephina, taken to live with the angels far too soon. No, she carefully omitted the tragic part of her history which was tied to Chauvin, and later, New Orleans, choosing instead to focus on the good moments of the past and those that were yet to come. Some stories, she thought, were meant to remain untold, dead and buried. She secretly hoped that her first husband had met with a tragic fate, a destiny which had come to him from a just universe, which doles out punishment based on actions and behavior. After all he had done to her, it seemed only fair.

Chapter Thirty-seven

Spring, 1866

For the third morning in a row, Angelique was up early and out in the fields while the dew was still on the grass. Terence stood near a plot of rich black dirt, shovel in hand.

"Morning, Miss Angelique," he said, tipping his hat. "If today goes like I think it will, we shore gonna be busy with the planting in the days ahead."

Angelique bent to watch him dig into the soil, testing the temperature and moisture with his hands not once, but twice. She wondered how many crops he had started in this same way and how many fields he had harvested after so many months of carefully nurturing the plants. It was a ritual shared with the many who lived in harmony with the land, coaxing Mother Nature to release her bounty, regardless of her fickle moods. Except this time he was doing it as a free man, the overseer of a plantation, and clearly in charge.

"Uh huh," he said, holding out a palm full of Louisiana soil for her to touch. "Warm enough, with just a bit of moisture. Looks like the good Lord is smiling on us today."

The fields had been in disrepair, overgrown with weeds and underbrush after being neglected for years, and Angelique wondered if they would ever be productive again. But she had underestimated Terence.

He had worked tirelessly to coax the earth back to life, finally preparing the ground weeks ago as he had hooked up the rusty plow to the lone mule and tilled the dirt, making uniform mounds to accommodate the seed. Angelique had placed a fat pouch of money in his hand on that first day. "Use this to hire the help you will need. And find dependable men who will be loyal to you. Trust is most important." But it hasn't surprised her to see that he had taken much of the responsibility and work load upon himself, wanting it to be done right this first time.

And so, the next morning, Angelique roused the children earlier than usual. "Planting time," she whispered. Aimee and Aida giggled. "We are going to make the cotton grow."

"Indeed we are!"

Andrew was waiting for her on front veranda. He handed her a steaming cup of black coffee, which she gratefully accepted.

"It is daunting, terrifying, but somehow doing this thing which scares me has made me more alive than I have ever been before."

"Here's to having your dream realized, my darling," he said, toasting her with his cup.

"I hope it will be our dream, Andrew."

The silence hung between them as he sat wordlessly, scanning the predawn sky for a sign of rain.

Franklin appeared, grinning. He held up a glass jar.

"What's that?" Angelique asked.

"The seeds we picked out of the cotton that day we sat under the tree at Maison Blanche."

Angelique gasped, her eyes filled with tears. "You kept those?"

"Sure did," Franklin said proudly.

She moved to hug the boy. "I have always said that you are the most resourceful person I know, Franklin. How smart of you to save them so that we can have a bit of the Bourgeois family with us always."

He beamed. "And I think we should plant them closest to the house so that we can see how they are faring from here."

"Good idea. Now, go find Terence and tell him of your plan."

And as the morning sun grew brighter, the family joined the hired hands to carefully plant the cotton seeds.

Within the hour, Aimee and Aida were complaining that their backs hurt. Angelique sent them to sit on a blanket to watch. Franklin and Andrew worked side by side, having created a rhythm to the work. Even Jubilee joined in.

"Never thought I would be out working in the fields, Miss Angelique. If my momma could see me now, she wouldn't believe her eyes."

"Isn't it amazing what a person will do for love?"

Jubilee sighed. "Not sure if you are referring to Terence or yourself, but yes, this is labor born out of pure affection. Nothing more."

"But think of how proud your husband is going to be when the first crop is harvested and brought to market."

"Lord, that's all he talks about."

"He gets a share of whatever we make. And then, there's the land I promised you. Someday, I hope that Chauvin is going to provide all of us with a good living."

"As long as I have that man, I am already enjoying a good living."

Angelique smiled. "Nice to see that you are still on your honeymoon, Jubliee."

"Guess I hadn't planned on this as being a part of it." She paused to rub the back of her neck.

"Life can take us down some unlikely roads. Never say never. Remember that." Both women laughed as though sharing some sort of private joke.

As Angelique bent to drop a seed into soil, she could hear her father's voice, cautioning her to cover it well. She remembered her days as a child in this same field on planting day. His speech was always the same. "Soon the green sprouts will break the ground, the flowers will casually chat with the rain. And if the Good Lord is willing each seed will fulfill its destiny, growing into what it can."

And as she shielded her eyes to survey the scene, she certainly hoped that would be true. She needed it to be true.

Chapter Thirty- eight

The transition period of consolidating the two churches had taken longer than expected and Jean Paul was glad for the reprieve, the extra months of sanctuary that living at the religious compound had provided. He tried to use the time wisely, to map out a plan for his future, but the uncertainty loomed large. New Orleans was his destination. What happened when he arrived there remained to be seen, but he needed to be vigilant, prepared for the worst which he hoped would never happen. And as he purchased his one way ticket on that foggy April morning, he wondered if he needed one for his traveling companion, fear, which most certainly accompanied him on his journey.

The trip from Richmond was relatively uneventful, with fewer stops than he had anticipated. He ate the bread and cheese that cook had handed him as he had bid his tearful goodbyes. And careful of how he spent his limited funds, he bought only what was necessary to keep the hunger at bay. He slept fitfully, dreaming of monsters from the swamp determined to devour his soul. And once, he had a nightmare that Aimee had fallen into the river. Try as he might, he couldn't save her from drowning. After that, he avoided sleep, afraid of where his overwrought mind might take him. By the time the train pulled into the city station, he was physically and emotionally exhausted.

The streets of New Orleans were familiar as were the sounds and smells, the sensory attack bringing with it a flood of memories. He held tight to his threadbare satchel as though it could somehow anchor him, keep him grounded; otherwise, he wondered if he would simply float away. Orienting himself, he began his walk, knowing that he could only afford a room in the seedy part of town, avoiding the fancy areas he had frequented in his previous life as Jean Paul Latour, plantation owner, successful gambler. He had thrown away, lost in one hand of cards, more money than he presently carried in his pocket. It was an irony he tried not to ponder as he quickened his pace.

By midafternoon, he had found a rundown boarding house in a less than desirable neighborhood. He was shown to a tiny room, ironically not much bigger than the closet he had occupied at the rectory, which he figured would suit him just fine. He tried not to notice the overwhelming smell of whiskey, rotting food, and sewage that came up from the alley below. And he hoped that the constant noise, the dueling music and sounds of folks arguing, yelling obscenities at each other, wouldn't be too difficult to bear after the quiet serenity of the church. As he spied the bed with its filthy mattress, and one leg shorter than the other, giving it a rather comical lopsided appearance, he reminded himself that this was temporary. He paid for a week, which took the majority of his funds, and he prayed that he would find work sooner than later.

The kindly priest had written him a letter of introduction, a testament to his work ethic and character. And so, the next morning, he carefully placed it in his pocket as he donned his best suit, terribly out of fashion and faded at the collar, and set out to look for a job.

A church seemed the most logical choice, and so he began at St. Patrick's where he was politely told that there were no open positions. He visited St. Joseph's and St. Vincent de Paul's, asking to speak to the priest in the hopes that his letter might make a difference. But in both places, he was refused. He even sought out the sisters at the Ursuline Convent on the assumption that they might require regular assistance, but he was turned down point blank and told that they had already given as much as possible to the downtrodden in the name of Christian charity.

He finally made his way to St. Louis Cathedral, figuring that it took a large staff to maintain a house of worship of that size. He was turned away by the head housekeeper, who refused to let him past the front gate. As he turned to walk away, wondering what his next plan of action night be, she called him back.

"Are you willing to do anything?" she asked.

He nodded. "I am desperate, ma'am."

"Go around the back to the groundskeeper's office. It is a separate building, not hard to spot. Tell him that I sent you. I think he may have something."

Jean Paul tipped his hat. "Thank you."

He knocked tentatively at the door of the small brick building. With no sign or means of identification, he hoped he was in the right place. When, there was no answer, he knocked again, more urgently this time.

The door was answered by a burly man whose thick eyebrows had managed to grow together into one dark horizontal line across the top of his face. Jean Paul thought it made him look constantly surprised, and he tried not to stare. "Yeah?" the man barked.

Jean Paul cleared his throat. "The housekeeper sent me to see you, sir. I am in need of a job and having worked most recently at St. Luke's in Richmond. I hoped that perhaps you might have something for me.

The man sized him up without uttering a word. The silence was awkward.

"My name is Jean Paul Latour," he said, offering his hand. "I have reference letters from Father Jones if you'd like to read them."

He reached in his pocket to remove the letters, which he held out.

But the man ignored them. Finally, he spoke. "You willing to do anything?"

It struck Jean Paul as odd as it was the same question that the housekeeper had posed.

"I am."

The man nodded. He removed a large skeleton key from the hook inside the door and muttered, "Come with me." He motioned to the stables across the street, where a simple wagon was hitched to a pair of horses. Jean Paul followed. The man climbed into the driver's seat and in one shift motion, coaxed the horses into action as they made their way through the streets of the French Quarter. Six blocks later, they pulled into St. Louis cemetery, dubbed the first because it was the original home to the dead. Slowly, they followed the gravel path until they reached the farthest edge. There, stood a solitary wooden shed, a strange contrast to the marble and granite tombs which surrounded it. As the man dismounted, he used the key for the large padlock on the door.

"Here. Come in."

Jean Paul was still confused, but did as he was told. The inside of the shed was damp, the air thick from the Louisiana humidity. His leg immediately began to throb in response, a painful reminder of the afternoon when Angelique aimed a pistol at him and fired in unbridled anger. He absented mindedly rubbed it as he looked around. A small window near the door was shut tight and a big black spider happily spun a web across the panes. Beams of sunlight broke through the clapboard, which had been hastily constructed and not weatherproof by any means. Jean Paul struggled to breathe. There was a small desk which also served as a table. Papers and an inkwell were on top, along with a chipped coffee cup. In the corner of the room was a sagging cot, which looked like it had been pressed into service after the war.

"This here is the watchman's cottage. It is where you will spend your days and nights, except for Tuesday afternoons when someone will come to relieve you. You are to report to me at that time to receive your pay and instructions. The cemetery gate is to be locked nightly at dusk and reopened at six the next morning." He held up the key. "Same one as used for this door. Guard it carefully."

"So am I hired?" Jean Paul asked, not sure what to make of the experience.

"Wouldn't have brought you out here otherwise," the man replied. "And don't think this is going to be an easy job. You are to remove spent flowers to the pile there." He pointed to a mound behind the shack. "And you are to patrol the premises once an hour."

It seemed reasonable.

"Understand that there are grave robbers. Unseemly men, although there is an occasional woman, who will prowl the new graves looking to steal jewelry from the deceased. And then, there are the voo doo priests, who can often do the unthinkable out here. You will need to remain alert."

Jean Paul wondered if the man was trying to scare him or make him aware of the dangers of the job. Either way, he had no choice.

"There are ghosts, too, the unsettled spirits who wander through the night. You may see things you never thought you would. Three men took this on before you just in the past two months. One left without his pay. Let's see what you are made of."

But Jean Paul Latour had seen many ghouls in his lifetime, fought many battles against demons both real and perceived. He would not be intimidated by the phantoms who haunted the cemetery or the thieves looking for easy money. It had nothing to do with being brave.

The man handed him a pistol and key before returning to the wagon. "Move in as soon as possible. Darkness comes all too quickly."

And Jean Paul simply nodded. Perhaps it was appropriate to learn how to live again while dwelling among the dead, he thought. After all, the resurrection began in a tomb. For indeed, we all write a book which is the story of our lives, he thought, and this, would be quite an interesting chapter.

Chapter Thirty-nine

Summer, 1866

With the cotton growing higher by the day, Angelique set her sights on the cane crop. She often thought it was a more lucrative investment of time and land since it was far less finicky. But in a post-war world, there was a bigger demand for cotton and its magical ability to be transformed into cloth than there was for the sweet stuff. At least for now. Even Mr. Lincoln had acknowledged that potential, calling the area near the river "Louisiana's Sugar Coast." It was all the encouragement she needed.

Angelique loved the cane's ability to regrow once it was harvested, rewarding the farmer with its sweet abundance. It thrived under conditions that would have ruined the cotton in a matter of days. Cane was a survivor. And so, on a hot June morning, she followed Terence into the fields, carefully wielding her way through the rows of tall reeds as he methodically wielded the knife, cutting a seed piece from each. She watched with interest, placing the shoots into her basket. If she was to work this land, she wanted to understand every facet of what it took to bring the crops to harvest. She learned long ago that the key to feeling safe was to never be dependent on anyone, ever.

She stopped to examine a tall stalk. "This row should be ready in a month or so," she said to Terrance.

"Good eye, Miss Angelique."

There was a peace that accompanied the work, the sweat and grime caking her palms. She wiped her forehead with the back of her hand. "My daddy would be pleased."

"We should all be pleased, ma'am. I have never seen a finer field."

"But it is such work. Like a new baby, these plants require almost constant attention. Maybe we should change the name of the plantation from Chauvin to Hardscrabble."

"Might not be a bad idea, although we both know that this effort is gonna pay off in the long haul. Just you wait and see."

Angelique smiled. "I sure do hope so. Guess I will go back to the house and check on the children. There are peas from the garden if you and Jubilee want some."

"Sounds good. I am sure she will be mighty grateful."

Terence shook his head in wonder. He had seen many Southern women in his lifetime, a fashion parade of pampered belles whose idea of work was pouring tea. But this one had earned his respect. Indeed, she had.

Angelique slowly walked up the front steps. She was tired and wondered if she had time for a quick nap before lunch. Andrew was on the veranda, book in hand. She hadn't even noticed him until he spoke.

"I hope all is well in the fields."

"Goodness, you startled me. I think I was in my own little world."

"You have been since planting day. That crop seems to occupy most of your thoughts and all of your energy."

"Do you truly think so?"

"I know so. Ask your daughters. They will confirm it."

Angelique's face grew serious as she furrowed her brow. "That is troubling, Andrew."

"For me as well. All you seem to care about is this place."

She moved to him and knelt by his chair. "That isn't true. Why, I am doing this for all of us, for our future, to realize our dream."

He interrupted her. "This is your dream, your life. I am no farmer and never will be."

She swallowed hard and her face flushed. It hadn't occurred to her that he was unhappy. She should have noticed. He certainly would have seen her discontent.

"I'm so sorry, Andrew," she whispered. "I will do better for you, for the whole family. We harvest the cotton in a matter of weeks. After that, I will be all yours."

He nodded, and she hoped that he believed her. He turned his attention to his book, which she realized was not printed, but written in his own hand.

"What's this?' she asked.

"Nothing really. I've been recording cloud formations, weather conditions. I've done it since we first moved to Chauvin."

"And?"

"Not much more to add. I had hoped to see a pattern, for example, days of intense heat brings about rain, but so far it is all speculation."

She reached for his hand. "You should write a book. There is such power in the written word and so much that can be recorded for future generations."

He laughed. "Goodness, Angelique, what would I write about?"

"Write what you know, of course. Write about the storm."

Chapter Forty

Fall, 1866

Angelique was searching for the girls. After she had checked the usual places, she crossed the yard to the kitchen. There they were, huddled near the work table, and curious as to what they might be up to, she stood near the door, watching. Aida removed the cover from the bowl, licked her finger and scooped up a little. She spit it out immediately. "It's salt," she cried.

Aimee, who had been waiting for her turn, made a face.

Angelique laughed as she stepped forward to take the dish from her daughter's hands. "Well, now, there's a lesson to be learned. Never rely on what you see, little girl. Salt looks just like sugar."

"And it is terrible," Aida agreed, sticking out her tongue.

"You girls are growing older, but you have already witnessed so much in your young lives. We learn who and what to trust and how to believe because of experience."

"What do you mean, Momma?" Aimee asked.

"I think it is safe to say that from this point on neither of you girls will ever assume that any white powder in a bowl is sugar, right?"

Both girls nodded their heads.

"And not all people are nice," Aida added.

The comment was surprising, and Angelique wondered if she was referring to the fiendish Jean Paul who had kidnapped her sister or the Yankee soldiers who had taken over Maison Blanche. Not everyone is nice. It was among the hardest of lessons, one she had hoped her children wouldn't learn until they were older. "Yes, but there are many wonderful, kind people in this world. Just as you must test that bowl to determine if it is sugar or salt, so must you give people time to show you who they are. Do you understand?"

"Like Franklin?" Aimee asked.

"Franklin is a perfect example. He might have appeared to be just another boy when you met him, but he proved to be strong and brave and loyal."

"And now, our brother."

"Indeed. Speaking of Franklin, do you know where he is? I have something important to speak to all three of you about."

"I would say that he is out with the animals. The barn maybe? Or the pasture? He does so love them."

"And he is very good with them, too. Let's go look."

And they found Franklin sitting under a tree, feeding a baby bird droplets of a milky mixture he had concocted.

"What are you doing," Aimee asked, moving in for a closer look.

"This little one fell out of the nest. Just trying to keep it from starving."

"What's in the jar?" Aida asked.

"Sugar water."

Aida and Aimee looked at each other and giggled.

"What's so funny?" he asked.

"Nothing," Aida replied.

Angelique sat next to him and patted the ground for the girls to do likewise. "I have some news," she said. "You children are going to school."

"Real school?" Aimee asked.

"Yes. They have reopened the school down the road, hired a teacher from New Orleans, too."

The girls clapped their hands.

"It is time that you three get a proper education. You never know when it might be useful." She winked at Aida, who smiled.

Chapter Forty-one

It was Tuesday afternoon and Jean Paul's replacement was twenty minutes late. He tried to be patient as he paced outside the shack that had become his home, but he had things to do and a limited amount of time. And so, when he was finally able to leave the confines of the cemetery an hour later, he was flustered and in a hurry.

His first stop was the groundskeeper's office to pick up his pay. It wasn't much, but Jean Paul had already determined that his needs were simple. The long days and nights alone weren't easy, even if he did have regular duties to perform, and his mission for the day, in addition to getting some food, was to find a bookstore. Something to read would make a big difference for him, quelling the emptiness that he felt. The priest had given him a prayer book as a parting gift, and Jean Paul had read through it at least a dozen times, memorizing the litanies of petition and praise that he recited daily. But he figured that even God was growing tired of the words repeated over and over, and a diversion more secular in nature would be welcomed.

He had only walked a few blocks when he heard the laughter and shouting, the metallic twang of a piano being played with gusto. Something stirred deep inside, a feeling that was comforting and familiar. He followed the sound, which led him to one of the many taverns along Bourbon Street, pausing at the door before entering.

It took his eyes a moment to adjust to the dimly lit room, and he struggled to focus. There was a bar, of course, and the mirrored back seemed to double it in size. There were a few people casually chatting at tables, but the action seemed to be happening in the back of the room, where a group of men laughed as they cursed under their breath. He slowly made his way to where they sat, listening to the seductive sound as the dealer expertly shuffled the cards. He simply stood and watched as they played, the betting growing more feverish with each round. His fingers began to twitch.

The men, suddenly aware of his presence, sized him up, his old dirty clothes and long hair giving him the appearance of a beggar.

"Help you?" one of them asked.

He shook his head, but continued to stare at the cards and money on the table. Another pointed to the empty chair. "You in?"

Jean Paul quickly calculated how much money he had in his pocket. It was a week's pay, money he couldn't afford to lose. But winning was always a possibility and he could double, maybe even triple it, in a matter of minutes. He nodded.

The dealer handled the cards again and Jean Paul sat, staring at the five placed before him. The others had placed an initial bet in the middle of the table, and they looked at him in anticipation. He touched the cards. His hands began to tremble as he reached in his pocket to withdraw a coin.

"Is this who you want to be?" the voice asked.

He sat stone still. "Did you hear that?" he asked the men.

"What?"

The voice asked again. "Will you repeat the mistakes of the past?"

He shook his head. "No."

"You crazy?" one asked.

But Jean Paul didn't answer as he got up from the table and walked out into the street. He squinted in the glare of the bright sunshine that hurt his eyes, but it also cheered him a bit, and he quickened his pace until he reached the bookstore.

He could imagine the kindly priest congratulating him on passing his first test, while admonishing him that there would be more to come. For good measure, he whispered "lead me not into temptation," hoping that the Lord would help him remain on the path to redemption. He was learning what a difficult road it was.

Chapter Forty-two

Spring, 1867

Angelique found it hard to believe that it was planting time again and that an entire year had passed. The thought of repeating the success they had enjoyed the previous season had her itching to get out into the fields once more. Chauvin was proving to be a wise financial investment as well as a sentimental wish fulfilled.

She awoke well before dawn and was surprised to see that Andrew had not yet gone to bed, as he sat at the desk in the library, the lamplight glowing in the darkness.

"Have you been writing all night?" she asked.

He nodded, stopping to rub his eyes. "I guess the time got away from me," he said.

"Then, I take that as a good sign."

"I hope so. It has been challenging to go back to that time, especially without any of my notes, so much of what I am writing is narrative, rather than statistical."

"Meaning?"

"More like telling what happened instead of listing facts."

"I see. And that would make for more interesting reading, I would think."

"I hope so, although goodness knows to whom this book might appeal, Angelique. And I have tried to avoid the temptation to insert my own emotional account of the human toll, the fear and anxiety on the island as we waited and watched. I have to remember than I am writing a scientific book and not a story."

Angelique picked up a sheet of paper among the many covering the top of the desk. She leaned into the light and read one and then another and another.

"Andrew," she whispered "it is wonderful. Yes, it is a book based on science, but there is more to it than that, and I can most certainly appreciate the sensitivity with which you describe the events. I can't wait to read it in its entirety."

"Well, I am almost done, at least, I think I am."

"And then what?"

"Is it arrogant to think that perhaps a publisher might be interested in it?"

"Of course not. That is why a person writes a book in the first place. Any idea where to begin?"

"I will send some inquiry letters, of course. I do still have friends at the Smithsonian with ties to the right people. I would assume that I would have to look to the North for such a thing, since it is more industrialized, which means more printing presses, but you never know."

For a fleeting moment, Angelique panicked. She hoped that Andrew didn't have his sights set on moving back to Washington or New York, even, especially since the plantation was doing so well. But she wouldn't court trouble by bringing the subject up. "Well, I just know that any publisher with a lick of sense would be foolish not to produce it."

He kissed her cheek. "My supportive wife."

"Goodness, Andrew, don't you think I could say the same about you? You put your ambitions aside for mine for far too long. I just want for you to be successful."

He nodded. "Well, we shall see how the success part goes. For now, yes, the work gives me a new purpose, and I like that. I need it."

"Keep at it, then."

"And I assume you will be off to the fields soon?"

"Big day. Planting time."

"And the children?"

"They are to go to school as they normally would. Aida and Aimee have no real interest in it. Franklin would prefer tending to the animals instead of planting a crop. Besides, they are thriving and learning so much in the process. I found the girls in the library looking through the books that Henry had given me from Maison Blanche. They are enamored with reading. Franklin is, too. It has been good for them."

"Education is always a worthy endeavor, as my daddy used to say."

"And your daddy was right. He raised an important scientist, soon to be an author."

Andrew smiled. "Guess he would have been proud."

"Indeed." Angelique kissed him on the forehead before donning her straw hat. She tied the thick crimson ribbon under her chin and turned to face him. "And so am I. Truly."

Chapter Forty-three

Summer, 1867

It was one of those beautiful summer days. The infamous Louisiana heat and humidity had been kept at bay, and an occasional breeze rustled through the trees. Angelique had spent the morning walking through the fields, while the twins picked blackberries that grew wild nearby.

"For a pie," Aida told her mother as she presented the bowl of ripened berries.

"Only if you help," Angelique said.

Both girls nodded enthusiastically.

And so, after lunch, the trio took to the kitchen to roll out the dough and place it in a pie pan that Angelique looked at so lovingly that the girls thought perhaps it was lined in gold.

"Such memories. Hannah used to make the most delicious pies you could ever imagine and this was what she always used. She never allowed me to do much other than watch, but I thought she was magical, creating such sweet treats for us to enjoy."

"I thought that she was your nanny, like Jubilee is ours."

"Well, she was, but the whole family depended on her, even my mother, who was a most elegant lady and clearly in charge of the running of the home. And we had a cook, of course, but Hannah used to spoil us with special dishes that she would whip up as a surprise. Oh, how we loved that."

Aimee pointed to Jubilee who was tending to her kitchen garden. "Is Jubilee much like her? She does take care of us, although not as much now that we are almost grown."

Angelique laughed. "You two have a long way to go before you are grown."

"Well, we are getting there," Aida added. "I know that Jubilee always made us feel like she cared for us."

"She did. Well, she still does. And very soon, she will have a baby of her own to love."

Aimee clapped her hands. "Won't it be fun to have a baby around?"

"It will be, although you have to promise that you won't be a nuisance. There is a reason why she and Terence have their own place far away from the main house. "

"We are going to help her."

Angelique rolled her eyes. She had seen these two when they thought they were assisting. In fact, as she looked around the kitchen with flour covering the table and floor, she shook her head at just how helpful they could be.

"I am going to give Sarah to the baby." Aimee announced.

"Really?" Angelique asked, moved by her daughter's kindness. "And what made you decide on that?"

"Just did. I am growing older and have little need for dolls, so maybe the baby will like her."

Angelique wondered if somehow Sarah reminded Aimee of her time with Jean Paul or Uncle Gaston as she had called him. After all, he had given her the gift, no doubt to gain her trust. Perhaps this was her way of leaving that part of her young life behind, a step toward healing.

"I think it is a lovely idea, Aimee. And I am sure that the baby will love having Sarah. Now, let's bake this masterpiece, shall we?"

Angelique had just slipped the pie in the oven when she saw Jubilee walking toward the house.

"Some berries left if you want them," she called.

"No berries for me. I think I have a baby coming."

"Truly? How long ago did it start?"

"About half an hour."

"I'll send Franklin to find Terence so he can get the midwife."

She nodded, a mask of pain covering her face.

"In the meantime, let's get you home." Angelique remembered her sudden labor with the twins and how important it was to her to have her babies in her own bed. She was sure that Jubilee felt the same way.

They slowly made their way the two hundred yards or so to the overseer's cottage where Jubilee and Terence lived. The twins' incessant chatter was unnerving, and Angelique tried to think of some chore of perceived importance that she could assign to them just to keep them out of the way.

"Go and stand by the front door and keep your eye out for Terence. Let me know if you see him coming."

"We will. Don't you worry," they said in unison.

Angelique turned her attention to Jubilee, whose contractions were occurring with regularity.

"Looks like you are going to have a fast birth, Jubilee," she said, helping her into the bed. "If so, you will be lucky, this being your first."

Jubilee started to speak, but her face contorted as the pain swept through her.

"Terence will be here soon, along with some help." Angelique whispered.

Jubilee stared at some unmarked spot on the ceiling as though it held the secret to the fear and hurt. Her breathing grew more frantic with each contraction.

It seemed like hours had passed before Terence appeared, his face solemn.

"Where is the midwife?" Angelique asked, noting that only Franklin accompanied him.

"Gone. Her house was empty, like she up and moved or something. Not sure what I am supposed to do."

Angelique took a deep breath. She had brought three children into the world. Surely, she was capable of helping Jubilee. "I'm here. I will do what I can. Start by getting me some rags. Clean ones. And a fresh bowl of water."

Terence nodded. "Yes, ma'am. Right away. Much obliged to you." He moved to his wife's bedside, taking her hand in his. "It is going to be alright, honey. We gonna have us a baby."

But Jubilee couldn't answer. She simply offered a weak smile. "Soon, I hope."

As the sun set, Angelique began to worry. She calculated that Jubilee had been in labor for close to six hours and seemed to be making no progress. She had sent Andrew back to the house with the girls earlier. Terence and Franklin waited on the tiny porch.

"Franklin, you go on home now. Not anything you can do here but wait. Even I feel useless. This is a place for the women," Terence said.

"I think I will stay a while, if you don't mind. Could get mighty lonely out here."

Hours passed. Jubilee seemed no closer to delivery than she had been earlier. As the night turned into day and the sun appeared on the horizon, Angelique grew concerned. First babies could be incredibly stubborn, taking their time to make an appearance in the world, but this felt more serious. Jubilee had grown weak, her breathing shallow at times, while her body, wracked with pain twisted on the bed. And the child seemed unwilling to be born. Angelique wasn't sure what to do.

She walked out onto the front porch, rubbing her eyes, hoping to keep the fatigue at bay. Terence and Franklin were sleeping. Men sometimes seemed to have an easier time at life, she thought.

"I am worried about Jubilee," she whispered to Terence. "It has been too long, and I don't know what to do to comfort her."

Terence sat up, the worry etched in his face. "Is it serious?"

Angelique nodded. "It is. Are you sure you don't have another midwife? I could write a note and you can go and fetch Dr. Hornsby."

"Would he come?"

It was a difficult question to answer and the unspoken reasons hung in the air between them. "I don't know."

Franklin, who had sat quietly by, cleared his throat. "I can help."

Angelique smiled. "I know that you mean well, but how on earth do you think you can help, son?"

"The milk cow. Remember? She had the same problem. The calf had twisted inside of her and couldn't come out. Could be the issue here."

Suddenly, Franklin appeared older, wiser, more of a man than a boy.

"Terence? She is your wife. Will you let Franklin try?" Angelique asked.

Terence shook his head. "Not sure about this. I suppose I will always view Franklin as a child. It is hard to trust, but I am afraid of what might happen if we do nothing. I can't let my wife and baby die. Yes, let him try."

Franklin entered the small bedroom where Jubilee lay. Beads of sweat formed on her brow, her face contorted.

Franklin sensed his mother's apprehension. "I have done this before. The anatomy is similar. First, I need to feel for the baby."

Angelique nodded. She was aware of the need to preserve Jubilee's modesty as she draped the sheet over her legs and abdomen. "Now, Franklin."

He felt under the covering until he located the spot, the look of calm concentration on his face.

"Well?" Angelique asked.

"Feet. I feel feet."

"The baby is breech," Angelique whispered.

"I can try to turn it."

Angelique looked at him in horror. "How on earth would you accomplish such a thing?"

"Carefully, of course, but it is the only option. Did it once with a mare."

Angelique had no idea of the extent of Franklin's knowledge. "You did? Jubilee is not a horse, you know. But, yes, you must try. Be gentle, son. And hurry."

Jubilee screamed in pain as Franklin slowly and methodically turned the baby within her womb. After several agonizing minutes, he was done.

"I think I did it. Now, let's see what happens."

Angelique stood in wonder at the bravery of her son. "Stay with me until the end."

He nodded.

Jubilee opened her eyes as though the Lord above had suddenly given her the energy reserves necessary for the task ahead. "Oh. I think it is time. I need to push."

Franklin supported Jubilee's back as Angelique coached her through the pushing, the sheer force it takes to bring life into this world.

"Again," she said as one contraction flowed into another.

And as though some dam had broken, releasing the ocean that it held, the infant came into the world, a cry accompanying its first breath.

Angelique scooped up the baby and wrapped him in a clean blanket before placing him in Jubilee's arms. "You have a son," she whispered, "a beautiful boy."

Terence heard the cries and rushed into the room. He fell to his knees, weeping tears of joy. "I got me a son," he said proudly.

"Indeed, you have. And now, let us give the three of you a little time alone," Angelique said, as she and Franklin moved to the porch.

"I can't believe you did that," she said. "I am so proud of you."

Franklin blushed. "So glad I could help."

"You did more than that, son. You saved two lives today. That was brave."

"I guess all of that time with the animals taught me something. I have studied them for so long with a plan in mind."

"A plan?"

"I want to be a physician, momma, a healer."

Angelique moved to hug him. "And you will be a most excellent one."

Chapter Forty-four

Winter, 1868

Angelique sat at the same desk that her father had used to tally the final crop totals. She carefully copied the numbers into the ledger book, first the expenses, then, the profits. She leaned back in the chair and smiled. "Poppa would be proud," she said.

Terence had been waiting for her on the veranda. He stood, hat in hand, trying hard not to pace as he waited for the numbers.

Angelique finally appeared, smiling. "Come in," she said, pointing to the library. She held the book open for him, running her finger down the lines. "Here is what we spent and here is what we made."

He whistled low, "I never thought that we would be here so fast. I mean, you gotta admit, them fields were pretty sorry when you took over the place."

"Agreed. But you have been a miracle worker when it comes to rehabilitating the land, getting the crops to grow. I couldn't have done it without you."

"You would have found somebody else, Miss Angelique. Lots of newly freed men out there looking for an opportunity. They know the soil, and they are willing to work for money after being in bondage for so many years."

"You may be right, but none would have been as loyal as you."

"Well, ma'am, you did deliver me a wife. And now, I got me a son. Guess that gratitude works both ways."

"And he is a fine boy, too."

"Jubilee and I are proud, that's for sure. Nothing like having your own family, one you know can't be bought or sold, to show you what life is all about."

"I guess you are right, Terence. Lots of big changes for you in the past few years, including citizenship, I hear."

"All blessings, for sure."

Angelique handed him a wallet filled with bills. "Your share. And I haven't forgotten about the land I promised. The cottage and now two additional acres are yours. Here is the deed made out in your name."

Terence swallowed hard. "This was just a dream for a man like me, Miss Angelique. If I was to die tomorrow, I would have told the Lord thank you for giving me all that I ever wanted."

"You earned it, Terence. I have always thought that good things should come to good people."

He nodded. "And I thank you for that. Guess I will go and share the good news with Jubilee."

"Indeed, you should. And give Jacob a kiss for me."

"Will do, ma'am," he said, placing his hat on his head.

"And Terence?"

"Yes?"

"This year we will do even greater."

"With the Lord's help, we sure will."

Angelique stared out the window. The cypress and fir trees were still green in spite of the cold. The sight comforted her, as though they defied all odds to remain alive. When she reflected on all she had been through, Jean Paul's deception, the storm, Aimee's kidnapping, the war, she felt that she too had defied the odds, survived and thrived in spite of the obstacles. It was hard not to think of Jean Paul, even after so much time had passed. She wondered if the hatred, the need for vengeance that churned deep inside of her soul would ever go away. She had been blessed, that much was certain, so much of what she had lost restored. And she always wanted to live in a place of gratitude. But she couldn't help but wonder if Jean Paul lived or if a righteous God had struck him down for his sins just as she wanted to do. It was a question that remained in her mind, haunted her when sleep escaped, and yet one, she figured, would never be answered.

"A penny for your thoughts." Andrew moved to the fireplace to stoke the logs. "Cold in here."

"I guess I hadn't noticed."

"You seem to be thinking about something serious."

"No, not really. Just pleased with the final numbers on the harvest."

"So there is a profit?"

"Indeed. A substantial one, I might add."

"I am so proud of you, Angelique. Truly, you amaze me. I figured that you were strong that first moment when we met, but you have proved it to me every day since."

"Most Southern women are, Andrew. It is how we were raised. We may appear to be all sweet and fragile on the outside, but inside, we are tough as nails. The need for swoon bottles among us is highly exaggerated, but then, that's part of the game. It makes it easy to be underestimated."

He laughed. "I wouldn't disagree, especially after having spent more time here."

"Why, there were whispers all through the South that the only reason that Sherman spared Savannah when he burned most of Georgia in his march to the sea is that he had a mistress there, one who was quite persuasive, I might add," she said with a wink.

"I would never underestimate the power of feminine charm. Especially yours." He moved closer to put his arms around her. "I also have some good news to share."

She titled her head ever so slightly to look into his eyes. "Do you?"

"I think so. I just received a letter. My book has been accepted for publication."

"Oh, Andrew, I am so happy for you. And what will that entail?"

"I'm not sure, but I would suppose it means some recognition, perhaps in the scientific community. Assuming, of course, that anybody reads it."

Angelique smiled and moved to put her arms around him. "Lots of people will be moved by your words. I am so proud."

"And I think this calls for a toast," he said, pointing to the decanter of brandy.

He poured her some and raised his glass. "Here's to our success. It has been a long time coming."

"Here, here," she said taking a sip. "But to our happiness, too, because without that there is no success."

"My eloquent wife. To happiness."

Chapter Forty-five

Angelique was up early. She was on a mission, one which required a trip to the big city to accomplish. Terrence had offered to drive her, but in the end, she figured he was needed at home, and enlisted his cousin, Samuel, hired shortly after the big move. She gave Andrew a vague excuse about going to meet with potential cotton buyers, and when he pushed with more questions, she changed the subject.

"Sometimes, a woman needs to go shopping, sugar," she said. And it wasn't entirely a lie.

That seemed to satisfy his curiosity. And so, he bid her goodbye that morning with a kiss on the cheek and his best wishes that she have a successful day.

"I'm counting on it," she said with a wink.

By midmorning, they were in busy downtown New Orleans. The sounds and smells accosted her senses, which had become accustomed to the peace and tranquility of life on the plantation. What a contrast between the two paths her life in Louisiana had taken. Angelique considered a visit to the St. Charles, but then, after remembering that Mr. Wilson was no longer there, saw no point it in. Big change could be wonderful, but sometimes, it made her sad.

They made their way to the Quarter, where she instructed Samuel to water the horses and wait for her.

"Not sure how long this will take, but if I am not back by sunset, you come looking for me."

He laughed, assuming that it was meant to be funny, but she simply turned on her heels and waved goodbye.

***

So much of Jean Paul's life had become routine, a regular rhythm of responsibilities, punctuated by Tuesday afternoon outings. But the structure had been good for him, keeping his mind focused on purging his soul of the sins of the past. Someday, he hoped to be rid of the memories that haunted him and become worthy of a real life, one complete with laughter and perhaps, pride.

For now, he was satisfied with the books that had become his companions, occupying the empty places in his heart and mind. He was grateful that his father had insisted that he receive an education befitting a gentleman. Learning how to read as a child was a priceless gift to him now as the stories took him on a journey outside of the realm of possibilities, a sweet escape from the dismal world that had become his reality. And he was building quite a library in the process, the guard shack that was his home was littered with stacks of books in every inch of free space.

He had been to the groundskeeper's office for his pay, bought bread at the bakery, and was on his way to the bookstore, anxious to see what new volumes awaited him. He crossed the street to avoid passing in front of the gambling hall. It seemed foolish after all this time, but the music, the laughter of men hoping for a win, always triggered something deep inside of him. Like Odysseus, lured by the sound of the Sirens, he simply had to avoid the temptation at all cost.

Jean Paul had turned the corner when he saw her. He rubbed his eyes in disbelief, but there was no mistaking the cascade of dark hair that hung from beneath her bonnet as it swept back and forth in the rhythm to her gait. She carried a parasol to shade her delicate skin from the brutal sun, but he could still see her tilt her head in that familiar way, when she saw something which, no doubt, brought her great delight.

Something stirred deep inside of him. Could it possibly be Angelique? It defied all logic, of course. She lived in Charleston, not New Orleans. Perhaps, he thought, the memories of walking these same cobblestone streets with her so long ago had triggered his emotions. This was where they had begun their lives as newly married couple. And in spite of all of the troubles that had eventually transpired between them, those had been good times.

He followed her for six blocks, compelled to see where she was going, hoping for a glance at her beautiful face. At one time, she had been his charming wife, her affection and devotion unquestioned. He had loved her. Truly. But he had destroyed the life and fondness they shared, squandered the time. It was a lifetime ago.

Jean Paul had no intention of speaking to her. What would he possibly say? There were no words to make amends for all that he had done. But if he could, he would tell her how sorry he was for everything, especially taking Aimee. Of all of his sins, that one haunted him the most.

She reached the millinery shop, stopping to close the parasol before entering. She turned to him, her face a mixture of pity and distain as she clutched her handbag tightly to her chest. Quickly, she pushed the door open and slipped into the shop.

He stood on the sidewalk and laughed out loud. What tricks the mind can play on its unsuspecting victims, he thought. It wasn't Angelique. Didn't look one bit like her either. A part of him was disappointed, saddened that he had no assurance that she was alive and well, but a part of him was also greatly relieved as he doubled back to the bookstore.

***

Angelique had treated herself to a late lunch at Antoine's. And it bothered her not that she was an unaccompanied woman sitting alone in one of the finest restaurants in the city. She savored the freedom of her own company along with the food.

She took one last glimpse at her purchase, pleased that she had located exactly what she wanted at the price she was willing to pay. It had been a productive day, and as she made her way back to the waiting Samuel for the long journey home, she was well pleased. Well pleased indeed.

Chapter Forty-six

Angelique had just finished tying the ribbon around the box. The twins stood nearby, with Aida eyeing the cake that had been placed in the middle of the table. When nobody was looking, she ran her finger around the edge of the porcelain plate, scooping up the vanilla icing. Aimee gave her a stern look and whispered, "Stop. Wait for Poppa to get home." But Aida merely shrugged.

"It a special day, girls."

"Cause Poppa gets his book?"

"Yes. He has worked so very hard to make this happen, and we should all be very pleased for him."

"I am," Aida said. "We can put it in the library, so if visitors would like to read it, they can."

"That's certainly an idea. And, of course, Poppa hopes that someday his book will be in libraries all over the country, maybe even the world."

"The world?" Aimee asked. "Do you mean in faraway places like France?"

Angelique's world stood still. At one time, the country had held a lovely romantic appeal. It was, after all, the home of her ancestors, but now, all she could think about was Jean Paul and his plot to take her child there, his arrogance in believing he had the right to snatch her, turning their world upside down in the process. It was a terrible crime for which he hadn't paid, and that was unsettling.

"Momma? Are you alright?" Aimee asked, reaching for her hand.

"Of course. Just imagining how surprised Poppa will be when he gets home." She clinched her fist behind her back. It angered her that thoughts of Jean Paul threatened the happy mood that she wanted more than anything to preserve. No, she vowed, the cad had already robbed her and her family of enough joy. She would not give him the power to take anything else.

Aida ran to the window. "Poppa's coming and Franklin, too."

The twins ran to either side of their mother, unable to control the giggles. "And when he comes in, what do we say?" Aimee asked.

"Just say 'hooray' because he did something great."

"Hooray?" Aimee repeated, rolling her eyes. "That's silly. How about 'congratulations?'"

And the trio agreed just about the time they could hear Andrew's footsteps on the porch.

"Congratulations," they yelled in unison.

He smiled, holding up the first copy of the book. Angelique took it.

"*A First Hand Account of the Last Island Hurricane from a Meteorological Perspective.*" Aida read the title aloud, stumbling over the last two words. "What does that mean?"

"It is a book about the storm that your mother and I survived when we first met. We don't know much about hurricanes, so the fact that I was there and can share the experience will make the book interesting, I hope."

"We have cake," Aida offered, anxious for a piece.

"I see that."

"And a present, too," Aimee said.

"Goodness. This is like a birthday party."

After the cake had been cut and the children were happily occupied with eating, Angelique held up the box. "For you, from me. This was the reason for my special errand in the city."

Andrew smiled. "This is not necessary, but I certainly do appreciate it." He untied the ribbon.

For a long time he simply stared. Nestled inside was a gold watch, engraved with his initials. "It is beautiful, Angelique. I so appreciate your thoughtfulness."

She swallowed hard, her eyes filling with tears. "I know that you have done without one since our days at the St. Charles. I was simply glad to be able to make it up to you."

He smiled, taking her hand. "You noticed? I thought I was being so clever."

"You are always clever, Andrew, but it is the sacrificing for us, your family that means so much."

"I would do anything for you and the girls. Now and always."

She moved to him. "I think that this is the happiest moment of my life."

"Mine as well."

And although neither said what was on their minds, they both thought of the elusive nature of happiness, threatened at every turn by unknown forces that plot to destroy it.

"Let's just enjoy it, shall we?" she said.

Chapter Forty-seven

Half an hour before sunset ushered in the darkness, Jean Paul lit the lantern and began making his way to the entry gate. It was a long walk, and he altered his route every morning and evening, just to make it interesting. Although he had lasted longer than any other watchman, according to his boss, he still hadn't explored all of the neighborhoods, as he called them, in the city of the dead.

Some streets seemed more traveled than others, wider, with gravel paths that crunched under the weight of his boots. And others, more secluded, were overgrown with a tumble of vines and fallen bricks which had come dislodged from random tombs. There was no order to the design, with trails from one grave site suddenly exiting at another or leading into nothing at all. It could be disorienting, maze-like, and confusing to navigate. And even after he had spent so much time here, he tried to have the gate locked right at dusk, counting on the last bit of fading light to guide him back to the safety of his shack.

He sometimes wondered why the church fathers felt the need to employ a full time watchman since he had witnessed very little out of the ordinary since he had arrived. Occasionally, he had to send a group of teenagers playing some sort of hiding game on their way. And once, he caught a couple in a rather compromising position between two imposing vaults on a warm spring afternoon. But he had only spotted one threatening situation from a group he suspected to be grave robbers. And all he had to do was fire one shot in the air from the pistol, and they ran like they were being chased by the devil himself. But perhaps it was the common knowledge of his presence that prevented more situations from occurring. After all, protecting the bodies and possessions of the dead has a long history, going back to the Egyptians, who shared the Southern reverence for the deceased. At any rate, it was honest work, kept him occupied and allowed him to support himself. He was grateful for it.

There were lavish bouquets of flowers that had been left earlier in the day. Porcelain baby dolls, their eyes fixed as they stared straight ahead, marked the resting place of several young girls. One tomb had a bottle of whiskey propped against it, and Jean Paul made a mental note to check if it was still there in a day or two. So many angels adorned the crypts that when the wind blew, it was said that it sounded like a chorus of heavenly voices. Unlike in so many places, the dead were not forgotten in New Orleans, the connection between the dearly departed and those who lived, not severed, but merely altered by the finality which separated them.

He hummed a little tune to himself, quickening his pace to match the cadence of the music. And he had almost reached the gate when he heard the low murmur of voices. He wasn't sure if they were visitors, unaware of the time, or something more threatening, but he made his way in their direction, expecting the worst. He rounded one corner and then another. No one to be found. He stood and quietly listened. Silence. Finally, he returned to the gate and locked it with the skeleton key he kept on a string long enough to wear around his neck.

Halfway back to his shack, he heard the voices again. Darkness was closing in, and he questioned stumbling around with so many obstacles littering each path, but protecting the cemetery was his job, and the responsibilities included those which could be dangerous. He lifted the lantern and followed the sound, which was now impossible to ignore. And then, it stopped, replaced by the chirping of the crickets who had come to welcome the night. Thirty minutes later, he confirmed that whatever he had heard was gone, and he shrugged as he considered that it was possibly his imagination. He turned in the direction of where he believed his shack was, but having lost his bearings, was unable to site the landmarks he had so often used to navigate through the cemetery. Where was he? Taking a deep breath, he tried not to panic.

He made his way down one lane and then reaching the end, looked one way and then the next, hoping for a sign. Continuing toward the southern edge of the property, he searched for the border fence to guide him, but it remained hidden behind rows and rows of tombs and mausoleums. His throat was parched, dry as a desert, making swallowing difficult. He wondered if the oil in the lantern would last long enough for him to find his way back.

After an hour of wandering aimlessly, he shifted his focus. Perhaps he should stop and rest until sunrise. It seemed futile to continue down the circuitous paths without getting lost any further. And while he certainly didn't want to sleep braced against a cold granite grave, he didn't see that he had much choice. The flickering lamp light, confirmed his decision.

He slowly lowered himself to the step of the closest tomb. It seemed wide enough to hold his body if he felt the need to lie down. And before he extinguished the lantern, he raised it to see who his bed partner for the night would be. His mouth opened, the need to scream primal and urgent, but there was no sound, not even a whimper as he silently read:

JEAN PAUL LATOUR
BORN: NOVEMER 18, 1821
DIED: JANUARY 6, 1856

JOSEPHINA MARIE LATOUR
BORN: OCTOBER 3, 1852
DIED: DECEMBER 1, 1855

RESTING WITH THE ANGELS

Chapter Forty-eight

His breathing returned to normal once reason and logic had eliminated the fear. In fact, he laughed out loud as he considered the irony that he had lived in close proximity to his own final resting place for so many months, unaware that the two worlds could have easily collided on any given day. Life, he thought, has a way of tapping us on the shoulder, reminding us of the demons we try to outrun in our minds. And this was a very tangible reminder, indeed, a monument, one built of granite and marble.

Jean Paul remembered sweet Josephina, whose remains lay so very near to where he sat. He had not thought of her in so very long, not allowing himself the luxury of bringing her back into existence, even if only in his mind. The memories of her short life, although joyful, generated waves of grief that he had not yet resolved, much less accepted, even after the passing of so many years.

Her untimely death at such a tender age had triggered his downward spiral into a deep abyss of despair which manifested itself in his grievous behavior, the irrational choices he never thought he would have made. He stopped caring about anyone or anything, including the woman he loved, the child's mother, who, most certainly, was battling her own sorrow. And when he had readily destroyed everything, he grew numb to it all, especially, the pain.

Over the years, he had become stoic, an expert at avoiding feeling anything akin to emotion. Or so he thought. Aimee had awakened something in him, her sweet innocence and blind devotion restoring a portion of that which had vanished long ago. And when he lost her, admittedly through his own fault, it caused a crack in the dam. The sentiment, deep and raw, flooded his heart and mind when he least expected it, drowning him in the sorrow. Tears ran down his cheeks. Aimee had only been a year or so older than Josephina, whose earthly existence had been frozen in time when she passed. For a moment, he imagined the anguish, the utter despair he might have felt had his daughter disappeared suddenly, without a trace. He wept for the heartache he had brought to Angelique, who deserved none of the suffering she had experienced at his hands. And this was his cross to bear, the truth that he would have to live with for the remainder of his days. There was no way to erase the past transgressions, no prayers he could say, no penance he could do. Nothing at all.

The priest had spent months preaching of God's infinite forgiveness, the grace extended to sinners all. But he wondered if some people were unredeemable, damned to the fires of hell for all eternity for transgressions even the Lord Himself found unpardonable. And he questioned if he was one of those people. If so, it was a righteous punishment. In spite of his efforts, he still felt tainted, his polluted soul festering deep inside of him. Would he ever feel pure, absolved, worthy? These were the philosophical and theological questions that could never be fully answered while here on earth, he figured. Like so many of life's mysteries, it would only be revealed at the hour of his own death.

His thoughts returned to his beautiful daughter. She had been his angel on earth and now she was, most certainly, an angel in heaven. Perhaps she would intercede on his behalf, help him to find peace as she rested here, so close. And somehow, the thought brought him a strange comfort as he began to talk to her. Deep into the night, he spoke the words from his heart into the grave. Perhaps help for his restless soul lay here among the dead. With Josephina.

Chapter Forty-nine

Summer, 1870

Angelique lifted the porcelain tea pot, and carefully poured a cup for Andrew, then herself. She spooned a little sugar into his and gently stirred before handing it to him.

"I am glad that we have started to do this, Andrew. It gives us a bit of alone time to catch up."

"It does. And makes me feel positively British in the process."

"It reminds me of Monsieur Muggah, who thought it was the most civilized of customs. I was glad it was part of his routine when he stayed at the St. Charles. I suppose I owe my arrival at Last Island to it."

"And since that's where you and I connected, I guess you could say that tea is the ultimate match-making drink."

She laughed. "I suppose that we should be drinking champagne instead to celebrate the success of your book."

He raised his eyebrows. "It has been the most amazing surprise."

"And I am so proud of you. The second one will be equally as well-received, I'm sure."

"If I get it written. The research alone takes so much time since I have limited resources."

"It may require that you spend a day in the city from time to time. Perhaps at the university library?"

"I will do that, in all probability, which brings up a subject that I'd like to discuss with you."

"Sounds serious."

"It is." He reached into the pocket of his waistcoat and removed an envelope. "This came yesterday, but I wanted a day to think about it before we spoke."

She tilted her head, fixing her steel blue eyes on his. He had her complete attention. "Go ahead."

"It is a job offer. A very exciting one, I might add."

"A job? I didn't realize that you had been looking for one."

"I hadn't. This just came to me because of the book."

"And?"

"It is from the University of Louisiana. They are expanding their science department to include meteorology. And they want me to join the faculty as a full professor."

Angelique could feel her heart racing as her mind tried to process the implications. But she hadn't forgotten his support when she chased her dreams, even though they didn't align with his. She would be a loyal partner, no matter what. He deserved that.

"My goodness, Andrew, how exciting. And what an incredible vote of confidence. But I never imagined you as a teacher."

"I never saw myself in that role either, but I find the idea of sharing what I have learned exciting. Besides, the position comes with a rather generous research grant."

"Which means what?"

"A chance for me to learn as well. I have been away from my field since that dreadful day at Fort Sumter. The war put much of the weather study on hold, so this is a chance to continue that, based on what we know. I miss it, Angelique, the challenge, the discovery."

She smiled, taking his hand. "Of course you do. This is your life's work. I remember the look of excitement in your eyes when you talked about cloud formations and barometric pressure."

He laughed. "I sound rather boring. How on earth did I manage to woo a beautiful woman like you?"

"Because in addition to your brilliant mind, you have a kind heart. I'm afraid that I was smitten by both."

He kissed her palm. "Then you think I should consider it?"

"Consider it? I think you should accept it, Andrew. It is time that you get to realize your dreams as well."

"Then, come with me into the library so that we can draft a letter."

"You begin, and I will join you shortly."

He nodded. "And we need to think about an apartment in New Orleans, perhaps even a small house near the campus. The prospects for the twin's education will much more varied there, too, which I hope they will find exciting. Franklin is a year overdue in entering college. I think that this will be good for all of us."

But Angelique didn't answer. This was his moment, and she certainly didn't want to spoil it, but she had no intention of leaving Chauvin Plantation or moving to New Orleans. Not now. Not ever.

Chapter Fifty

Fall, 1870

Terence had loaded the trunks onto the wagon and stood nearby, waiting. The plan had been to leave for New Orleans shortly after daybreak, and it was already well past that. He tried not to think of the fact this was an important time of year for the crops, and he hated to be away. But his employer had insisted that he do the driving, and he would refuse her nothing after all she had done for him and his family.

Franklin, dressed in his finest suit, joined him.

Terence whistled low. "Looking good. Big day for you, Franklin,"

"Sure is. When I was a boy, I never imagined that I would be off to college one day."

"I guess neither of us imagined what kind of dreams Miss Angelique would make come true."

Franklin grinned. "You are right, of course. She literally rescued me from the streets. Gave me a family and a whole lot of love. I am grateful to her for all she has done for me."

"She's good at that. Taking care of folks, I mean."

Franklin nodded. He leaned against the wagon. "Not sure how much longer it's going to be."

Terence shrugged. "I got all the time in the world."

Inside the house, Andrew paced, trying to conceal his growing agitation. "I'm sorry, but it makes no sense to me, Angelique. We fought so hard to avoid being separated. I thought once we reunited in the lobby of the St. Charles, we would never be apart again."

"I understand how you feel, Andrew, truly, I do. But it is temporary."

"Is it?"

"Of course, it is. And besides, this is very different."

"How?"

"Well, for one thing, there isn't a war going on. And I know exactly where you are. New Orleans is close enough that I can visit whenever I choose. When you get tired of the hustle and bustle of the city, you can come here, to the quiet of the country."

"And do you think that is going to happen? Will you and I make the journey to see each other for a brief moment or will it just be easier to go on with life?"

"I suppose I am much more optimistic about our commitment."

The comment stung. "And I suppose I underestimated how stubborn you are."

She wanted to laugh. Surely, her husband knew precisely how stubborn she was. "As soon as the harvest is over, the girls and I will join you in the city. I simply can't leave right now."

"I hope that after the crops are brought to market, you won't find some other excuse."

"I prefer the word reason, but I don't foresee a deferment."

"And will you write to me?"

"I will. You will be busy, more occupied than you might think with your new professional responsibilities. Franklin will need your support as he adjusts to college. The time will pass quickly. You'll see."

He left out a deep sigh. "I can tell that this discussion is going nowhere, so I will bid you goodbye. We are already running late."

Angelique hooked her arm into his. "Let me walk you to the wagon."

Andrew swallowed hard. "I will miss you."

"And I will miss you, too, darling." She looked deep into his eyes. "Never forget."

"You, too. Until we see each other again."

And within minutes, the wagon was headed down the drive, taking the two most important men in Angelique's life to a new adventure. Sometime, she thought, the wisest decisions were the most difficult to make. And she hoped that she was being wise.

Chapter Fifty-one

For the fifth day in a row, Angelique was in the fields. She had learned that she wanted to be in the thick of it all come harvest time, to see the sugar cane being cut, the wagons loaded higher and higher as the workers tossed it into random piles in a rhythm that they clearly understood. Terence had asked her to stand to the side, casually observe. He was worried that she might get hurt, but she dismissed him as she often did when she had made up her mind about something, and he had learned not to argue.

It was hot, even for a Louisiana fall, and Angelique adjusted her hat to shield her face from the sun. She was gleaning, gathering the dropped cane to bring home to the girls. It lasted for months stored properly in the kitchen, and they loved peeling away the husk to chew on it, something they had done since that first introduction to its sweetness in the fields of Maison Blanche.

Angelique found it hard not to be nostalgic with so much around her having changed. Although Franklin and Andrew had been gone for close to two months, she still had a difficult time adjusting to their absence, even though it had been her choice to stay behind. Letters came. They were doing well. Andrew's new position was a challenge, but exciting. Franklin was adapting to college life, excelling in his studies. The girls were growing, too. The school had expanded, which gave them better opportunities and more friends. They had little need for mothering these days. Even Jubilee was busy with her own home and child. Angelique had never been one for visiting with the women from nearby plantations, sipping tea and exchanging idle gossip as they stitched on some fancy needlepoint. But she wondered if that had been a mistake since her life sometimes felt unsettled. She was at a crossroads with more change to come. That much she knew.

It was a temporary state of being, she thought, a fleeting moment of discontent. The harvest would be over soon. She and the twins would join the rest of the family in New Orleans. Of course, the girls would protest over being uprooted in the middle of the school term. And she would need to remain at the helm until the crop had been brought to market and the books reconciled for both the cotton and cane. Then, the holidays would be upon them. It simply wouldn't be Christmas if they celebrated anywhere but at Chauvin with the big cypress tree decorated with the origami ornaments that meant so much. Once winter had passed, it would be time to sort the seeds and orchestrate the planting. Perhaps she might need to remain at Chauvin until summer. But she knew that was impossible. If Andrew was hell bent on living in New Orleans, so was she. There was a compelling reason, more important than crops or school or holiday celebrations. More important than anything.

Angelique was walking down the most recently cultivated row when the pain came. It took her by surprise, and she caught her breath, stopping for a moment until it subsided. Sweat dripped down her back as the cotton bodice of her dress stuck to her skin. She wondered if it was fleeting, indigestion perhaps, as she tightened her hold on the cane. But it gripped her again. Dropping the bundle, she willed herself not to panic.

There was an urgency in her step as she hurried home. She regretted having walked instead of taking her horse, but she had thought it to be a wiser decision. Besides, she had no idea how the day would transpire that morning. By the time she had reached the steps of the veranda, she knew what was happening as sadness washed over her, gripping her soul.

She hadn't been sure that she was pregnant the day that Andrew left for New Orleans, although she suspected as much. There was no need to tell him, to get his hopes up if it was simply a miscalculation. Two weeks later, when her monthly time failed to materialize, she was reasonably certain. It was hard not to conceal her joy, not to dash off a telegram to him with the news. But she wanted to wait, to be sure. Especially this time.

They had rarely spoken of the failed attempts to expand their family. Having children was all that Angelique ever wanted, but the twins' birth had been a difficult one, and she often wondered if that altered her chances to conceive again. Each passing month was disappointing, so they simply stopped anticipating that it would happen. Twice, when they were so filled with hope, the life had slipped from her womb within weeks of conception.

This time felt different. She was stronger, healthier. And even though she was older, she was optimistic that the Lord had deemed her worthy to have another baby. This time, she thought, it would happen.

The tears flowed as freely as the blood as she sat and waited for it to be over. It was her own fault, she thought. She had no business being in the fields in her delicate condition. To jeopardize her baby for her own ego and foolish pride was unpardonable. She wanted another chance. She wanted her mother, who would stroke her hair and tell her that all would be well, to reassure her that she didn't have to always be strong. But she was painfully alone, left only with her thoughts of sadness and guilt. And she knew with a reasonable certainty, that she would keep this secret close to her heart, bearing the sole burden of grief for a child that was never to be. Andrew would never know because to see the look of despair on his face would be unbearable, compounding the pain. No, the sadness would remain a part of her, along with so many moments that had become the story of her life.

She told the girls that she didn't feel well and needed to go to bed early. Cook gave them dinner. Afterwards, they found ways to entertain each other. Angelique lay awake thinking about what mattered most. And while the plantation was the realization of a dream, the restoration of what she had lost because of Jean Paul, it had cost her dearly. Her obsession was clearly an example of misplaced priorities. The place was made of bricks and boards. Hadn't she already witnessed how easily such things could be broken, snapped like branches in a storm? Somehow, she had lost sight of what was significant. Sure, she had been scratched and bruised by life. Hadn't everyone? But she had also been incredibly blessed, saved over and over again by the protective arms of the angels and the love of a wonderful man. A man who patiently waited for her.

Chapter Fifty-two

Three days later, Angelique felt strong enough to think about the move. The twins were less than enthusiastic when she proposed it until she described the opportunity for adventure that the city presented. "There are parks, libraries, stores, restaurants."

"And the bakeries are amazing," she added, "with pastries of every imaginable description."

Aida laughed, "I know that you think I am a child, easily swayed by the thought of cookies, but as you can see, Aimee and I are growing up."

Angelique felt her heart respond. She was right. The girls were at an age of self-discovery, navigating the transition between childhood and young adulthood. These years were important, and she didn't want to be too busy, too preoccupied, to miss a moment of the time that she had left with them. "Of course you are, although you can't blame me for wanting you to stay little forever."

Aida rolled her eyes while Aimee moved to take her mother's hand. "We will always be close, Momma. Always."

"And I know that Poppa and Franklin miss you. Our family has been apart for too long."

Somehow, when Angelique said it out loud, it solidified her feelings and confirmed that moving to

New Orleans was the right decision for all of them. "Now please help with the packing. We have so much to do."

"And will we never return here?" Aimee asked, looking around the parlor.

"Of course we will. This will always be our family home. New Orleans is close enough for us to spend holidays, vacations here. And I will come back at planting and harvest time. It will be a perfect balance. You'll see."

***

Saying goodbye to Jubilee was the hardest.

"My goodness," Angelique said, "it feels so strange to be leaving you behind. You have moved with us from Washington to Charleston to New Orleans to here. It is hard for me to remember a time when you weren't a part of our family."

"We have seen lots together, Miss Angelique. And traveling that path with you has brought me to this life. I wouldn't trade my man or my son for anything in the world."

"Even if it means being a farmer's wife?"

Jubilee laughed. "Sometimes, what you think you don't want is exactly what you need."

"I think that is the wisdom of the universe as it gently pushes you toward happiness."

"That is certainly true. And I have plans for the future. When you come back to visit, I hope that they will be in place."

"Really?"

"Jacob is getting older, and I want for him to have an education. There are so many children like him, sons and daughters of field workers both here and at neighboring plantations. I always saw myself as a teacher. I am going to build a school."

Angelique smiled. "Oh, Jubilee, what a noble idea,, and much needed as well. My goodness, you were born to be a teacher. I know that Aida and Aimee learned so much from you. Let me know when you break ground. I will do what I can to help you with the funding."

"I'd be so grateful, Miss Angelique. And if you don't mind, maybe I could borrow some of those books from the library as I need them?"

"Of course."

"Especially that book about the stars. I want those children to be able to look up into the sky and understand what they see, the vast beauty of the heavens above them."

"You are starting to sound like Andrew."

"I guess that he influenced me, too."

"I can bring you others from the city when I return. Write to me with your needs. You will write to me, won't you?"

"Of course I will. Terence will want for me to keep you informed on plantation business anyway."

"I'm leaving the place in good hands. That makes it easier."

"You know he will do his best to see to it that things are done right." She pointed. "And here he is himself."

"Wagon is loaded, Miss Angelique." Terence said. "Ready when you are."

Aida and Aimee moved in to bid their goodbyes to Jubilee.

"We will see you again soon," Aimee said, wiping away a tear.

"Going to miss you and little Jacob," Aida said.

"And I am going to miss you girls, too. Guess you will always be my babies, even when you insist that you are grown women."

"We are," they said in unison.

"Safe travels, Miss Angelique," Jubilee whispered. "If anybody deserves to be happy, you do."

The two women embraced. "It is time for both of us to start something, I guess, to trust the magic of new beginnings," Angelique said.

"I like that. Let's hope we both find that magic."

Chapter Fifty-three

It didn't take long for Angelique to realize that Andrew's apartment near the university was far too small to accommodate the five of them. Even with Franklin gone, off to class or studying most of the time, it still felt cramped. The girls complained about tripping over books, and Andrew had to use the campus library to write just for the quiet it afforded. The conditions were less than ideal.

But the twins had happily settled into their new school, declaring it better than the one they left behind. It pleased Angelique to hear them giggling as they whispered secrets about new friends and boys they deemed "dreamy." Only she was restless in the new place, not yet at home, although surrounded by those she loved. It was disconcerting, as though her life had been upturned as she searched for the pieces.

Each morning, Angelique poured over *The Picayune*, pursuing the ads for a suitable home. They had set relatively specific criteria, which limited the choices. And while location was important, Angelique also insisted that it have a little bit of green space. After so many years of growing cotton and sugar cane, she wanted to be surrounded by flowers, ones that she cultivated herself. She needed a little project to occupy her time.

When nothing materialized on the pages of the newspaper, she took matters into her own hands and began combing the neighborhoods, often on foot. Sometimes, she would walk for what seemed like miles without even realizing it, taking in the sights, examining the blocks of townhouses and cottages, punctuated by produce stands and restaurants. She had forgotten how alive these areas were, with people sitting on their tiny porches waving a greeting to passersby, music and smells wafting from homes and businesses alike. And yet, interestingly enough, one street over the atmosphere was obviously more affluent, with grand homes made of brick and stone, impressive structures built to demonstrate wealth and position in a flamboyant city. Angelique wanted something in between, large enough to accommodate their family, but not ostentatious. She would search until she found it.

One morning, when the apartment felt emptier than it normally did, she tied the ribbon of her bonnet under her chin and set off to explore another part of the city. She had learned to navigate the streetcar, memorizing the routes within a few miles of the university. If there was transportation readily available, she figured that she could expand her search of suitable areas. And perhaps, she could keep the girls in their new school and still make it convenient for Andrew and Franklin. House hunting had become her own personal challenge, and she had already come to realize that she never liked things that came to her too easily anyway.

She strolled along the sidewalks, admiring the flowers that still bloomed in spite of the impending winter. There was a familiarity to this area, and she wondered if she had passed through the district with Robert when she was so desperately looking for Aimee. As she turned north, she began to recognize street names. Her mind told her to stop, to turn and walk the other way, but she felt compelled to go on, drawn by a strange mixture of curiosity and dread.

She could hear the sound of her boots as they marked a rhythm, each step bringing her closer, but she could also hear her heart as it beat wildly in her chest. Minutes later she silently stood, observing the home where she had once lived, the cottage where Jean Paul had gallantly carried her over the threshold as a blushing bride, where Josephina had been born and tragically died, and where she had tearfully bid goodbye to Hannah one foggy morning. The ghosts spoke to her, reminding her of a life she once led, one so filled with promise. This place held a lifetime of events to recall, created only yesterday. But she had lived so much in the subsequent time that had passed that it felt like a hundred years ago. Much of it was best left dead and buried, except for one recollection, a bittersweet one. She thought of the morning when all that she owned was auctioned off to the highest bidder and how a shy budding meteorologist had purchased her most prized possession, a blue and white clock that had accidently been thrown into the mix. And she smiled as she recalled how sensing her distress, he had returned it to her. She had been immediately smitten. And when fate brought him back into her life, her heart was ready, open to the possibilities.

Angelique wondered how a place could have at one time held both her past and her future, but this one certainly did. Such irony. And indeed, the days spent there, both good and bad, had taught her lessons, brought her happiness, and given her memories. It was in this house that she learned to be strong, to stand on her own two feet as she faced whatever came her way. As she turned to catch the streetcar back to the apartment, she had a new resolve to find her family a home, one that they could share together. And she prayed that heartbreak would never cross the threshold.

Chapter Fifty-four

Angelique had been unusually quiet over dinner. The twins chattered on and on about school and the newest fashions. Andrew was questioning Franklin about one of his courses, while offering advice about the best way to study. No one seemed to notice her disengagement, which was probably best. It would have been difficult to explain the emotions she had experienced that afternoon after stumbling upon the house she had shared with Jean Paul. The children had no idea of the life she had led before the one with Andrew, and she preferred to keep it that way.

As she was clearing the table, Andrew put his arms around her. "Good dinner, darling. You have been so wonderful about doing the cooking. And when we get a proper house, I promise that we will hire help."

Angelique shrugged. "No need for that. I don't mind, really. It gives me something to do."

He put his hand under her chin raising her face until her eyes met his. "I know that this is an adjustment for you. You have gone from the business of running a plantation to the role of idle housewife. The latter doesn't suit you. I sense your discontent."

"Maybe when we find a house, it will be different. I can pursue some of my own interests. For now, life seems to be on hold."

"And I know you have shouldered this burden as well. I promise to help you with the search. After this week, my schedule should be a little more flexible."

"What is happening that will make such a difference?"

"I am ending one research project with a group of students. And I am about to begin another, one that I think will be most exciting."

"I'm interested if you can explain it in nonscientific terms. I am afraid that I tend to lose the ability to concentrate when you start with the complicated jargon."

He laughed. "I was thinking that you might help me."

"Help you? What on earth can I do besides record your data or stand in the corner and smile sweetly?"

"I am going on a field study tomorrow. It will be a day trip, but a long one. I had hoped that you might accompany me. It would get you out of the house, and I think you might find it interesting. And perhaps your observations might prove valuable."

"My observations? Where are you going?"

"That, my dear, is a surprise."

She clapped her hands. "I do love surprises. Yes, I will go with you. Should I pack us a lunch?"

"That would be wonderful. We leave early in the morning and won't return until sunset."

She nodded. "Then, I must choose what I am to wear for our little adventure."

"Adventure is a perfect way to describe it."

***

The next morning, they were at the station just as the sun was breaking the horizon. Andrew carried the picnic basket and his satchel with ink and paper to record notes. Angelique was unable to conceal her excitement as they boarded the train. "And our destination is still a secret?"

"It is."

She took the window seat and stared out at the low-lying Louisiana landscape. "I do think that the moss covered cypress trees are beautiful. The marsh looks so other worldly. There really is no place like it."

"Indeed. It is an interesting eco system. So much wildlife contained there."

Two hours later, when the train pulled into Bayou Bouef, Angelique raised an eyebrow. Andrew offered his hand as he escorted her to the waiting boat.

"Are we going where I think we are going?" she asked.

"Shall I spoil the surprise?"

She shook her head and swallowed hard. A range of emotions from apprehension to curiosity to elation flooded her mind. She was unsure of how she felt about Andrew's surprise. But regardless, they were headed toward the Gulf of Mexico. They were going to Last Island.

Chapter Fifty-five

There was a slight chill in the air, and Angelique was glad that she had brought her cloak. "I don't understand," she said as the steam engines started and the boat slowly pulled away from the shore.

"I have been commissioned to write a summation article about conditions on the island. It has been fourteen years since the hurricane destroyed most of what was there. The assumption is that the topography has changed based on the periodical storm activity and other metrological factors."

"You are speaking scientist again."

He laughed. "I am doing research on how different the island is now as a follow up to the book."

She nodded, but said nothing else, staring out into the wide expanse of the Gulf.

"You seem to be in deep thought," he said.

"I just never thought I would ever return here. I have mixed feelings, that's all."

"Understood. And maybe seeing it again will give you closure, help you to understand that survival brought out a strength in you that you didn't know you had."

"Perhaps. I had such happy moments there, yet overwhelming fear and sadness, too."

She tried not to think of Jean Paul, how easily she could have killed him that day, and what future heartache she might have spared them had she done it.

Andrew reached for her hand. They were quiet for the rest of the trip. But when the island came into view, she stood straight and tall, gripping the rail tightly with both hands.

"We are almost there," he whispered.

The hull of *The Star* lay weathered and decaying in the sand, a weary sentinel. The days following the storm had been played out there near the wreckage, when desperation and anguish surrounded them. It was hard not to recall the sadness, the loss that hung in the humid air like a dense fog.

As soon as Angelique's feet landed on the sandy soil, the world spun around her, the dizziness overwhelming, and she thought that she would faint at any moment. Oh, how she detested such weak women, damsels in distress who swooned at the slightest provocation. But she felt like one of them as she stood on the beach, surveying the island. It was all so overwhelming, too enormous to comprehend.

There was scattered debris. Pilings from homes long swept away and random rotting pieces of wood littered the landscape. The island, once filled with music from the hotel, the laughter of children dancing in the surf was eerily silent. Hand in hand, Andrew and Angelique walked the shore, looking for something recognizable, something that would point them to a place which was familiar and significant. There were bricks half buried in the sand, many in an arranged pattern that suggested that they were once steps.

Andrew pointed. "Do you think that is where the Ocean view was? Could that possibly be the entrance to the veranda?"

Angelique shrugged. This was much less of an archeological expedition for her as it was an emotional return. It mattered not where buildings once stood. What was important was that people lived here and loved here and died here. A terrible hurricane came and took most everything with it. And for some reason, they were spared.

Andrew stopped to take notes, quickly filling page after page in his book. A photographer from the university had set up his tripod and began to take shots of the desolate place, the remnants of a bygone time that would never come again. Angelique shuddered.

Wiping the tears from her eyes, the ghosts of the hundreds who were lost spoke to her through the breeze. She whispered a prayer for their immortal souls, a peaceful rest, and, for good measure, added a special petition for the Countess, whose kindness had gotten her through those early days at the resort and whose generosity continued to bless her daily.

As she stood and gazed out into the water, the waves crashing to the shore, she wondered about her life and the path she had chosen. Survival can bring with it a heavy burden to bear, a need to prove a worthiness for not perishing like so many others. Perhaps this is why she often felt restless and unsettled. Had she lived an honorable life since the winds blew and the waters rose taking so much with it? And would she ever be able to let go of the inexplicable pain she carried around like a sack of cotton, the ache that she concealed from everyone, even herself?

Andrew put his arms around her waist. "This is where we began, darling."

"It is. And while it has been hard to revisit, I think it was good for me. Perhaps it was time for me to think about this memory that I had tried so hard to forget. I didn't realize how much of the sadness of that time I still feel. Until now."

The wind blew harder as the sand swirled around them. Andrew pulled her closer. "Looking back can be hard, but important. We have had a series of unfortunate events to overcome, but life has a way of showing us how to be brave. You certainly are."

She nodded. And she wanted to add that much of the heartache could be traced back to Jean Paul, but she remained silent.

"I suppose we should be leaving if we are to keep to our time schedule," he said.

And as they walked back to the waiting boat, Angelique wondered how her thinking might have changed. On the return trip, she took a deep breath and closed her eyes, hoping to feel at peace. While she had so much to be grateful for, abundant blessings, a beautiful family, she, most certainly, had a troubled heart. And she couldn't quite understand why.

Chapter Fifty-six

After a long search, Angelique had finally located a suitable home in the Garden District of the city. The butcher had mentioned that it was about to be up for sale one morning when she was shopping for pork chops for dinner. And the next day, when the sign went up in the front yard of the raised cottage, she was the first to knock on the door to ask for a tour. It seemed ideal for her family. Located only four blocks from the university, it had a large parlor and adjacent dining room, three spacious bedrooms, attached kitchen and a full bath. Best of all, it had a lovely courtyard with a bit of green space in the back. When Andrew readily agreed, they made an offer on the spot and within a week, they were moving in.

Having a home helped them all feel more settled in the city. The girls loved their room which faced the street. They sat at the big window for hours, people watching, giggling away the summer afternoons. And when they discovered the park two blocks away, they met their friends there for gossip. It was hard for Angelique to imagine that they were already in their second to last year of school, young women on the precipice of adulthood. Franklin had distinguished himself as a student, and in fact, had managed to double his class load. Angelique admired his ambition and drive, although she worried about how he would survive. But he did, holding steadfast to the goal of becoming a physician. And Andrew's book had been nationally recognized as a remarkable combination of scientific facts and poignant human accounts. His research grant money had been increased as he began to delve into the idea of publishing daily weather reports, based on a set of predictors that he had compiled. He was excited about the possibilities that existed with his work.

Angelique had begun to garden, turning the backyard into an oasis of color, the fragrant flowers filling the air with a sweetness that made its way into the house through the open windows. She had learned to propagate her own varieties of roses, and when she wasn't digging in the soil, weeding or watering, she was out searching for something new to plant. And this gave her an opportunity to explore the neighborhood, chat with like-minded people, some with postage stamp sized front yards and others with more impressive plots. Many had full time gardeners and merely supervised the work or cut the flowers for bouquets. But Angelique loved the feeling of the soil in her hands, which took her back to her childhood on Chauvin Plantation when her father had given her a tiny plot of land and allowed her to plant whatever struck her fancy. She had ended up with tomato bushes intertwined with daisies and zinnias, but as the plants grew and blossomed, she thought it was magical. She still did.

At the suggestion of one of her neighbors, she took the streetcar downtown and into the French Quarter.

Every Thursday afternoon, several of the homeowners opened their secret gardens for tours. Angelique had always wondered what lay beyond the wooden gates and brick walls which concealed the enchanted grounds of such homes. And she was not disappointed as she went from place to place, trying to memorize the combination of flowers in a container or bed that caught her eye.

It was a lovely afternoon and not as hot or humid as a typical Louisiana summer, so she decided to explore a little more before returning home. As she reached the edge of the Quarter and crossed over onto Basin Street, a riotous display of color two blocks away came into view. Climbing roses, she guessed, as she was drawn to the sight.

She stood in front of the iron fence, reaching over to smell the fragrance of the bright red blossoms, and curious, she looked beyond. Peering through the greenery, she spotted the whitewashed tombs. The cemetery. She had never been here on foot, having had Robert to deliver her on those mornings when she visited with regularity so long ago. It looked different from this vantage point, changed over the years. But then, she had changed as well.

Her first instinct was to turn and walk away, not subject herself to the painful memories that lie beyond the gate, but something tugged at her heart. Her sweet baby rested so close. How could she not visit her?

She swallowed hard as she stood at the entrance. The location of Josephina's grave had been etched into her mind, and she was not surprised to have remembered it clearly. Second row from the left, six down. She crossed one path where a worker tended to a tomb. He paused, brush in hand, and she thought, gratefully, that the graveyard had not fallen into decay and neglect like so many others. Slowly, she made her way to the place she sought, the marble angel still marking where Josephina lay. It had been recently washed, the weeds removed. And she wondered why that meant so much to her. Her eyes filled with tears and her hands shook as she gently touched the engraving. It had been so long. Grief settles into a person's soul, finds a place to reside forever. But standing there, reopened the wound, causing a flood of emotion that came with such a force that she stifled a scream as if the sheer act would help release the pain. She had forgotten for a moment how final and absolute death was, not only robbing those left behind of the physical presence of the one lost, but exacting an emotional price, a debt that could never be paid.

Josephina's death had been the beginning of the days of sadness for her, the unraveling of her life with Jean Paul. It was as though her tiny spirit had kept them together, and when she departed, there was nothing left except for emptiness and sorrow, which neither could share. And she wondered if his misdeeds, his reckless behavior had somehow stemmed from the loss of their baby, so tragically taken from them. But then, as he looked at the engraving of his name and faked date of death on that same tomb, the anger resurfaced. Life is always about choice, and he chose to gamble, to lie and steal. Worst of all, he chose to kidnap Aimee, take her from her family. There were no justifiable reasons to explain what he had done, and certainly no forgiveness in her heart.

She wiped her eyes and kissed the tomb. "Rest in peace, my angel," she whispered. "You have two sisters. Watch over them. And until we meet again in heaven, know that I love you, and I always will."

Taking a deep breath, she adjusted her bonnet and made her way to the gate. Perhaps she would take a carriage home instead of walking the four blocks to the streetcar. It had been an unusual day, one occupied with flowers and remembrance. Symbols of life and death. As always, life was a contradiction, a paradox of moments of joy peppered with melancholy. And there is no real choice other than to go on, hoping the days which follow will be better than those past. Without that, there is nothing. And while the New Orleans house represented so much, the restoration of all that she had lost, she wondered why she still felt restless. Peace, it seemed, was elusive, hard won. And somehow, she knew the answer lie somewhere between revenge and forgiveness.

Two rows over, Jean Paul paused from his task of white washing a tomb. He removed his hat and wiped the sweat from his brow with a bandana he kept in his back pocket. A woman was leaving, having visited the grave of someone she loved, no doubt. He was accustomed to the parade of mourners, some who visited daily, others whom he saw once and never again. As he studied her, watching as she walked away, he thought that she reminded him of Angelique, the familiar gait, the tilt of her head. For a moment, he considered running after her just to see. And then, he remembered the day in the business district when he followed the stranger for blocks thinking it was she. He laughed at his foolhardiness. Angelique was in Charleston. And he prayed that she had found some joy in spite of the pain he had caused her.

Chapter Fifty-seven

Spring, 1872

Angelique was arranging flowers in a cut glass vase. She hummed a song that she had learned as a child, having long forgotten the words. It had been quite some time since she had prepared for a party. Was it the masquerade ball at the Oceanview, she wondered? And for a moment, she recalled that lovely night of excitement and romance in the middle of the Gulf of Mexico. Admittedly, there had been little to celebrate since. But life is a dynamic force and when the difficult days pass, moments of joy often follow. This was certainly one of those.

It was the happiest of occasions, a time to remember. All three of the children were graduating. The girls had completed high school, and Franklin had earned a medical degree. Angelique had spent months planning the celebration, sparing no detail. It was a proud moment.

Franklin entered the kitchen. "What smells so good?"

"Gumbo, of course. I hadn't forgotten how much you love it, Dr. Slater."

He walked over to the stove and lifted the lid on the cast iron pot. When Angelique wasn't looking, he tasted a spoonful. "Guess it is going to take me a while to get used to being called that."

"Well, you have certainly earned the title, son. I can't begin to describe the pride I feel."

He leaned against the cupboard, "Oh, Momma, my life would have been so different had I not met you that day in the park. I was nobody, had nothing, belonged to no one. What future did I have? I owe everything to you. You took a chance on me, and I never wanted for you to regret it."

"Goodness, Franklin, I never did. In fact, it is I who felt grateful to you. " She wiped the tear that rolled down her cheek with the corner of her apron. "I have always been fascinated by how life works. You are the only good thing that came from the tragedy of Aimee's kidnapping. And certainly, without you, we would have never found her. I can't even begin to fathom how that would have altered my life as well."

"I guess it is one of the grand mysteries. Some things we will never understand."

"And I would say that you were meant to be a part of this family."

"In order to have bratty little sisters," he teased, pointing to Aida and Aimee as they entered the room.

Aida crossed to him, punching him in the arm. "Hey, I heard that. You may be Dr. Fancypants to some, but I do believe that I can still give you a hard time."

He laughed. "And I wouldn't have it any other way."

"You look lovely," Angelique said, moving to hug them, noting that they no longer dressed alike. "Are you excited about your party?"

"I know that I am. All of my friends are coming." Aida said, and Angelique was struck by the fact that it had been a long time since she spoke for her sister.

"And you, Aimee?" Angelique asked.

"Of course. This is an important day, I suppose. In the eyes of the world, we are no longer children."

Angelique smiled, trying hard to put on a brave face. "It is difficult for me to believe that you two will be in college in just a few months. Where did the time go?"

"It is inevitable, Momma," Aimee said. "The seasons pass, children grow up. Time waits for no one."

"That was almost poetic," Aida said as she dipped a spoon into the bowl of potato salad.

Aimee rolled her eyes. "Sarcasm doesn't become you, sister dear. You are already sounding like somebody itching to study the law with that fine-tuned waggishness of yours."

Aida sighed, "And it is so unfair that just because I am a woman those doors are closed to me. I am as smart as any man. Maybe even smarter. Do they truly think that if they give us rights theirs will somehow be threatened? Insecure fools! It is high time that America realizes that we are not a weak-minded gender. Surely, if we are resilient enough and clever enough to have the babies and then raise them to adulthood, we should be able to vote. I shudder to think what would happen if the roles were reversed and men were responsible for bringing life into this world."

Franklin laughed. "I am sure that there would be fewer births, for starters. I have worked in obstetrics. I remember that night with Jubilee. The whole birthing experience strikes me as rather painful. It takes a lot more courage to be a mother than it does to be a father."

"My point exactly. We are, by far, the stronger sex."

"Not sure that I can argue with that, or if I'd be willing to try," Franklin said. "But I can still pick you up and twirl you around."

"And I can still talk you into a corner."

He nodded. "No disagreement there. I hope that by the time you finish your studies as a legal assistant, law school will be open to you. If I ever end up in jail, I sure would want you on my side."

"I do, too," she whispered, the disappointment on her face obvious. "I have a lot of fight in me, I suppose."

"As for you," he said, moving close to Aimee. "The fact that you have chosen nursing pleases me to no end. Perhaps when you are done with training, you will join me. I have big plans for my medical practice. I could use your help."

"We shall see, Franklin. I am determined to become the Florence Nightingale of New Orleans, you know."

"And I have no doubt that you will," he said.

Angelique stood quietly, listening to the banter between her children. They were bright, responsible young adults. She couldn't imagine anything more fulfilling. There may have been difficult times in her life, moments when all hope was lost, but this one instance made all of the struggle worth it. In their success, she found hers.

Andrew called from the parlor. "Hey, where are you guys? Looks like the guests are arriving."

And the family made their way to the front door to greet them. It was time for a party.

Chapter Fifty-eight

Andrew had weeks of writing ahead of him. The publisher had set a deadline for the second book, and he was feeling the pressure.

"I was thinking that maybe we could spend some time at Chauvin," he suggested that night as they got ready for bed.

Angelique had been brushing her hair and stopped short at his suggestion. "Truly?"

"I remember the solitude it provided when I wrote the first book. I do love the hustle and bustle of the city, but it is often distracting, which makes concentrating difficult. Even the library at the university can be chaotic as groups of students gather to share study questions. I think it would give me the quiet I need to finish this."

She was pleased. It was less than enjoyable to make the trips back on her own while he stayed behind for work and to supervise the girls. And even though the plantation was in Terence's capable hands, she still needed to visit. It was, after all, her business, and the profits, along with her money from the Countess helped to fund their life in New Orleans as well as their children's college education. She wasn't so foolish as to ignore the responsibilities that accompanied such a large enterprise, especially as Terence had tamed the back forty acres that her father had always deemed unplantable. And she couldn't wait to see what he had done with the plot of land.

"And maybe it is isn't as wet there. This has been such a rainy spring. "

"That would be nice. I have never witnessed so much precipitation, although it fascinates me from a meteorological perspective. Some folks are worried about flooding if the river gets any higher."

Angelique was alarmed. She knew what that could mean, although she tried not to consider the possibilities. She changed the subject. "So when shall we leave?"

"I'd say by the end of the week if you are in agreement."

She moved to kiss him. "I am absolutely in agreement."

***

Three days later they were making the familiar trip away from the city and up the river road toward Chauvin.

As the levees came into view, Angelique peered out to gauge the level of the water. It was obvious by the puddles which dotted the road that rain had been an issue here, too. She hoped that it hadn't washed away the newly planted seed. That could be a disaster.

Terence greeted them with a half-smile, his brow furrowed from worry. "Rain's been bad, Miss Angelique. The ground has taken about all that it can hold."

"And the seed?"

"Not sure yet. The good thing is that it is early. It will be hard, but we can replant if we have to."

"And costly."

"Well, yes, but better than losing an entire season. A later crop is better than none."

Angelique agreed. "Let's go out in the morning and inspect the fields."

"Sure enough, Miss Angelique."

The next morning as Andrew settled in with his manuscript, Angelique and Terence mounted the horses and made their way to examine the grounds. It was worse than she had imagined. Rivulets had formed between the tilled rows and the earth bulged from the water that had no place to go. Much of it was impassable, so they could only speculate as to the damage.

"We won't know until the sun comes out and dries it up a bit. Until then, we wait."

"I wonder how long that will take?" Angelique asked, impatient, as always.

Terence laughed. "If I knew that, I would be a weather expert. But we do have one here. Why don't we ask him?"

Back at the house, Angelique softly knocked on the door of the library. "We hate to interrupt you, Andrew, but we have some questions that maybe you can answer."

Angelique was serious. She stood near the desk pinching her hands, a habit she had developed long ago when forced to face something she deemed painful.

"Of course, how can I help?"

"The weather. Any idea when the rain will end, and more importantly, when the sun will come out and dry things out."

"As you might well imagine, it is virtually impossible to pinpoint the conditions in the atmosphere, which are ever-changing. But sometimes, we can see a pattern, especially in the clouds."

"And?" Angelique was anxious for answers, not explanations.

"Cumulonimbus clouds. Notice how they look like cauliflower, something I always thought amusing. They indicate rain, more than likely a mature thunderstorm. Come, I will show you."

The trio stood on the veranda as Andrew pointed to the white wisps in the sky. "I am afraid that it isn't over."

Angelique swallowed hard. "Bad news for the crops."

"Let me see if I have an old barometer here. If I can take some regular readings, maybe I can give you better news. It we can see a rapid rise in pressure, that means improving conditions and clearing skies. We will keep our fingers crossed."

"Sure will, Mr. Andrew," Terence said. "That's about all we can do."

But Angelique was less resigned to the inevitable. She had lived on the river for much of her life, and she knew that losing a sprouting crop was the least serious consequence to come from the incessant rain. Andrew might have been the scientist, but she was well versed in the concept of cause and effect. And the possibility of this one, scared her more than she would admit.

Chapter Fifty-nine

The rain had slowed to a drizzle by the next morning, but the dampness hung in the thick air. And the ground, which was already saturated, tried to accept more. It was as though Mother Earth was drowning and desperate to save herself, tried in vain to divert the water to other places as gullies formed and quickly became streams.

As Andrew worked, Angelique stood at the window, trying to process the scene. She examined the clouds for a ray of sunshine, but when none was forthcoming, simply wondered how much longer it would be. By mid-afternoon, when it began to pour again, she had given up hope.

She was so lost in thought that she hadn't noticed the men who arrived on horseback until they knocked on her door.

"Howdy, ma'am," one said, tipping his hat, which dripped water onto his shoulders. "Wondering if we could have a word."

"Of course. Come in."

They stood in the hall, the water from their rain soaked clothing trickling down onto the crimson rug that her mother had so carefully chosen to accentuate the space as visitors were welcomed into the stately home. "Sorry about the mess," he said.

"Unavoidable, I'm afraid. How can I help you? You wouldn't be out in this unless it was a matter of importance."

"That's for sure. I'm Joseph Bergeron. I live about a mile down the road. Moved in about six months ago. These men are my neighbors. I guess you know some of them."

"Yes, of course. How are you, Stephen? Jefferson?" The men nodded in recognition.

"Is your husband home, ma'am? This is something that needs to be discussed with him, I'm afraid."

Angelique narrowed her eyes. Unless this man was here to ask about weather conditions, his business was with her, not Andrew. "He is. But you should know that this is my family plantation. I make the decisions here. So say what's on your mind."

His face flushed and he cleared his throat. "I understand. But would you invite your husband to listen to what we have to say?"

Angelique sighed. And before she could ask Andrew to join them, he appeared. "What's going on? I overheard some of the conversation. Are there some concerns, gentlemen?"

Joseph nodded. "Trouble, I'm afraid."

"What kind of trouble?"

"Stephen here heard some commotion last night and went out to investigate. His house is closest to the levees."

"And?"

"Let him tell it."

"Saw some men prowling around the levees," Stephen said. "Can't say for certain, but I have reason to believe they are from New Orleans."

Angelique held her breath. She knew what that meant. "Lord, help us," she whispered.

"I don't understand," Andrew said. "Why would men from New Orleans be a concern?"

"They want to blow up the levees, divert the water," Angelique said. "It means the city is in danger. And they will readily sacrifice us to save themselves."

"Flood us instead?" he asked.

She nodded. "There are a few plantations, but it is mostly smaller homes, poorer country folks. Somehow, to those in power, we don't seem nearly as valuable."

"But that's unconscionable."

"People have no conscious when it comes to their own safety. Surely the war taught you that," she said.

"Yes, of course. So what can we do? Anything?"

"That's why we are here," Joseph said. "We have to defend our homes, our families."

"And what are you proposing?" Andrew asked.

"A watch. Tonight and every night until this is over."

"Count me in," Andrew said.

"Are you sure?" Angelique asked.

"Why wouldn't I be? This is our home, your legacy. I will protect it and you."

"It could get ugly," Joseph said. "You will need a weapon, and be prepared to use it."

"I understand. And if Terence is willing, he can come, too. He has as much at stake here as we do."

"I will speak with him," Angelique said. "Jubilee and Jacob can stay here with me."

"We have divided the levee into sections. If each of us covers a portion, we will have secured the entire area."

"Agreed," Andrew said. "Let's hope that the rain stops and the water recedes before anybody gets hurt."

"It is what we always hope for," Stephen said, "but unfortunately, we have to be prepared for the worse."

Chapter Sixty

Thankfully, the rain had stopped. The air was thick and heavy, with fog cloaking the levee like a gossamer blanket. For the third night in a row, Andrew and Terence stood watch, waiting for visitors who were hell-bent on destruction.

"See anything?" Andrew whispered to Terence?

"No, but I think that's a good thing. If we have guns, I would imagine that they do, too. Don't think that either of us are looking to get shot tonight or any night."

"Not if we can help it, that's for sure."

They sat in silence for another hour when a dim light in the distance caught Andrew's eye. He put his index finger over his mouth and pointed. Terence nodded.

Andrew cocked the rifle. The light grew closer, then went out. A man carrying a burlap bag over his shoulder looked around and then stopped, placing the bag on the ground. He reached in and pulled out a long thin object, then another, and another. Sticking each one in the wet earth, he struck a match, poised to light them.

"Cover me," Andrew said to Terence as he swiftly moved to the man.

"Don't do anything that will get you killed," he said to the man as he shoved the barrel of the gun into his ribs and blew out the match. With his left foot, he kicked away the dynamite. "You have two choices, fight or flight. The way I see it, I have a gun, so it would be unwise for you not to choose the latter."

The clouds parted and a sliver of moonlight illuminated the scene. The man narrowed his eyes at Andrew. Without uttering a word, he reached for the pistol in his waistband. Andrew fired.

As though in slow motion, the man fell, gasping for breath as the blood flowed from the gaping wound.

Within minutes, the other men had joined them, surveying the scene. "We heard the shot," Stephen said. "What a fool."

"Just a desperate man, I guess," Andrew said, "like so many of us. Guess he underestimated what we would do to protect our homes."

"Wonder if he was a hired mercenary?" Joseph asked.

"In all probability. Politicians don't like to get their hands dirty. They hire folks to do their bidding so that they can claim no knowledge of things when they happen. I have lived long enough to see how power works. And ultimately, it corrupts."

The men nodded in agreement. "Guess the only advantage to the wet soil is that it won't be difficult to dig this man a grave."

"And if it is alright with you, Mr. Andrew, I have just the spot on the edge of the fields. Nobody will be the wiser," Terence said.

"Then let's do it now. And we all agree that this never happened," Joseph said.

And the men shook on it. "It never happened," they repeated in unison.

***

As night turned into day, the sun rose in the East. By mid-afternoon, the water had begun to recede. Andrew had reported an uneventful night on the levee, for which Angelique was grateful. And three days later, the fields were dry enough for Terence and Angelique to ride out once more. Terence reached into the soil first one place and then another. He moved to the next row and gently pushed the dirt aside.

"All gone, I'm afraid," he said.

"I expected as much. How long before we can reseed?"

"If it stays dry, next week. It will put us behind, but only by a few weeks."

"Then, we will do what we must," she said. "We will replant because sometimes, you just have to begin all over again." And as he led her horse back to the house, she smiled. It was a lesson she had learned through experience. After the storm, the rebuilding begins. And sometimes, a new start is exactly what is needed.

Chapter Sixty-one

Fall, 1873

Just as Terence predicted, the crop had been delayed by a few weeks, and while the replanting had cost a bit in time and money, the profits from the harvest had more than made up for any losses. He beamed with pride as they went over the numbers.

"None of this would have been possible without you," Angelique said.

"Nah. I've already said that you would have found you a good hand to run the place."

"I don't think so, Terence. Not one who cared."

"Well, this is more than a job to me, Miss Angelique. Thanks to you, it is also a home for me and my family. Our future is here."

Angelique handed him a piece of paper. "And this will add to that future. It's another two acres."

"If you keep this up, you won't have much of a plantation left," he said.

"Nonsense. I have plenty of land. I have to do what I can to keep you."

"No worries, Miss Angelique. Jubilee wouldn't let us leave here anyway. She sure is happy with that school."

"I visited yesterday. It is really remarkable. She was born to be a teacher. Which reminds me, I have some books in the carriage for her. Will you see to it that she gets them?"

"I sure will. Yup, I am mighty proud of her. And she is doing good by those children who might never learn to read or write."

"It is noble work, Terence. Jubilee is quite a woman."

"Well, she once told me that her life changed the day she knocked on your door to be the nanny of those girls. I think you taught her a thing or two about how to be strong, to not back down, even when times get hard."

Angelique swallowed hard. "That is kind of you. Jubilee was by my side through some of the most difficult moments in my life."

"I always thought it funny how life works. People get to be brought into your life for one reason or another, but usually to help you in some way. I know that might sound funny coming from me since I spent most of my life as a slave, but I have seen it over and over again. One of the house servants at Maison Blanche taught me how to read. She had learned from her mistress as a child. I guess what I mean is that you just never know."

"I agree. Absolutely."

"And the day you arrived at the Bourgeois house with your husband and three children, little did I know that mine was going to be changed. For sure."

Angelique laughed. "Guess that is the truth."

He tipped his hat. "I need to be getting back to work now. And I will get those books out the wagon for Jubilee."

"I am leaving in the morning. You make sure that things are under control while I am gone."

"Will do, Miss Angelique. This place is safe with me."

"I know it, Terence. And it brings me great comfort."

Chapter Sixty-two

Angelique had not even considered venturing from the house. She had added another log to the fire and settled down with a book. Andrew wouldn't be home until five, and the girls had back to back classes. She had hours until dinner, an afternoon to herself.

Franklin, she hoped, wouldn't be late. He had been so busy with his work at Charity Hospital, that he was rarely home. When she had expressed her concerns about his need for rest, he winked and said that he usually slept on a cot in the physician's lounge.

"But that can't be comfortable," she had protested.

"It isn't," he said, "but if I am there when the most interesting cases come in, I get them. I have learned more in the months I have spent on the wards then all of my time in a college classroom. There are so many people in need, Momma. If I can help, I must."

"You make it hard to argue with that," she had said.

But ultimately, she had made him agree to come home for dinner at least once a week. "Let's make Wednesday family night, no matter what."

Those evenings were always a special occasion, a meal that had been carefully planned, a good bottle of wine. She looked forward to the table conversation as her children chattered away, sharing the news of their busy lives.

Putting her book aside, she went into the kitchen to check on the bread that was rising. The roast would go into the oven in a couple of hours, and she would peel the potatoes and carrots after that. She searched for the ingredients so that they would be at the ready later, but was unable to find potatoes. Thinking back to the last time she cooked them, she remembered using the few that were left three days earlier. Unable to find a suitable substitute in the cupboard, she sighed as she grabbed her cloak and gloves from the hall tree and headed toward the neighborhood market.

The wind was stronger than she thought, and she shivered as she pulled the wrap around her neck. It was foolish not to have been prepared. In the distance, she could see what appeared to be a child, a little girl, alone. She seemed to be lost. The image was puzzling, and Angelique wondered if she was imagining it. She quickened her pace to get closer.

For a moment, she thought she was watching Aimee, her long black hair bouncing with each step. The stab to her heart was swift and painful. This child was about the age that her daughter had been when she was taken, abducted by Jean Paul. If the girl needed help, she had to come to her aid.

"Stop," she called, "I won't hurt you."

But the child began to run, turning down a side street and into an alley.

Angelique followed.

"Please," she said. "Let me help you. I have two little girls of my own at home."

And the girl continued to run, darting in and out of secluded places, around corners. Angelique struggled to keep up until, finally, she disappeared out of sight.

The experience was unsettling. Angelique wondered if she had been bewitched by some voodoo spell or had suddenly developed an otherworldly sixth sense, but the encounter was real. So was the child. That much she knew for sure.

She had almost forgotten about the potatoes and had to double back to the market. But once back home, could not shake the feeling of bewilderment about the experience. Perhaps the child was an orphan who saw Angelique as one of those well-meaning women who were meant to save such children, but only brought them to a place of misery and despair. She recalled Aimee and Franklin's account of Sister Bertha and Brother Nelson, who had taken them against their will with the promise of a better life. When she thought of the orphanage where she had found Aimee, a filthy, overcrowded home of hopelessness, tears filled her eyes. These were children. Surely, they deserved something more than a cot on which to sleep and a bit of questionable food. What kind of future could they ever hope for in such a place?

As she peeled the potatoes, she thought about the rains that had washed away the cotton seed. The idea of starting anew had filled her with optimism. And yet, she had fallen back into the rhythm of her life, the daily routine as she ignored the signs. Perhaps that is what happening upon the child was meant to give her. It felt like a gentle nudge into a different direction with her life, a divine signpost, guiding her to where she was supposed to be.

By the time the roast was cooked and the family had gathered around the table, she had the answer. The undoubtable certainty came from deep within her soul. Suddenly, she had an answer to the question she didn't know how to ask, and it was deeply satisfying.

"I have an announcement to make," she said as she raised her glass to make the first toast.

"What is it, Momma?" Aida asked.

"I am going to open an orphanage."

"A what?" Andrew asked.

"An orphanage. I have no idea where or when or how. But it will happen."

"I have no doubt of your determination, but why that and why now?"

She looked at Aimee and winked. "Because it is what I am meant to do. And because, quite frankly, I can."

Andrew had no words, having learned long ago that once his wife had decided, it was hard to alter that decision. "I hope you will give this some thought before you do anything."

"I have. My mind is made up. It is important to me, Andrew."

"Then, you certainly have my support."

Aimee whispered something to Aida who nodded. "We'll be right back," they said, running upstairs to their bedroom.

"Close your eyes," they said in unison when they returned.

Angelique obliged.

"Now open them."

There in front of her was a black velvet box. "A present from all of us, although Franklin put in the most." Aida said. "We were waiting for the best time to give it to you. This is it."

"I don't understand," Angelique said.

"You will," Aimee said.

Angelique slowly opened the box to reveal a blue enamel butterfly pin with gold antennae and sapphire eyes. She began to cry. "It is lovely. Just so beautiful. Thank you for such a thoughtful gift."

"We thought you needed an angel of your own, a reminder of what a loving mother you are. Follow your dreams just as you have taught us to follow ours."

Perhaps it was time for her to spread her wings and fly, she thought. In that defining moment, Angelique was able to finally comprehend what had stood between her and true peace. And she intended to shatter those walls.

Chapter Sixty-three

Spring, 1874

Angelique took the streetcar to the French Market. She needed to find the one person who could help her. Robert. She breathed a sigh of relief when she found him, sitting on a bench in the square.

"Robert!" she said. "I was afraid that you wouldn't be here." He was older, the lines etched in his face more pronounced, his hair greying around the temples.

"Miss Angelique," he said, obviously pleased to see her. "My goodness, it has been a long time. How are you? Are you in town for a visit?"

She hadn't considered how much time had passed since he delivered her family to Maison Blanche. One year tends to run into the next erasing some things and reclaiming others. "I have much to tell you, I suppose. But no, we live here now, near the university where Andrew currently works."

"That's wonderful. So glad to see you are so happy."

"Thank you, Robert. I still have you to thank for helping to reunite my family. I will never forget your kindness."

"I was happy to do so. You know that."

"I came here specifically looking for you. I need your help once more."

"Anything I can do for you, as always."

"I need for you to take me someplace."

"Gladly. But you came all this way for a ride?"

"It is a place that only you would know how to find."

"Now, you are sounding mysterious. Yes, of course. I will take you anywhere. Come, meet my new horses." He led her to his waiting carriage.

Time had taken its toll on many things, including the horses she had given him eighteen years earlier. She was pleased to hear that they were retired, living out their days at a friend's farm, with children who delighted in riding them daily.

Perhaps it was this sudden realization of the fleeting nature of life that strengthened her resolve. "Take me to the female orphanage. Remember the place we went to when we were looking for Aimee?"

"The one that was abandoned and in such a dismal state?"

"Yes. There."

He shook his head. "Are you sure? I can't imagine that anyone has done anything with it since your visit."

"That is what I am counting on," she said.

He was confused, but willing to oblige. "Then there we shall go," he said.

The trip hadn't taken as long as she had recalled. Perhaps it was closer than she thought. And so, twenty minutes later, Robert coaxed the horses to the curb. She sat there, peering out the window. She tried to process the image.

As he opened the door, he offered his hand, "It is worse than I remembered it."

"I see that," she whispered. The brick façade was crumbling. Wild vines climbed up the walls and snaked into the broken windows. Part of the roof was missing. The iron fence was rusting, sections completely decomposed.

"Do you think we can get inside?"

"It's possible, although it might be dangerous. If you don't mind me asking, why so interested in this particular building?"

"This is where I first knew that Aimee was alive and that finding her was a possibility. I felt hope standing on these steps. And I won't soon forget that. But I have been blessed, Robert. And now, I have the means to do something good, noble. I can't imagine a better place to begin than here."

He nodded. "Kind of you, as always, Miss Angelique. And what are your plans?"

"This is going to be an orphanage, a place where children who have no family will be nurtured and loved, where they will know that they can have dreams."

"It is going to take a lot of time and money to turn that into a reality."

"Granted. But we both know that time passes regardless. So you can't give up on a goal just because of that. I am determined."

"Then, let's see if we can get inside to have a look."

He had managed to find an unlocked window and crawled inside. "I am sure that this is considered illegal," he said, opening the door for her.

"Probably. But you can always blame me. It was, after all, my idea."

"Nevertheless, I suggest we look around as quickly as possible."

They slowly made their way down the darkened corridor. There were several small rooms on either side, all in a similar state of disrepair. The paint was peeling, the floors were unleveled, with random boards missing. Dust hung in the air like a thick blanket, making breathing difficult. A small pool of foul smelling water had accumulated near a shattered window. The kitchen was a filthy mess. Animal droppings covered every surface while rusty pots hung from the overhead rack. Robert looked at the staircase and deemed it unsafe. So whatever the second floor held was a mystery.

"We need to go," he whispered.

Back on the sidewalk, Angelique took deep breaths in an effort to clear her lungs. "It is as bad as I thought."

"Still determined?" Robert asked.

"Even more so. Can you imagine being a child having to exist in such a terrible place?" She shuddered to think of Aimee there, even if it was short-lived.

"Any idea who owns the building?"

"The church, I think. It was run by the Sisters of Charity. They took over the new children's orphanage. I suppose I would begin would be a meeting with the Bishop if I were you."

"Then, I will do that as soon as possible. And if you wouldn't mind delivering me home, you will know where to fetch me when I need you again."

"As always, I am here to help," he said.

"I am counting on that, Robert," she said. "You have been a source of support for me for a very long time."

"Happy to do so, ma'am. Always."

Chapter Sixty-four

Angelique wasted no time in trying to see the bishop. It wasn't like people were lined up, desperate to buy the run-down building, but she was afraid that if she thought about it rationally, factored in all of the work that needed to be done, she would lose some of that resolve which kept her motivated. So she moved forward as soon as possible.

She arrived on a Tuesday afternoon, unannounced and with no appointment, but before making her way to the offices, she stopped into the cathedral, just to have a little chat with God. The St. Louis was massive, designed in the style of French European churches, with a main altar and two smaller ones on either side. The hand painted ceiling soared for at least fifty feet, with walnut beams providing architectural interest. It wasn't her regular church since its location in the French Quarter was farther from her home than she would have liked, but whenever she had the occasion to visit, she did. Somehow, because it was the seat of the diocese for the entire city, it felt important, as though God viewed it as His base of operations, too.

After lighting a candle, she slipped into a pew. "Lord," she prayed, "if this is Your will, then, let it happen easily. And give me the courage and stamina to see it through."

Taking a deep breath, she made her way through the iron gate at the side alley and onto the rear courtyard, searching for the heavy white door labeled as the office. She walked in and approached the priest who sat behind the reception desk. "I would very much like to see the Bishop on a matter of upmost importance."

The young priest cleared his throat. "Do you have an appointment, Madame? As you might well imagine, the Bishop is a very busy man."

"I understand that. But for me to make the trip here to simply arrange a time, then, to return at that time seems rather inefficient. I had hoped that you might extend a kindness and allow me a brief audience with him. I can assure you that he will be most pleased with what I have to propose."

"It may take a while."

"I will wait."

For the next hour, Angelique studied the picture of the sacred heart of Jesus along with the portrait of the Pope which hung in the waiting area. She wondered if it was true that Jesus chose the Pope or if that was just a bit of church wisdom used to influence the congregation. Regardless, she decided that he had a kind face and was probably a good man, with a huge responsibility on his shoulders. Perhaps because she was about to assume one as well, she felt a kinship with him. She wondered if she would ever travel to Italy. If she did, she decided, she would very much like to meet the Pope. And so, lost in thought, she failed to hear the priest call her name until he appeared by her side.

"His Excellency will see you now," he simply said, ushering her into the well-appointed book-lined office where the bishop sat behind a massive walnut desk.

"Mrs. Slater," he said, pointing to the empty chair. "Please sit. I understand that you have a pressing matter to discuss with me."

Angelique cleared her throat. She had carefully rehearsed her speech that morning, but now, faced with the decision-maker, a man of such importance, she had forgotten the words. "Yes, Your Excellency, I uh. I mean that…"

He smiled. "Relax, my child. Simply tell me what is on your mind."

She exhaled. "The building on Camp Street that used to house the Female Orphan Asylum has been abandoned for the past twelve years. It was in deplorable condition before that. Now, you can only imagine the state of disrepair it is in."

"I am only slightly familiar with it. Go on."

"Prior to the move, my daughter was there for a brief time. She had been kidnapped, unfortunately, and through a twist of fate was rescued by a group of missionaries, who brought her there. In my search for her, I came to truly understand the plight of the orphans in our city. It is a tragic, heartbreaking situation. And the war has left many more, I am sure."

"First of all, I am so sorry to hear of your experience. I assume that you were reunited with your daughter in due time?

"Yes, happily. Thank God."

"Please know that we do what we can to help those unfortunate souls, Mrs. Slater. It is never enough, of course, but we are proud of what we are able to accomplish."

She blushed. "Of course, Father. I am ever so grateful for the care given to my Aimee. And perhaps I didn't make my intentions clear. I want to help with that mission. In fact, I would very much like to buy that old building from the church with the intention of restoring it and turning it into an orphanage."

He sat back in his chair. "Buy it?"

"Indeed, assuming that it is within the realm of possibilities as far as my pocketbook is concerned."

"I see."

He moved to an adjacent cabinet and took out a leger, searching until he found the page. "Here it is, listed among the church holdings."

"Mrs. Slater, I believe that your intentions are honorable. But are you prepared to oversee such a massive undertaking? Create a private orphanage? May I remind you that you are a woman and that construction is very much a man's realm?"

"And may I remind you that when God calls us to do something that we must step out in faith?" She had worried that she had transgressed with her words which might be considered insubordinate. That wouldn't help her cause one bit. "I'm sorry if that sounded insolent. I meant no disrespect. I am afraid I am rather passionate about this."

He nodded.

"Besides," she said. "The caring for orphan children has always fallen to the good sisters. Women are born to nurture, I think. Our Lord Himself was gently guided to manhood by Mother Mary, was he not? That

264

is where the heart of the cause lies. The building is just a place."

"You do make a rather persuasive case, especially since the asset is currently more like a liability to us. For some reason, I feel compelled to help you."

"God's gentle prodding, perhaps?"

"Perhaps. I will propose your idea to the council for their consideration. If they are in agreement, we will set a price for you. Then, it will be up to you to determine if it is acceptable."

"That sounds fair."

"Come again next Tuesday at this same time. Please bring your husband for an additional signature in accordance with the law. I am optimistic that we can come to an agreement. For the good of the children, of course."

"Certainly. I am grateful for your consideration."

Angelique left the office feeling positive and hopeful. She stood in the square and smiled, humming a little as she made her the way to the streetcar.

And twenty feet away, Jean Paul swung open the wrought iron gate on his way to the groundskeeper's. Tuesday afternoon was, after all, payday.

Chapter Sixty-five

"**A**re you sure that this is what you want to do Angelique?" Andrew asked as they boarded the streetcar for the cathedral and their appointment with the bishop.

She tried not to laugh. "My answer is the same as it was the first ten times you asked. Yes, I am certain. This is my purpose, I think, as well as the future for so many waiting children."

"I swear that I am not trying to be discouraging. But this is going to take a great deal of time and money. The process will be fraught with frustration and obstacles. It is going to get difficult. I want for you to be prepared for that."

"Well, I can't do anything about the time factor, but if I had a dollar for every time someone warned me of the expense, I would have at least half of the project funded. I need your support with this, Andrew. I know that you can't possibly understand my motivation, but if you had visited those orphanages as I did, seen the look of utter hopelessness on the faces of those children, you would be equally as committed."

He nodded. "I will help as I can, of course. The college of architecture at the university has some talented folks, who will more than likely give you advice, find you some craftsmen. I will speak to someone about it tomorrow."

"Assuming that all goes well today. The bishop may very well give us an exorbitant price, which will derail the entire project before it begins. There is a great deal riding on this meeting."

"Agreed. We shall see what happens."

They arrived at St. Louis Cathedral just as a service was ending. It seemed like a strange time for daily mass, and Angelique wondered what the occasion might have been as she and Andrew made their way through the crowd to the massive iron gate emblazoned with a cross. And here, there were more people than usual making their way to the various offices. It was, it seemed, a busy day for church business.

Andrew followed Angelique with a quiet curiosity. He was surprised to see so many outbuildings surrounding the courtyard, which seemed almost like a small city unto itself. She pointed to the largest door, attached to the rear of the cathedral, and he nodded. For the briefest of moments, he locked eyes with a man, a vagrant no doubt, judging by his threadbare clothes and dirty face. He felt a pang of pity. So many found themselves in that same position, unable to earn a reasonable living in a city that seemed too busy to notice. But there was something oddly familiar about him, as though he knew him, although he couldn't imagine how. His was just another face of the lost and the downtrodden And Andrew suddenly understood why Angelique felt compelled to help the children. Perhaps a stable start in life, decent food and an education, would make a difference to them. It was too late for this man.

They were ushered into the bishop's office right away. And Angelique was happy that not only did he remember her, but he seemed genuinely pleased to see her.

"May I introduce my husband, Andrew, Your Excellency?"

"Nice to meet you, Mr. Slater," he said, as he motioned to the empty chairs. "I suppose you already know how determined and persuasive your wife can be."

Andrew chuckled. "Indeed I do. Her strength is one of her greatest assets."

"That's good because she is going to need it in the months ahead."

"Does that mean that the council has approved my request to buy the orphanage?"

"They have. In fact, the support was overwhelming."

"I am so happy to hear it. And the price?"

"I think you will be delighted to hear that to facilitate your work, they are prepared to sell it to you for one hundred dollars."

"Seriously? That is wonderful, a miracle in my mind."

"With one stipulation."

"Which is?"

"If the project is not completed and the orphanage fully functional one year from today, the property reverts back to the diocese. And that stipulation is in the document presented here for you and your husband to sign."

"That seems fair."

"Then, the rest is a matter of formality," he said, passing the pen first to Angelique and then, to Andrew.

"Congratulations, Mrs. Slater. And may God bless you in this endeavor. I am most anxious to see what you accomplish. Somehow, I think you will do great things."

"I certainly hope so. That is my intention."

Angelique chattered nonstop all the way to the streetcar, her voice high-pitched and filled with excitement. Andrew smiled, offering his arm. Two blocks from the cathedral, he spotted the stranger again. He had a noticeable limp, and Andrew wondered what might have happened to him. A war injury, no doubt. And then, the man entered the bakery. Hunger unites us all, Andrew thought.

Chapter Sixty-six

Angelique tried to visit the construction site daily, just to check on the progress, pleased when she heard the sound of busy workers echoing through the air. She often made her way through the rooms, speaking French to many of the craftsmen who were painstakingly repairing molding and damaged doors. It did her heart good to hear the melodious sound of the language fill the air, especially since so many were discouraged from speaking it after the war. Nevertheless, she felt that it gave her a certain kinship with the men, whom she felt worked twice as hard on her behalf as a result.

Admittedly, the bishop's deadline gave the project a sense of urgency, and she breathed a sigh of relief to see the progress. Andrew had made good on his promise to find her some help from the pool of talent at the university, and students often showed up to work for an hour or two most afternoons, free of charge. The architect had donated his professional services, deeming it a worthy endeavor, and when he announced that they were weeks ahead of schedule, she clapped her hands with delight. The idea of a nondenominational orphanage removed any barriers, which somehow gave the community a sense of ownership, and it so wasn't unusual to find random strangers wielding a paint brush or sweeping away sawdust. It was all overwhelming and wonderful at the same time.

But that's not to say that everything went smoothly. There was the family of squirrels who had taken up residence in the walls of what used to be the office. They didn't take too kindly to being evicted, and in the end, it became an ongoing battle, a game of chase in order to relocate them to a nearby park. A snake was discovered coiled around the vines outside the building and the poor worker who happened upon it, fell off the ladder and broke his arm. Plaster that they had thought was acceptable, crumbled at the touch, and gas lines had developed dangerous leaks. But these became the story of a building coming back to life after so many years of neglect, a page in the scrapbook of what was to become a place of hope.

Standing at the foot of the stairs, she paused to take it all in. The walls had been repaired, years of dirt and grime washed away, replaced with bright white paint that made the space look bright and cheerful. The wooden floors were restored and polished to a brilliant shine. And the mended roof meant that rain no longer poured into the building. The kitchen, which was the most time-intensive, remained to be done. The crew had determined that they would renovate the upstairs dormitories as funds allowed, even though it might not house children for a year or two. Angelique wanted to start small, to do it right by providing the best of care for the first group who came to live there. Slowly, she would utilize the entire space and turn the structure into a real home for those who never had one.

The foreman had announced that the building would be completed earlier than they had originally anticipated, thanks to the extra hands. Angelique thought of how the bishop had questioned her resolve, her ability to oversee such a massive undertaking. And while she hated to admit it, she doubted herself as well, second-guessing her decision daily. But the Lord, she determined, had removed many of the obstacles and sent her hammer-wielding angels to help. As she surveyed the progress, she could only deem it a miracle.

And the staffing decisions were ever-present. Angelique was determined to assemble a group of innovative teachers and compassionate caretakers. She remembered the steady stream of detached, yet efficient nannies who had applied for the position that ultimately went to Jubilee. She didn't want workers who were merely competent; she wanted a group of people who cared from the heart. And she would search until she found them.

Fortunately, Aimee was able to find some worthy candidates among her college friends, recent graduates in the nursing program. And one of her teachers named Anne, a jovial woman, who had once been a missionary to the Congo, expressed an interest in being the administrator. After two meetings, Angelique was convinced that she was perfect and hired her immediately. And so, the two women worked together in the final stages of the building to insure that every room would accommodate the needs of the children.

With the finishing point looming large, Angelique set about to plan the dedication. She had already commissioned the sign to be erected outside the building. Naming it would be significant, a way to honor the person whose generosity made the entire endeavor possible. And so, seeing the Countess Maria de la Martinique Children's Home take form, was gratifying, exciting in ways she could not have imagined only a year ago, and certainly the opening would be worth celebrating.

Angelique carefully drafted the guest list. All of those who had helped turn the dream into a reality would be invited, of course, along with the bishop and other city dignitaries. But the most important invitation was extended to the Countess' oldest son. She was grateful to Mr. Davidson, who had graciously given her the address when she wrote to him, describing her plans for the orphanage and her intention to honor the countess. And she spent the better part of one afternoon penning a letter to the Count, whom she had never met, but somehow felt a kinship to, asking him to come to see the place, explaining how much it would mean to her.

And so, three weeks later, when she received his reply that he was honored to have been invited and even more touched by the fact that the building would be named for his dear mother and that yes, he would love to attend, along with his eldest grandson, Angelique was both elated and nervous. She would have to visit the library to learn the protocol for a visitor with a title, she thought. And she would need to make arrangements for their accommodations. But most of all, she wanted him to be proud of the

Countess' legacy, which would make a difference for so many children in the future.

A letter of regret came from Mr. Wilson. He was happily settled in Texas, but the logistics of such a trip made difficult by arthritis in his knees, deemed it impossible. However, he did send a generous check with the implicit instructions to buy books and toys with the money. Angelique had always thought that he was magic, like Santa himself. That hadn't changed over the years.

She looked forward to the special day with great anticipation. It would be a time of abundant blessings and new beginnings. Angelique closed her eyes. The sounds of construction filled the air. This is what building a miracle sounds like, she thought. And in a matter of a few months, it will all take form, rising from the rubble much like the mythological wonder. She could hardly wait.

Chapter Sixty-seven

Winter/Spring 1875

The line of carriages stretched for several blocks as the guests made their way to the reception and dedication of the Countess Maria Children's Home as it soon came to be called. Angelique proudly stood near the front door to greet each person in attendance, shake each and every hand of those who had donated time or money to the cause. This was their celebration as much as it was hers.

The bishop was among the first to arrive. "My dear Mrs. Slater," he said, pausing to take in the sight of the transformed building, "I must admit that I underestimated you. I am truly surprised and inspired by what you have managed to accomplish here."

"Thank you, Your Excellency. I had a great deal of help and support."

"Which only serves as a testament to your ability to rally the troops on behalf of a worthy cause."

"Well, for now, it is only a building. Our first children arrive next week, and I do hope that you will return in a few months when the place is alive with their laughter."

"It will be my pleasure," he said.

Angelique pointed to the adjacent rooms. "Please do have a look at the rest of the facility. The architect is available for questions. And you remember Andrew, of course. He is directing the tours."

"Still supportive, I see."

"Indeed he is. I am blessed."

"I would not argue with that, Mrs. Slater, as are the orphans who will benefit from your generous spirit," he said as he made his way to the recreation room.

Angelique was pleased when the children joined her. "Mother," Aimee whispered. "I remember being brought here so long ago. And even though it was for a short while, those memories stayed with me. It was a place of sadness, then. Now, it is utterly transformed. It is as though the spirit of love and hope was infused into these walls. I am so proud of you."

"My precious girl," Angelique said, turning to hug her daughter. "It is because of your courage that this happened. It is truly the manifestation of the gratitude I feel for the day when your sister and I stood on those stairs, and we knew that you lived. There is something very empowering about being able to turn a sad time into a moment of triumph. Never forget that."

Aimee nodded. "One of the many lessons you have taught me, Momma."

When she saw the tall gentleman accompanied by a young man, coming up the stairs, she knew right away that it was the count. She reached over to squeeze Aida's hand. "Here come the guests of honor," she whispered.

His eyes, amber in color like his mother's, were warm and kind. And although he was older, with hair the color of a winter snow, he was exceedingly handsome with a youthful zest that belied his years.

Angelique could feel her heart flutter, as though being in the presence of the son of her dearly departed friend brought her a strange comfort, an unexpected connection. She thought of the Countess' clairvoyance, her gift of the spirit and wondered if perhaps her son had the same powerful connection to the unexplainable.

"And so, Mrs. Slater," he said, bowing to kiss her extended hand, "we finally meet."

"Count de la Martinque," she said, attempting to curtsey, "I cannot begin to tell you how much I appreciate your presence, what an honor it is to have you here."

"Please, call me Jacques. I already feel as though I know you. I think our implied history makes titles unnecessary."

Angelique blushed. "Certainly. And you must call me Angelique."

"With pleasure."

"I take it that the trip here wasn't too long or arduous?"

"No. Your location meant a pleasurable journey by ship from New York. Besides, I wouldn't have missed this occasion for the world."

"I am so pleased. Your mother was the most remarkable woman I have ever known. I miss her still."

"I can't disagree."

"She certainly changed my life. I shudder to think the path I might have taken without her guidance. I will always be grateful to her for her kindness."

"You know, she wrote to me of you that last summer she spent on Last Island. She did care for you so dearly. I think in many ways, she viewed you as the daughter she never had."

"What a lovely thought! And I cared for her. I am just so happy that I am now able to honor her memory."

"Which would have pleased her more than you can imagine. She did so love children, especially the babies. And, of course, you must know the pride she would have felt in your work here."

Angelique swallowed hard as she blinked away the tears. It wasn't easy to control the emotion she felt as she stood there with the son of the woman who had shaped her destiny and restored her hope. It was overwhelming, but lovely.

"Please forgive me, Jacques. I have not introduced my children. These are my daughters Aida and Aimee and my son, Franklin."

"So happy to meet you, of course. And may I present my grandson, Michel. He was kind enough to accompany me when I mentioned that I was bound for New Orleans."

Franklin extended his hand. "Great for you to join us. I hope you will be here for a few days at the very least."

"My pleasure. And yes, that is the plan."

Aida's blue eyes sparkled as she smiled at the younger man. "My sister and I will gladly show you around the orphanage, if you'd like. And we would love to take you on a tour of the city, too, if you would like. "

He nodded, duly charmed, and she slipped her hand into the crook of his arm as they made their way down the hall to tour the sleeping rooms for the children. "I would enjoy that very much," he said.

The guests had assembled into the largest of the rooms set aside for the recreational needs of the children. Champagne flowed freely and a three-piece orchestra played in the background. The sound of laughter, punctuated with conversation, filled the air. Angelique allowed herself a brief moment of pure joy. This night was the culmination of an optimistic idea, a vision that she could only hope to someday realize. More importantly, it was just the beginning of a better life for so many children.

Franklin had come to get her, extending his hand for her. "Mother," he said. "What an amazing feat you have accomplished. And just as you rescued me so many years ago, gave me a future I never thought possible, you will do the same for so many others. I am so very proud of you. Now, let's go and greet your guests."

She entered the room just as Andrew raised his class. "I would like to propose a toast to the courageous woman whose foresight and determination has made this evening possible, a woman whom I am most fortunate to call my wife. Here's to you, Angelique, to making dreams come true."

The color rose in her cheeks as all eyes turned to her. "Here, here," the crowd pronounced. "To Angelique."

Chapter Sixty-eight

Angelique considered taking the Count and his grandson Michel to a nice restaurant. They were, after all, only in town for a few days, and so many of the culinary destinations in New Orleans were legendary. But in the end, she followed Andrew's suggestion and penned a note to be delivered to their hotel, inviting them for dinner at her home. He was right: it was a more intimate setting for conversation and a more personal way to connect.

She had sent the girls to the market with a list and explicit instructions on how to choose the freshest seafood and produce. While they were away, she set the table with her finest linen tablecloth and her mother's porcelain china and silver, which she had managed to recover when she purchased Chauvin. She had buckets of greenery to be arranged and regretted that the winter season meant her garden lay dormant. Nevertheless, when it was all complete and she stood back to admire her handiwork, she was pleased.

The girls joined their mother in the kitchen as they chatted on about the evening. Angelique put them to work peeling vegetables, and Aida complained furiously when she had been assigned the task of chopping onions. Tears ran down her cheeks as she finished the last one.

"I shall marry well enough," she announced, "to hire a cook so that I never have to be a scullery maid for anyone."

Angelique stopped stirring the roux for the gumbo and removed the pot from the stove. Calmly, she crossed the room to where Aida sat at the kitchen table.

"Look at me," she said, leveling her steel blue eyes on her daughter. "I married quite well, thank you. And might I remind you that without that marriage, you would not be sitting here, disrespecting your mother. I am no scullery maid, dear girl. I choose to take care of my family because it brings me joy to do so. Perhaps you may grow to be a woman who is able to save the world. If that is what you want to do, then, I support you wholeheartedly. But I hope to never hear you belittling another's choices because they don't align with yours. In light of your rather progressive views, that seems rather old fashioned and outdated to me."

Aida sat quietly as Angelique returned to the stove. The silence hung in the air like a dense fog. Aimee hummed to herself as she peeled the last of the potatoes.

"You are right, of course, Momma," Aida said, after a few minutes. "Freedom means being able to choose. I think I had forgotten that."

Angelique said nothing, resisting the urge to cheer at the small victory. She continued to blend the flour and oil, cooking it as it slowly turned the dark brown of a pecan shell. Carefully, she dropped the chopped onion, celery and peppers into the hot roux. It sizzled, filling the kitchen with an enticing aroma.

"There goes the trinity, girls. It is the magic that releases the flavor and makes everything come together, creating the basis for our Louisiana cooking. And families are like that, too. No one stands alone. It is the composition and unity that releases the spice, the structure of what we are. Remember that."

The girls nodded in unison like they did when they were young. Angelique smiled. She wondered how the time had passed so quickly, turning her babies into young women overnight. It too, was magic. And it had happened right before her very eyes.

By seven, the candles had been lit, the wine poured and everyone was seated at the table. Angelique proudly ladled the gumbo from the bone china tureen into the bowls that her mother had used for that same purpose.

"What a treat," the Count pronounced when Angelique said that she had made it herself. "I so wanted to try some authentic food while I am here."

"Perhaps tomorrow night you will allow us to show you what the restaurants in the area are able to offer. I can assure you that you will not have a finer meal, even in New York City," Andrew said.

"I think I am having a pretty fine meal right here."

"I am so pleased that you like it, Count," Angelique said.

"I thought we had agreed to dispense with the formalities. It's Jacques."

"Of course. I am glad that you are enjoying it, Jacques."

Michel turned to Aida, "You did promise to show me the sights of the city. I intend to hold you to that."

"I have classes in the morning, but I am free for lunch and afterwards, if you would like."

"Classes? I didn't realize that you were a student."

"I am. In fact, both Aimee and I graduate in just a few months."

"And what are you studying?"

Aida sighed. "I would like to say that I am to be a lawyer, but I am most certainly, studying the law. I will work in an office until those doors open for me. And rest assured, they will be, even if I have to find and use the battering ram all by myself."

Michel smiled. "Somehow, Miss Slater, I don't doubt it for one minute. And I look forward to our afternoon together and getting to know you better."

Aida blushed as she raised her eyes to meet his. "Indeed, sir. I am quite the mystery."

And across the table, Aimee and Franklin stifled a giggle.

Chapter Sixty-nine

He was sweating. The dampness from his drenched clothing woke him with a start, and within minutes the night air sent chills through his body as he lay on the cot shaking uncontrollably. He prayed for it to be over soon, that a merciful God would send him a respite from the attack that took place far too regularly, leaving him weak and defenseless. He sat upright and took a deep breath. His chest rattled. Reaching for the nearby jug, he took a big gulp of water, hoping it would help. The pain, he had learned to live with, but the inability to rest had sapped his energy, and he wondered how long it would be before his condition would be discovered. That was what he feared the most.

For a long time, he simply sat there in the dark, motionless, his mind unable to form a coherent thought. The fatigue, chronic and unrelenting, had robbed him of the moments of clarity that the solitude of his work had given him. He missed the quiet creativity. As he attended to his daily chores, he had often made up stories about those who lay in permanent slumber, those whom he served. In fact, he knew the residents of the graveyard as he would neighbors, or perhaps, even family. Now, he was unable to recall even one name. And as the sun rose in the east, Jean Paul Latour wondered if he would be joining them soon.

***

Aida was pleased to discover that Michel was in a waiting carriage as she emerged from the law building on campus. He had already passed the first test. She admired punctuality, deeming it reflective of other moral qualities. A man who failed to value another's time, rarely valued other things as well. They would have this entire afternoon together, and she wondered how much she would learn of him. He was handsome, educated, refined, and titled, the type of man whom any women would deem a good catch. But something more attracted her, and she was determined to discover what it was during their outing of sightseeing.

"First, we have lunch," he said, clearly taking charge of the itinerary, "but you get to choose the destination."

She directed the driver to take them to Antoine's in the French Quarter. There, they were seated right away in the light-filled sunroom and after following her suggestion, he ordered baked oysters and crawfish bisque for the two of them.

"So, Miss Slater, I would like to know more about you. What secrets do you hold that you are willing to share?" he asked, focusing his amber colored eyes on her.

She blushed and took a deep breath. Rarely was she flustered. She prided herself on holding her own and was not easily intimidated by anyone, particularly a man. But suddenly, she felt like a silly giddy teenager, instead of the self-confident woman she considered herself to be. He was charming. She hadn't counted on that.

"It is no secret that I am most interested in the law, particularly woman's rights. For now, I have to resign myself to the fact that I must work in an office as an assistant, but someday, I will do more, be more."

"I don't doubt that for one minute. I can see that you are a tenacious woman with a lofty goal. I admire that. So tell me, what do you see as the most pressing issue?"

"Without a doubt, the right to vote. The fifteenth amendment has been on the books for quite some time. It gave all men, including former slaves, the ability to cast a ballot. Women are still denied that freedom."

"I see. And there has been no resistance to the Negro vote in the South?"

"Of course. There have been scare tactics as well as what they deem to be legal means like poll taxes and literacy tests. I'm afraid many a Southern man, who would never fail to call himself a gentleman, mourns the civilization that collapsed with the war."

"Sounds like a society stuck in the past rather than one set on embracing the future."

"Sadly, it is. And it relates to women on the most basic levels."

"How so?"

His interest made her bold. "It is such misguided thought. Some slave owners saw owning another human being as a form of protection, as they provided for the essential needs of these poor, illiterate workers, unable to care for themselves. It is almost like they expected the slaves to be grateful."

"Truly? That seems like quite a stretch in an effort to justify a practice most view as unacceptable."

"It is, of course, but that same idea is extended to women. As long as we are charming and delicate, cause no trouble, question nothing, we have the right to be protected by a male-dominated society. A woman's basic requirements will be met, and she can be assured of safety. In my idea, that sounds like a similar kind of bondage."

"My goodness, I never heard the argument presented in such a way. That's fascinating. The views in the North are relatively solid in regards to slavery, but I am afraid that I know many a man who view women in that same light. Perhaps it stems from a need to feel superior."

"That saddens me to hear, but I am not surprised. To some, the suffrage movement is the same as abolitionism. It won't be an easy war to win. Not many soldiers willing to fight for our glorious cause."

"I must admit that you are most impressive, Miss Slater. To what do you owe your progressive point of view? I see an indomitable spirit in you. That doesn't come naturally. It must be nurtured."

"One word, viscount. My mother. She has always been remarkable. She ran an entire plantation on her own, one she lost and managed to regain. Goodness, we were mere children when Momma took us out into the fields and taught us how to plant cotton seeds, explaining why it mattered. And you know, I look at the fact that she paid taxes on that land through the years, all the while being unable to vote. I seem to recall that the idea of taxation without representation is what founded this nation. Perhaps a revolution of a different kind is on the horizon."

He sat back in his chair studying her face. "You will make a wonderful lawyer, Miss Slater. You have a quick, analytical mind. And your mother should indeed be proud. Why I now understand why my great-grandma loved her so much."

"Truly. She is the strongest women I know. And we are all very blessed to have her in our lives. I am reminded of it daily when I look at Aimee. When my sister was kidnapped, she never gave up until she found her."

"Your sister was kidnapped?"

"She was. It is quite the story. Perhaps I will share that the next time we meet. I am afraid that I have already talked about myself far too much today."

"Nonsense. I find your words intriguing. And I would like that very much, both the story and the anticipation of meeting again."

The color flooded Aida's cheeks. "Me, too," she whispered.

The couple spent the remainder of the afternoon touring the city by carriage as Aida narrated. They stopped to stroll along the Mississippi and the French Market. When they turned onto Basin Street, Michel pointed to the walled cemetery.

"What's that?"

Aida raised her eyebrows. "Seriously? You don't know? It is a cemetery."

"But the tombs are above the ground, like grand monuments. I have seen nothing like that here in America."

"It is a necessity because New Orleans is below sea level. But our cities of the dead are quite unusual. Would you like to get out and look around a bit?"

"Absolutely."

The couple walked among the crypts, stopping to read the affectionate words engraved on many of the vaults. He asked for help in pronouncing the names and speculated on the life story of a few of the residents, who rested in eternal slumber. As he paused in front a large marble angel, he reached for Aida's trembling hand and kissed it lightly.

She wondered how a visit to a cemetery could rank among the best moments of her life, but it most certainly was. The viscount, was an extraordinary man. And try as she might, she was unable to control the fluttering of her heart.

***

In the shack at the rear of the graveyard, Jean Paul Latour packed the special books he intended to keep, along with the few articles of clothing and his other meager possessions. Shoving them into his threadbare satchel, he looked around one last time to be sure he hadn't missed anything. The visit from the groundskeeper had come as a surprise since he couldn't remember the last time he had actually seen him on the grounds. Unfortunately, he had fallen asleep early one evening and hadn't locked the gate, resulting in some minor vandalism. Jean Paul braced himself for the reprimand that was to come and hoped it was nothing more than that. He knew that on recent Tuesday afternoons when he went to retrieve his pay, the boss had asked about his health, the progression of his deteriorated appearance becoming more apparent with each passing week. Perhaps it was Jean Paul's current skeleton-like appearance, his hollow-looking eyes that was the critical cause for concern. But when he began to wheeze in his employer's presence, coughing up blood into an old soiled rag, he was fired on the spot and told to be off of the premises within the hour.

"Get yourself to Charity Hospital," the groundskeeper said, offering nothing more. "And pray that they can help you."

As he departed, several men with handkerchiefs covering their noses and mouths moved in with lye to disinfect the shack. And just like that, he had never existed, his presence washed away in an instant. It seemed ironic, he thought. As Jean Paul Latour, professional gambler, he was a force to be reckoned with as his reputation had often proceeded him at the tables. But this man, the one cleansed of his sins, living a life of atonement, was nobody, as disposable as the spent flowers that marked the graves. Perhaps that is the way it was meant to be, to sacrifice the ego for the good of the soul.

He made his way down the path to the place that had become so familiar and comforting. He touched the tomb. "Goodbye, Josephina, my angel," he whispered. "Until we meet again." And as he made his way to the gate, he paused to watch a young couple engaged in a tentative embrace before getting into a carriage. His heart clenched, and he swallowed hard.

At one time, I had such moments, he thought, a future filled with promise and love. Choice can bring us joy, and it can bring us sorrow. Such is life. And ultimately, death.

Chapter Seventy

For the next three days, Aida and the viscount were inseparable. They dined at the finest restaurants and explored the city. He asked all of the right questions as far as she was concerned and seemed genuinely interested in her rather progressive views of women's roles in a changing society.

On their second night together, Aida felt comfortable enough to inquire about his life, one she assumed was rife with pomp and circumstance that accompanied the title and privilege.

"I work," he simply said.

The nature of his job seemed a pivotal piece of information. She couldn't imagine him in a mundane profession, but her curiosity was piqued.

"Sounds rather cryptic. Would you care to explain?"

He smiled as he reached for her hand. "Perhaps it should remain it a secret, Miss Slater, just to keep you interested."

She was plenty interested, although she would have never admitted it to him. She narrowed her eyes, steel blue like her mother's. "Perhaps this is the way you court in the North, viscount, but we are very traditional here in the South. If there is cat-and-mouse game to be played, the women, I am afraid, are masters at it, particularly the part about being elusive and mysterious.

"He raised an eyebrow. "Are we?"

"Are we what?"

"Courting."

Her face turned a crimson red. Aimee had often warned her about speaking what was on her mind without considering the message. She should have listened. "My apologies. I am afraid that I misspoke. Please forgive me."

"Absolutely not."

"I beg your pardon?" He was toying with her. She took a deep breath. This was no time to let emotions overcome reason.

"I will not forgive you. In fact, I would love nothing more than to court you."

She didn't realize that she had been holding her breath until she exhaled, louder and more forceful than she had intended. "I don't understand."

"What could possibly be confusing, Miss Slater? I think that you are a fascinating woman. Unlike so many whom I have met, you aren't afraid to challenge me or my way of thinking. And you don't feel the need to hide your intelligence behind some bejeweled fan as you giggle and pretend to be some helpless damsel in distress. I find you most refreshing."

"You do?"

"Indeed, I do. So let's work out the logistics for a long-distance courtship. Perhaps you will honor my family and me with a visit to New York when you graduate.

Aida's head was spinning. It was the stuff of fairy tales. Here she sat in one of the most beautiful restaurants in New Orleans, having dinner with a handsome viscount, a man who was not only engaging and delightful, but interested in her. She searched for the right words. Aimee, she thought, would be proud.

"I am honored, sir, and most flattered by your attentiveness. I would like nothing more than to be courted by you, although I am sure that you realize the obstacles presented by the miles that separate us, will not be easily overcome."

"Nonsense. That's merely a possible hindrance. And perhaps, it means a shorter courtship."

She could feel the color returning to her cheeks. If she had been prone to fainting, she would have done so right there on the spot. "I do have one request, however."

"Anything."

"Will you ask my father for permission? I told you that we do tend to honor Southern customs, and this, most certainly, is one of them. I know that I am of age, but he would be offended if we did this without his blessing."

"I thought your father was from Baltimore."

"He is, but I am afraid he has been living in the South for most of his life. Took the Yankee right out of him. And besides, you can't possibly imagine my mother's influence."

"No, I can see how persuasive she might be. Then, yes, I will most certainly speak to him when I escort you home."

"Thank you, viscount."

"Actually, my father is the viscount. I just went along with the title when we were introduced. Besides, if we are to court, you should call me Michel, don't you think?"

She nodded. "And I am Aida, not Miss Slater. Forgive me if I ask you one more question."

"Of course. Anything." He gently caressed her hand.

"Your job? What do you do, Michel?"

His amber-colored eyes met hers. "I am a lawyer, Aida. A very good one, I might add."

And in that moment, Aida Slater fell madly in love.

***

When the time came for their departure, Aida insisted on accompanying Michel and the count to the dock to whisper her tearful goodbyes.

"I'll write, of course," he promised.

"And so will I."

"And you will come to New York in a few months?"

"Indeed. I am anxious to meet your mother and sister. And to see New York as well."

"And how about me?"

"That goes without saying. I will always and forever be anxious to see you."

He smiled before taking her hand in his and lightly kissed her palm. "I am so grateful to have found you, Aida. Time and distance will only make my heart grow fonder."

"Mine as well."

"Goodbye, my darling," he said before talking the long walk up the pier to the waiting boat. He paused to wave as Aida wiped the tears from her eyes.

"Goodbye, my love," she whispered into the wind. "Until we meet again."

Chapter Seventy-one

As she did on most mornings, Angelique arrived at the orphanage early enough to have breakfast with the children. This was a time of transition in her life, a shift from the way things used to be to what they were becoming. Aida and Aimee had graduated. Two days after receiving her diploma, Aida had left for New York, a move that Angelique questioned.

"It makes sense for me to go before I take a job, right?" Aida had said, and, as usual, it was hard not to argue with her logic. "And I will be well chaperoned once I am there."

Besides, it would have been impossible to keep her away from Michel, if the letters that had arrived daily were any indication of their growing affection. And so, it came as no surprise when a month later, Angelique and Andrew received a telegram from Aida announcing her engagement. She would be home soon to plan a fall wedding.

"It is a good thing that you are the consummate hostess. I am sure that this will be the wedding of the year, filled with pomp and circumstance if Aida has her way," Andrew said.

"Our daughter does like the spotlight. I suppose it is appropriate that she is marrying a man who will someday have a title. But I do like Michel. And I think

297

they make a good couple. I suppose the countess had no idea that someday she would be paying for her great-grandson's nuptials."

Andrew raised his eyebrows. "Now that's an interesting thought."

"Indeed it is. But it will be lovely, and the happiest of days if we can all survive Aida's big ideas, which are sure to include a small circus."

"Well, you have admit that her big ideas have been invaluable in raising money for the orphanage thanks to her friends in New York."

"And I don't discount that. She really has been a godsend in that regard. But the wedding will be a grandiose affair, I am sure."

"I expect nothing less for her. Something to anticipate."

Aimee had gone to work with Franklin at Charity, although the duo spent all of their free time in a makeshift clinic they had established for the poor behind the horse stables in the French Quarter. "So many in need," Franklin had declared when Angelique expressed her concerns about the safety of such an endeavor. "Besides, it is only two days a week, for now." But she was proud of the kind hearts that both of her children possessed, their steadfast drive to make a difference. Andrew had published his fourth book, having received wide acclaim for the first three. He had recently been promoted to head of the expanding meteorology department at the university. Her family was thriving. And so was she.

She took her place at the head of the long table, and they greeted her in unison, "Good morning, Momma."

It was the most special of titles, bestowed upon her by one of the first children who had come to live there. He had arrived dirty and in threadbare clothes, which were at least two sizes too small. Although much younger, he reminded her of Franklin when she encountered him in the Charleston park. And so, she felt an immediate connection to this boy as she kneeled in front of him.

"And what is your name?" she had asked, as she brushed the hair from his eyes.

"Charlie," he said.

"I like that name."

"And what is yours?" he had asked.

"I am Miss Angelique. And I do so hope that you will like it here."

He nodded. "Can I just call you 'Momma' instead?"

Her heart had immediately melted. "Of course you can. I would be honored."

"Good," he said as he looked around. "I think I am going to like it here just fine."

It hadn't taken long for the title to stick as the other children began to refer to her as "Momma," as well, and when she entered the orphanage, she proudly assumed the role of nurturing caretaker for so many beautiful children.

It seems that God most certainly gives us the desires of our heart, she thought, except that He multiples the blessings beyond the human limits of our imaginations. All she had ever wanted was a big family, children to care for and love. Ironically, with her own now grown and living lives of their own, she had that and more.

Following breakfast, she worked in her office for an hour. The administrative duties were tedious and endless, but thanks to the count's generous departure gift, she had the necessary funds to keep the place afloat for at least the first year. After that, she figured that the Lord and the countess and her fund-raising daughter would provide.

She looked forward to the mid-morning rounds. This is when the children were at their best, happily playing together or receiving instruction from the teacher on staff.

"Look, Momma. I can write my name," one of the girls announced, holding up her slate for Angelique to inspect.

"That's wonderful, Jeannette. And such a long name, too. You did so well."

When Angelique paused to give the girl a hug, she saw it, the tell-tale rash on her arm.

"Come with me, my precious girl," she said, taking her to the office, where she and Miss Martin, the headmistress, could inspect it closer.

"Do you think it is measles?" Angelique asked.

"No idea. But let's pray that it isn't. In such confined quarters, it will spread in a matter of days."

The girl began to cry and Angelique moved to hug her. "No worries. My big handsome son is a doctor. Did you know that? And he is going to come and look at your arm to make it all better. Can you be a brave girl for me?"

She nodded.

"Good. Then, we are going to move a cot into my office so that you can get some rest and keep me company while we wait for him. That will be kind of fun, won't it?"

She smiled.

Angelique hastily penned a note to Franklin and dispatched the driver to deliver it to him at Charity hospital.

"He isn't in residence, ma'am," the driver said when he returned an hour later.

"In the Quarter," she mumbled before giving instructions to look for him behind the horse stables.

***

By the time Aimee and Franklin had arrived at the clinic that morning, there was a long line of weary, dejected folks waiting in front of the repurposed army tent, seeking medical help. For some, this represented their only hope as they coughed fitfully or held onto painful wounds that would not heal. Charity Hospital was a fine facility with the best care offered in the state, but it was distressingly understaffed and woefully overcrowded. On any given day, more patients were turned away than were accepted. This bothered Franklin the most, and so he established the clinic, an improvised place where he could treat the sick. He had managed to get some of the most gravely ill into Charity, but it wasn't always possible, and often, much to his sadness he had to send some on their way with nothing more than the bits of medicine he had managed to pilfer from the hospital. Ultimately, he wanted to do more, but for now, he was limited by the resources available to him. At least, he had Aimee. She was invaluable, with good instincts. Best of all, she was fearless when it came to patient care. Perhaps that is what he admired most about her.

There were still another ten people waiting to be treated when the driver arrived with the message from Angelique.

"It is from Momma," he whispered to Aimee. "She has a sick child at the orphanage and needs us right away."

"But what about these people?" Aimee asked, pointing to the line, which had now grown to thirteen.

"That's why we need the extra help. I am working on a few doctors from Charity. But we are all so over tired. Not sure how much more any of us can do."

"I know. Hopefully, there will be a few. We can't give up now."

"And we won't. We will come back. Let's just give them a time to return."

Aimee nodded as she packed Franklin's medical bag, and he made the announcement to the crowd.

Within minutes, they were in the carriage and on their way to the orphanage.

"So relieved that you could come," Angelique said as she rung her hands. "What do you think?"

"Hello there," Franklin said, greeting the child. "And what is your name?"

"Jeannette."

"My goodness, that is such a pretty name. Can you show me your arm?"

She held it out for him to inspect.

"Does this itch you?"

She nodded.

"And can you tell me how long you have had it?"

She shrugged. "A few days, I think."

He turned to his mother. "I'd like to see the other children, too."

She brought him to the school first, where he discovered two more cases. One of the babies in the nursery had it, along with five toddlers playing in the recreation room.

"I'm worried. It seems to be spreading."

He nodded. "But the good news is that it isn't measles."

Angelique exhaled. "It isn't?"

"No. Can you take me to your laundry room?"

Angelique looked puzzled. "Why there?"

"I have a suspicion, that's all."

The laundry room was actually a separate building, and it took a staff of three, working all day, every day, just to keep up with the mountain of dirty clothes that seemed to multiply among children at play. One of the women was hanging sheets on the line, and Franklin asked if she was in charge. She shook her head and pointed. He entered the large room, a miserable place with the temperature being at least twenty degrees warmer than the already hot Louisiana climate. Steam from the iron formed a thick cloud that hung in the still air. He approached the second woman he encountered. "Are you the supervisor?"

She nodded, duly flattered that he had bestowed a title upon her.

"Can I ask you if you have made any recent changes, particularly in the soap that you use?"

She paused as though to think. "Yes, I have as a matter of fact. Had a man peddling something a week ago, claimed it was better than anything we buy. I managed to get him to give me a bag to try. Figured that if was good, he would make his money back 'cause we go through a lot of soap here."

"I see. And do you have any left?"

She pointed to the large cloth sack in the corner. "Over there."

Franklin stooped in front of the bag and scooped out a handful to smell. He made a face. Aimee moved in to smell it as well. "Whoa," she said, "not sure what it is in there, but it is mighty powerful."

"Agreed. Something harsh, like lye. And much too strong to use for bedding and clothes that touches the sensitive skin of babies and children."

"Do you think that is what it is?"

He nodded. "Happened once at Charity and we thought he had an epidemic. But when it only affected some people, we started eliminating the possible causes. Took us a month, but we traced it back to the laundry. Important lesson."

Angelique breathed a sigh of relief. "So grateful, son."

"I'm just glad that it was something simple."

As they stood near the front door, saying their goodbyes, Franklin pointed to the stairs. "And what are you doing with the second floor? Anything?"

"Nothing for now, although it will become more dormitory space as we expand. It will house the older children."

Aimee and Franklin looked at each other. She nodded. "Would you be willing to let us use it for the clinic? So many people who are ill with no place to go."

Angelique sighed. "I do appreciate your dedication to helping the unfortunate, truly I do. And I will support you as I can. You know that. But Franklin, I cannot bring sick people into this place, not with small children here. Don't you remember when the Yankees moved into Maison Blanche? They are as vulnerable as those you wish to help, and they are my first priority."

"You are right, of course. I understand. We are just so desperate. This began as a small endeavor, but in a matter of months, it has grown. The need is greater than I ever imagined."

There was silence as Angelique processed an idea. "You can't have the space upstairs, but I have another idea for you. And I am surprised that you didn't think of it yourself."

Confused, he followed her out the back door and through the courtyard to a large outbuilding that had once been used for storage.

"It needs to be cleaned, of course, but it is otherwise fine. You could adapt it to meet your needs over time. If you want it, you can have it."

Franklin broke into a wide grin as he moved to hug his mother. "You are the best. And yes, this will be perfect. We have access to all that we could possibly use. Probably can entice others from the hospital to help, too, now that this is about to be a real operation and not some crude tent. I can't wait to get started."

"Me, too," Aimee said. "You never cease to amaze me, Momma. Franklin and I are ever so grateful."

"Indeed, we are."

It wasn't even noon and already it had been a good day, Angelique thought. They had staved off a measles epidemic, and she had become the benefactor for a clinic for the poor. She had no idea all that would transpire when she woke that morning, but such is the beauty of life. Each day brings with it a realm of possibilities, and this one certainly did.

Chapter Seventy-two

Of course, Jean Paul knew the city well. It was two miles from Basin Street to Charity Hospital, but that unreachable distance might as well have been on the moon as far as he was concerned. But what choice was there? The hospital represented hope. He dare not think he could be cured, but a clean bed and compassionate care would bring him comfort in his remaining days. He had grabbed onto that thought and wouldn't let go. Once he had left the cemetery, in spite of his weakened condition, he was determined to make the trek one step at a time. Perhaps with a little food and water, he could make it. He had to try.

It had taken him a full day to reach the gates of the hospital and when he arrived, out of breath and sweating profusely, he barely had the strength to enter the lobby and present himself to the nurse on duty.

"I'm sorry, sir," she had said. "The hospital is currently full, and we are no longer able to accept new patients."

"But I am sick," he whispered.

She pointed to the room, filled with people, some outstretched on the floor, others, in a fetal position, moaning. Sounds of coughing filled the air. "These people are, too. They wait for a bed. I can put you on the list if you give me your name."

He nodded. "Jean Paul Latour."

She dipped the pen into the inkwell and wrote it on the ledger.

"How many before me?"

She consulted the list. "Eight-five, sir."

He staggered. It was hopeless, and he knew it. His choice was the sit among the doomed and wait for death or to return to the Quarter. At least there he could listen to the music and be among people who were alive, not sentenced to final days of pain. He slept under a tree on the hospital grounds after eating the last bit of bread he had saved. The next morning, he made the long walk back.

Jean Paul staggered rather than walked and passersby regarded him with utter disgust. He had lived on the street for close to two months, sleeping in doorways, begging for food. With nowhere to go and a paltry bit of money in his pocket that would need to last, he had few options. And survival, living just one more day, was all he could think of in spite of the conditions. The fact that the disease hadn't taken him yet seemed a miracle in itself.

"He's drunk," a woman commented. "He should be ashamed of himself."

And he was humiliated. He looked unhuman, the smell of his unwashed flesh over powering and disgusting. He had become unworthy of pity or kindness. Barely a man. And yet, like an unmoored ship, he was tossed about by circumstance, ill-fated timing, and a most uncooperative body. He sat on the curb outside of a barber shop. A breeze blew his hair. It wasn't altogether unpleasant. As long as he didn't begin to cough, he would be safe among the crowd, a place far too busy to notice one more vagrant.

A gentleman exited the barber shop, surrounded by the smell of powder and cologne. He paused, his golden tipped cane mere inches from Jean Paul, who braced himself for the blow he thought was to come. Instead, the man, dropped a gold coin into Jean Paul's lap. "Dinner's on me tonight," he simply said as he placed his hat on his newly groomed head and walked away.

For a long time, Jean Paul simply stared at the coin as though it had been tossed by the hand of God Himself. He was certain that it was more than ten times what he had in his satchel, the sum of his saved weekly wages, which he had guarded like a miser, a man who knew that even worse days lurked around the corner. The question as to how to best spend it loomed large. A decent meal would be wise. Goodness knows, his racked body cried out for nourishment. Perhaps he could get a room for a night, maybe even a hot bath. He closed his eyes as he imagined the feel of the water as it cleansed his body and restored his spirit. He turned the coin over in his hand. What if he could have both? What if he could turn this money into more? Those familiar feelings stirred something deep inside, something he thought had died, but really had simply lay dormant, waiting for the right time to resurface. He slowly made his way to the gambling hall.

Jean Paul entered the dimly lit tavern. He could feel the blood coursing through his veins, hear the sound of his own beating heart. For the first time in years, he felt alive. There were several tables with games in progress.

He watched from afar for a while, then chose the table he felt most drawn to, a tactic that had served him well in his heyday. As he approached the group, all eyes fell on him, their collective look of disgust reaffirmed what he already knew. He was a piteous sight.

"Room at this table?" he asked, his voice hoarse.

"Not for the likes of you," one of the men said as the others nodded in agreement. "You'd best be on your way."

He held up the gold coin. He had their attention.

Another of the men pointed to the empty chair. "One round. All or nothing for what you have in your hand."

Jean Paul closed his eyes. It had been so long, and he had forgotten the thrill, the anticipation of a big win. "If you fellas can match it, then, yes."

They all nodded as the dealer slowly shuffled the cards, giving each man five.

Slowly, Jean Paul looked at his hand. Except for the pair of threes, he had nothing much. But the discard might bring him something better. He waited and watched as the betting began, his gold coin, shining in the flickering gas light.

When the three random cards had been replaced by three more, equally as bad, he realized that unless the other men held even worse hands, he was going to lose. Beads of sweat formed on his brow, and the bitter taste of bile filled his mouth.

"So let's see what everybody's got," the dealer said.

And one by one, the players revealed their cards. The threes proved to be the lowest among them and the winner proudly displayed his full house with one hand while scooping up the pot with the other. He removed the gold coin from among the pile and held it up for inspection. "Lady Liberty sure is pretty."

Jean Paul's hands began to shake. He thought of the money in his satchel. It wasn't much, probably not even enough for one more round with these men, but he had to try.

"I have a little more," he said, reaching into his bag for the worn pouch.

"We sure hate to take all your money," one of the men said, "seeings as how you look like you really need it."

He nodded. "My choice." But before the next game could start, he could feel the rattling, the cough began from deep in his chest as it made its way to the upper part of his lungs. Closing his eyes, he willed it to stop, but his disobliging body simply began to shake as his throat clinched, like a hand gripped around him in a suffocating hold.

"Excuse me," he whispered, grabbing for the satchel. His chair fell on the wooden floor with a resounding bang as the room grew quiet and all eyes were on him. He stumbled to the door and out onto the street. The bright sunlight temporarily blinded him. Before he was able to take more than a few steps, Jean Paul fell, face first onto the sidewalk, unconscious and oblivious to the world around him.

Chapter Seventy-three

The men moved in swiftly. He was like them, part of the underbelly of New Orleans, belonging to no one or nothing. But they took care of each other as best they could, occasionally sharing a loaf of bread one might have been given from an altruistic passerby. They had spent many a rainy night together huddled in a doorway and often swapped stories about the way life used to be before whiskey or gambling or a woman had led to their downfall. Although each considered himself to be a loner, when one fell, they became a team. There was no dignity on the streets, no protection or respect, but they wouldn't hesitate to safeguard one of their own.

They carried him to the park, laying him the lush green grass of the square.

One of the men pointed to the cathedral. "Think I should get a priest?"

"You honestly think one of them will come out here for him? He ain't never put a dime in the collection plate. Don't suspect that any of them would waste their time on his immortal soul."

Another shook his head. "We gotta do something. Can't just leave him here."

"How about that doc behind the horses? He still there, you think?"

"Don't know. Haven't seen him, but I can go and check."

"You do that, and we will wait."

The youngest of the group made his way to the edge of the quarter. Two men were dismantling the tent. "Is this the place for the sick?"

One of the men nodded. "Was. Moving on to a real place now."

"I see. Either of you a doctor?"

"Both of us. Well, almost. Finishing medical school in three months."

"We got us a bona fide emergency over in the park. You think maybe you could take a look?"

"You finish here," one of the men said to the other. "I'll go. And I'll be back to help transport the tent to the clinic."

"Take me to the patient."

By the time they returned, Jean Paul had regained consciousness, but his hands were cold and clammy, although his forehead felt hot to the touch.

"What are your symptoms, sir?" the doctor asked.

"Cough. Sometimes, with blood. And I am awfully tired." He began to shiver, even though the sun glowed in the late afternoon sky.

"Consumption," the doctor pronounced. "You need to be at Charity. There is a whole ward dedicated to patients with the disease. Otherwise, this is going to kill you."

"I tried," he said. "I'm on the list, waiting for a bed, but who knows. People in my condition aren't exactly a priority."

"Nonsense," the doctor said. "If you men can help me get him to the wagon, we do have a clinic. At least he can lie down, have a meal. There is some medicine, too. Might make you more comfortable. The doctor who heads it works at Charity, as do we. Maybe he can use his influence."

"May God bless you for your kindness, sir. I can't express my gratitude in words."

And as they traveled to Franklin's clinic, Jean Paul's face brightened. For the first time, in a very long time, he felt hopeful. He bargained with God as he had so many times before. If his life was spared, he would be a better man. Help others. Go where the Holy Spirit led him.

But on Camp Street, the Slater family had no way of knowing who was headed their way.

Chapter Seventy-four

Aimee, Franklin, and their colleagues from the hospital had barely gotten the building clean enough to be acceptable when the patients began to line up. Angelique had a few extra beds that she had purchased for older children, who might find a home with her. But when she realized that they weren't being used, she happily donated them to Franklin's clinic. She also gave him a table. Several people in the neighborhood contributed odd chairs, along with their discarded bedding and towels. Aimee made pallets on the floor to use for examinations on those too weak to stand. Compared to what they had to work with in the tent, this felt like a real facility, a place of healing.

Franklin had seen his twentieth patient for the day and several more stood in the sun waiting their turn. His stomach growled in protest. He hadn't been able to stop long enough to eat all day, and he tried to will away the headache that was creeping in.

The wagon pulled onto the side street. "Looks like James and Stephen are back with the tent," Aimee said. Franklin was relieved. He would divert some of the waiting patients to them.

He was glad that they had retrieved the tent, which would be useful if he needed a mobile clinic or even to hold the overflow of patients, although he doubted that his mother would approve. The constant stream of people to the courtyard was already disconcerting. "Please watch them," she had requested. "I have precious young ones here. You don't know these people. And I have learned that some unscrupulous person can snatch a child in the blink of an eye."

He simply nodded. Her fear was not irrational, but rather, born from having lost young Aimee, snatched by a deranged stranger pretending to be her uncle. She was right, of course, and he did his best to keep the chaos under control. Some days were easier than others.

The men appeared at the door half-dragging a bone-thin man, who was unable to walk on his own. He was covered with dirt and grime. There was dried blood on his chin. His hair, matted and tangled, covered his face. The odor was overwhelming and Franklin covered his nose and mouth with his hand.

"This one," James said, "we couldn't leave behind. " Consumption, I think. Thought you could pull your weight and get him a bed at Charity."

"Not like that, I can't. I can't even let him into the building like that."

Franklin pointed to a washtub outside of the laundry building. "Can you bathe him? Aimee will give you some soap. We have some donated clothes, but anything should fit him. And for goodness sakes, burn what he is wearing now. Put him in the bed in the corner, behind the screen. It is the closest thing we have to a quarantine. Gee, guys. You sure know how to complicate the work here."

"I know you wouldn't have wanted us to ignore his pleas for help. The man could be dying, and we just might be able to save him. That's the whole point of this place, right? Aren't we dedicated to the brotherhood of healing?" James said.

Franklin softened. "No, of course we couldn't turn him away. You did the right thing. Just clean him up, for his own dignity. And does this man have a name? For our records, of course."

"I asked in the few moments that he was lucid, but I never did understand him. Is it important? For now, he can be Mr. X."

"As long as he has been scrubbed, you may call him whatever you'd like," Franklin said.

James and Stephen made quick work of it after flirting with the laundresses, who gladly gave them a kettle of hot water. They had draped a sheet between two trees, stripping away the man's soiled clothes as they gently placed him in the tub and scrubbed him. Franklin thought of how he had arrived at the pink house and how his mother had insisted that he be washed clean before he was allowed to sleep in the bed. But he also remembered how fresh and new it made him feel, like a true beginning. He hoped that this poor ill man would experience some hope as well.

By the end of the day, the foursome sat in the courtyard sipping tea that the cook had brought them. "Wish this was something stronger," Stephen said.

"I think we all do," Franklin said, "although one sip of whiskey would put me to sleep for three days. That's how tired I am."

"Agreed," Aimee said. "Fortunately, we only have four in beds overnight."

"I will make rounds and then stay the night. I have help coming in tomorrow."

"Franklin. You are exhausted already." She touched his cheek. "You have dark circles under your eyes. Truly, it won't be possible for you to keep up this pace for very long or you will end up in the hospital yourself."

He squeezed her hand. "We always look out for each other, don't we, Aimee? But I will be fine. I shudder to think what this might be like without good folks willing to give up some of their off time. As we add more volunteers to the staff, it will get easier, and we will be more productive."

Aimee nodded. "I hope so."

They departed, leaving Franklin to do one last patient check before settling down himself.

Slowly, he approached the man behind the screen. His eyes were closed and Franklin moved closer to listen to his labored breathing, the pronounced rattling in his chest. There was something oddly familiar about the man, and Franklin wondered if perhaps he had been a patient when all they had was an old army tent. He had placed his hand on the man's forehead to feel for a fever when he first saw it, the raised scar along his cheek. He brought the light closer as he studied the man's face.

"Oh, my God," he whispered. "Could it possibly be Aimee's Uncle Gaston? He looks so much like him, but coincidences are possible. Surely, this is an improbability."

And although exhausted beyond all point of reason, Franklin was unable to sleep. He sat in a chair most of the night trying to process the implications of what it meant to have the man who had kidnapped Aimee and hurt his mother, the man whose misdeeds had indirectly brought him to the Slater household asleep only a few feet away. He shuddered to think that he was quite possibly in the presence of the devil himself. And the question loomed large. What was he to do about it?

Chapter Seventy-five

An hour before sunrise, Franklin returned home. He crept up the stairs and into Aimee's bedroom. The moonlight cast an eerie shadow on the wall, but at least it provided a bit of illumination.

"Aimee," he whispered. She stirred, but didn't wake. He lightly touched her arm. Slowly, she opened her eyes as through trying to remember where she was.

She jumped. "Franklin? You startled me. What are you doing here in the middle of the night? Aren't you supposed to be at the clinic?"

"Shhhh," he said. "Get dressed. I will be waiting for you downstairs."

She poured water from the pitcher into the bowl on her washstand and splashed her face. Whatever Franklin was up to had better be important because every minute of sleep was precious after the long hours they had been working. As she passed the clock in the upstairs hall, she cursed under her breath. She would have to be on duty at the hospital in three hours.

"Why so mysterious, Franklin? I would appreciate it if you would share what's on your mind with me."

"In due time. I need your help with our new patient."

"The one with consumption? Goodness, no offense, but the sooner he can be moved into Charity the better. He puts all of our other patients at risk, not to mention you and me, as well as the other workers. We aren't equipped to handle such a serious illness. His condition is grave."

"I know all of this. But you will soon see what concerns me."

He wordlessly led her to the carriage as he guided the horses back to the orphanage.

She sat with her hands folded in her lap, trying to will the sleepiness away. Calculating the time in her mind, she wondered if she could make this visit a quick one and get back home in time to nap for an hour or so. Sometimes, Franklin could be incorrigible, relentless in something he deemed significant.

They reached the clinic in minutes, and Franklin held the lantern so that they could make their way through the darkened courtyard. Once inside the building, he lit another and handed it to Aimee.

Fortunately, the patients were all still sleeping. And she tried not to comment on the irony that their rest had not been interrupted like hers. But leaving them alone had been reckless since anything could have happened. Most life-threatening situations occur in the night, she had observed. It was one of the first things she had learned in nursing school.

Franklin slowly made his way to the back corner, where the mysterious man lay behind the screen. His breathing grew louder as they approached, the rattle more pronounced than it had been earlier.

"He sounds bad. Do you think he will make it through the night?"

Franklin nodded. "He is stronger than he appears. His heart is sound and the fever comes and goes." He held up the lantern, illuminating the man's face.

Aimee was growing impatient. "Why did you bring me here, Franklin?"

"Look at him."

She moved her lantern closer. "That scar. It is just like the one that belonged to...." She couldn't bring herself to say his name.

"Exactly. I need to know if I am imagining things or if could possibly be him."

Aimee took a deep breath and shifted the lantern. She examined his face once more before moving to his hands. Suddenly, she began to cry. "Franklin. This seems impossible, highly unlikely, but his hands are the same, a little more rough perhaps, certainly older, but most certainly the same."

The man shifted in the bed and Aimee could feel the dread, the rapid beating of her heart that she was unable to calm. "Do you think he would recognize me?"

"I doubt it. He is delirious from the illness. You were five the last time he saw you. And you are now a grown woman. If anything, he will see you as an angel of mercy."

"I am afraid that I am hardly that where he is concerned. I trusted him when I was a child, but now that I am older, I fully realize the gravity of what he did. You do realize, don't you, that had you not been in that park that day, I might have never seen my family again?" She wiped the tears with the back of her hand.

"He intended to keep me, Franklin, for whatever purpose suited him."

Franklin shuddered. They had never talked about that time in all of their years together. Aimee, he figured, was overdue to release all of those emotions.

"Were you ever afraid?"

"Of course. I had no idea what was happening when we boarded that train. He was a complete stranger to me, regardless of his claim of being my uncle. And I was so little, totally defenseless. I had no choice but to go along with him in spite of the fear. It's odd, but even after all this time, I can close my eyes and remember every detail of the day, how he smelled, the noise of the train, the vanilla ice cream he bought me when we reached Richmond. Some moments remain with you forever. It is interesting to me, but although I was a child, that experience changed me, altered my spirit. Sometimes, difficulty brings us to a new, rearranged form that results in life-long strength. I certainly feel that it did."

"My poor Aimee. I can't even begin to imagine. And all of those long days at the tavern, waiting. I felt sorry for you, although I must say, I had great admiration for you at the same time. You were a brave little soul."

She reached for his hand. "Thanks, Franklin. But much of that determination came from you. You saved me. Once I met you, I knew I had a friend, someone who would protect me. It was the only thing I could trust."

"And I would have. I tried."

"For me, to have a person I could tell if the situation with Uncle Gaston got scary was comforting. I knew that my momma would move heaven and earth to find me. It was just a matter of time."

"And she did."

"Only because of you. For the rest of my life, I will always be grateful to you. Guess I should have told you before now."

"Sometimes it is hard to revisit the past, particularly if it brings up those painful memories. And you have to know that meeting you changed the course of my life as well, Aimee. Goodness, Momma was willing to take me in, raise me as her own son. Before I met her, I had no chance for a future. I suppose I say it too often, but I don't want to forget how lucky I was. Maybe it is why I am so motivated to help others. In a way, I feel that I was given a responsibility when I was saved, a debt I am obliged to repay."

Aimee nodded. "Nonsense. We hope that we are able to gratefully receive what we need and accept what we have been given. It is a powerful lesson. But I think that it is because of our own suffering that we learn to comfort others."

"Very true. I think it is called empathy."

Aimee pointed to the withered man who lay before her. "Looks like Uncle Gaston altered both of our paths."

"And no doubt we would have been different people as a result, but a larger question remains, which we must discuss. It will be days, at the very least, before I can get him into the consumption ward at Charity. He will be here lying a few hundred yards from our mother. The thought of it gives me pause. Should we tell her?"

"Why would we? As far as she is concerned, Uncle Gaston is simply some lunatic who kidnapped her daughter. She doesn't know him. She wouldn't recognize him even if she did stumble in here and found herself at his bedside. Besides, after all these years, what purpose would it serve?"

"If it had been your daughter, what would you want? I am not certain if he will even regain consciousness, but do we have the right to deny her the opportunity to confront him, and at the very least to ask what motivated him to act in such a way? It just seems deceptive to me. And ultimately, what would we say to her if she if found out that we kept this from her?"

The questions rested between them until they took on a life of their own. Aimee simply stared in rapt fascination as the words danced in the early morning light. "I don't know," she whispered.

"I make the work schedule so I can be sure that you never have to see him again. It might be for the best. I doubt that he would recognize me anyway, so I am safe. But we must decide here and now if we share this with Momma. And then, we will never speak of it again."

Aimee sighed. "She deserves to know, I guess, but I can't bring myself to tell her. You must do it. As soon as possible."

"I agree with the timeline. But I also think you are right. Perhaps the truth of that terrible time will give her some closure."

"Then, let me get you home. We are both on duty in an hour. I will speak to her before Stephen comes to relieve me."

"Franklin? Thanks for telling me this. You could have kept it to yourself, and I would have been none the wiser."

"But that's not who we are, Aimee. Is it?"

"No, I guess not." She offered her hand as he walked her to the carriage.

"In a few days, this will all be over and done with. Such moments of strife are temporary. Remember that."

"I'll try."

Chapter Seventy-six

Franklin was grateful to find a large pot of hot coffee on the stove. He was tired after the long workday and subsequent night, but the thought of what lay ahead was even more overwhelming than the fatigue. He drank the cup quickly and returned to the clinic. His mother would be in soon for breakfast with the children.

Cook had given him tea for the patients, and he delivered it to each bedside, along with a thin slice of bread. He was grateful that he was able to use some of the provisions from the orphanage. His nonexistent budget was already spread too thin, and without their generosity, the people occupying those sick beds would most likely starve to death.

He approached the partition with trepidation. The cup rattled against the saucer in his hand. Telling his mother about Aimee's kidnapper would create a storm of emotion. Or worse. And what if they were wrong? What if this was an innocent vagrant whose body was racked with consumption? He and Aimee could be responsible for causing real harm to someone who didn't deserve it. No, before he said a word, he needed proof.

"Uncle Gaston?" he whispered. "I have brought you some tea."

The man's eyes fluttered and then opened as he stared at the ceiling.

"Uncle Gaston?" Franklin repeated.

"Aimee?" he said, his hoarse voice barely audible. "Aimee is that you?"

The hair on the back of Franklin's neck stood up, and he felt a cold chill run through his body like shock waves. Just to be sure he said the name once more. "Uncle Gaston?"

"Aimee. Have you lost Sarah?"

And there was the definitive answer to the question, the reassurance that he was doing what he must.

He was on his way out when Stephen appeared to relieve him. "You look terrible. No sleep at all?"

Franklin shook his head. "Difficult night. Your consumption patient is awake. There is tea and bread by his bed if you can coax him to eat. I have just a few minutes before I am expected at the hospital, and I need to see my mother. Don't be surprised if she comes to visit Mr. X. Strangely enough, they have a history."

"Truly? Then, maybe she can tell us his name."

"Oh, I can let you in on that. His name is Gaston. Gaston Marcel."

Franklin was waiting in the foyer for his mother, pacing to keep from falling asleep. He wondered how compromised he would be at work, but for now, this was more pressing. Somehow, he hoped that he was doing the right thing that this would help, rather than hurt, the woman who had given him so much.

She arrived right on time.

"Franklin! How wonderful to see you this morning. Are you alright? You look exhausted." She placed the palm of her hand on his cheek and brushed the hair from his face just as she had done when he was a boy. "I worry about you, son."

"I've had no sleep, but the reasons for that are what I am here to speak to you about."

"Really? That sounds important. Let's go into my office. I have a few minutes before I join the children."

He nodded. She pointed to the faded settee near the window. "Come and sit by me and tell me what is on your mind."

"We received a new patient late yesterday afternoon, a vagrant who had collapsed in the Quarter. As you know, Charity is unable to handle the sheer numbers of indigents in need of help. Stephen and James brought him to the clinic."

She looked puzzled, unsure what this had to do with her. He continued.

"The man was in dire condition, filthy, lice infested. It was obvious that he had lived on the streets for quite some time. We cleaned him up, placed him in a bed for the night. It was my turn to stay, so I made my rounds before preparing for sleep myself. It was only when I went in to examine the man that I realized who he is."

"Yes?"

Franklin took a deep breath and swallowed hard. "It is the man that Aimee called Uncle Gaston, Momma."

"Who?"

"Gaston." He paused, allowing her to process what he had just revealed. It was a helpless feeling, not unlike the one he had experienced many years ago in the park when he described Aimee's captor.

She was quiet for a very long time. "Are you sure?"

"I am. I would have never brought this to you otherwise. Aimee has confirmed it. Plus, it is a name he answered to when I spoke to him."

"And did you speak to him?"

"No. He is very ill, mostly in and out of consciousness."

"The diagnosis?"

"Consumption."

She nodded. "And how long will he be with you?"

"His days are numbered. But I am going to try to get him into Charity as soon as possible, for many reasons, not the least of which is to have him away from the premises. I don't want for his presence to upset you."

"Can I see him? I would like to look into the face of the man who brought me so much heartache and pain."

"Yes, if you would like. I wasn't sure that you would. I truly wrestled with the idea of keeping this from you, to spare you those memories of Aimee's abduction, but in the end, I thought it only fair that you decide."

Angelique reached for Franklin's hand. "And I appreciate it, son. I can imagine the weight of such a discovery, especially after all of this time has passed. He is probably the least likely person I would have expected to appear. But the universe has a way of showing us our past, sometimes in a painful way, in order to wipe the slate clean, to pave the way for a brighter future."

"I hope so."

"But I do have one request."

"Of course. Anything."

"Please don't tell your father of this. He is the most peaceful man I know, truly, but I fear what he might do. Men have a way of keeping their feelings concealed, locked away in a little compartment until the right moment comes and the door is open. Sometimes, when that happens emotion overcomes reason."

"I understand."

Angelique rose and opened her arms to embrace Franklin. "You get on to work now. And know that you did the right thing here today. You are a good son. Don't ever doubt it."

"Thanks, Momma."

When he had gone, she locked the door to her office. She closed her eyes, trying to identify the flood of emotions. What was she feeling? Like leaves falling in autumn, once they had collected on the ground, it was difficult to remember them as a part of the tree. But she had held onto the sorrow and pain her ex-husband had caused for so long that it had become a part of her, growing in her bones until she couldn't remember a time when it wasn't there, reminding her of the bitterness she bore.

After all of these years, Jean Paul was alive and ever so close. And she was going to have to kill him.

Chapter Seventy-seven

Angelique entered the dining hall just as the children were finishing their breakfast.

"Momma," they cheered.

"We were worried about you," one little girl said, appearing by her side.

"I am so sorry to have caused you concern," she said. "I had some important business to attend to, but I am here now."

"Will you come and play with us later?" a little boy asked.

"I will. And what shall we play?"

"Blind man's bluff!"

And Angelique smiled. "Of course." She wondered if she had been blind herself for so long, denying her feelings as she struggled to find a place of peace that had eluded her much like the blue butterfly that Aida and Aimee had been so enamored with as children. She had been resilient, strong, but she questioned if that was simply a complement to survival. What choice is any of us given when faced with circumstances that threaten our very existence, she thought? We fight the current, hold our chins above the water line because to give up means to drown. And yet, she had drowned in sorrow so often, that if she closed her eyes, she could taste the bitterness of those moments. And he had brought them into her life.

It was time to face the demon.

She crossed the courtyard to the outbuilding pressed into service as the clinic. It was simply a matter of a few feet that separated the two spaces, but it felt like a wide chasm, the distance huge, daunting. Each step transported her into the past, a place she thought she had left behind in thought and memory long ago. And yet, here it was, right in her own backyard. The feelings were achingly real. She was bound by the hatred which had kept her a prisoner, gripped her soul until at times, it threatened to squeeze the life from her as well. Although she had managed to keep it at bay, it was with her always and forever. And today, would be the showdown.

Although the midmorning sun shone brightly in the sky, the clinic was dark with shadows creeping along the walls. There was a man moaning heavily from one bed, while sounds of coughing echoed in the stillness. The thick smell of antiseptic and sepsis hung in the air. It was unnerving.

Stephen moved forward to greet her. "Mrs. Slater. How nice to see you. Franklin said you might be around to visit our newest patient."

She nodded. "Gaston?" The name stuck in her throat like bitter bile, foul and unpleasant.

Stephen pointed. "In the back behind the screen. I think he is asleep, although he wakes on occasion. Don't get too close, ma'am. He is, after all, contagious."

Angelique thought of the word, which somehow seemed perfect to describe him. He was infectious, his mere presence a threat to the harmony of those whose paths crossed his. Whatever disease had claimed his body would be nothing compared to the evil that had claimed his soul.

She took a deep breath and steeled herself for this moment of truth as she moved to his bedside. As she studied his face, it was like she was looking at a stranger. Only the identifying scar bore witness to his true identity. It had been twenty years since she had stood in the kitchen of his plantation, begging him not to go off to hunt, tearfully whispering her goodbyes when he insisted, the memory of that moment etched in her heart and mind forever. It had been the most dismal of times, and yet, she had no idea of the subsequent turmoil he would bring into her life over and over again.

It was hard not to wonder what had transpired once Aimee slipped through his fingers, disappeared from his life as she once had from hers. Had he been so overtaken by grief and loss that he had fallen into an abyss of despair? It was an idea filled with irony. The law of life often illustrates that what we do is returned to us in ways we might never have imagined. Perhaps this is what had happened to him. He had once been a fine gentleman with every opportunity for a happy life, but he had squandered his prospects, along with everything else that had any importance. Cards had been his true love all along.

His breathing was labored, and she thought perhaps that God would simply take him that morning, sparing her the burden of having to do it. But then, she considered that perhaps He had kept him alive so that she could take his life, exacting her revenge upon the man who had hurt her so. The idea was absurd, of course. The Lord had made it clear all the way back to Moses, when He carved out The Commandments, that he didn't condone killing. And for a moment, she wondered if she was insane to risk her own immortal soul for the sake of vengeance. A sin is a sin. Would hers be any less grave than those committed by Jean Paul? But she also knew that God offered limitless forgiveness, and she prayed for His mercy on her for what she was about to do.

She thought of simply placing the pillow over his face. He would struggle for an instant and then his breathing would cease, and he would exist no more. She still had the pistol the countess had given her, but using it would be foolhardy. And messy.

And then, as though he had read her mind, he provided her with the answer. "Tea," he whispered, his voice hoarse and unfamiliar.

"Indeed, Jean Paul," she whispered. "I will make you some tea."

Chapter Seventy-eight

The carriage made its way through the cobblestone streets into the French Quarter. Angelique peered through the window. The setting sun illuminated the sky, which was ablaze with color. "Red sky at night, sailor's delight," she whispered. And, as always, thoughts of the weather reminded her of Andrew. She was wrong not to tell him that Jean Paul had resurfaced. And he had a right to know of her plans where her cowardly ex-husband was concerned, especially since he had lived through so much of the turmoil that had been wrought on them by the man. The scar that Andrew bore on his shoulder was a testament to that. But ultimately, it was her battle, although she knew that he would gladly don his knightly armor and fight the dragon for her. The slaying of the beast rested firmly in her hands. And she would be the one to wield the death blow.

"Take the levee near the ferry," she told the driver.

They passed the river, commanding by its very nature. She watched as the light twinkled upon the surface, dancing and shimmering as though touched by the spirit, powerful and very much alive. The riverbed and its banks gently caressed the water in an intimate symphony. And perhaps, she thought, that is the way it has come to be with anger as we remember the ways we have been hurt or betrayed, the feelings flowing through us as we become the home, the host for them. She had certainly harbored a lifetime of emotion.

When they were two blocks from her destination, she quietly told the driver to wait for her. Such clandestine meetings needed no witnesses. Quickening her step, she opened the iron gate and made her way down the alley. She knocked on the door, which had once been painted a bright red, but had faded in the Louisiana sun. When there was no answer, she knocked again.

An old woman answered, "Yes?"

"I need something," Angelique said, "which only you can provide."

"Indeed? And what might that be?"

"A tool."

The old woman raised an eyebrow. "For the purpose of good or evil?"

"To right a wrong."

"I see. Come in."

The room was aglow with candles burning in every nook and cranny. A sweet smell of lavender perfumed the air. "How much do you need?"

"Enough to accomplish the task for which it was intended. One dose. No more."

"Do you know how to use it?" She asked as she moved to a wooden cupboard. "It can be dangerous in the hands of a fool."

"I am not foolish, I can assure you. And I will follow whatever instructions you give me."

She held the packet up for Angelique to inspect. "Inside, you will find fern-like leaves, with purple spots on the stems. You must handle it carefully. Use old gloves. Place them in the bottom of the cup and pour the boiling water over them. Steep for three minutes. You are to secure the spent leaves, preferably burying them in the ground, for they retain their poison for many hours afterwards. A child who might inadvertently touch one will most surely die."

Angelique shuddered. "And the name for this?"

"Hemlock, dear. A most powerful instrument, used for centuries. Are you sure that this is what you wish?"

Angelique nodded. "I am."

"Then, take this, and may you be protected."

"And payment? How much do I owe you?"

"Not a penny. To sell death means to court it. We coexist, the grim reaper and I. It is my intention to keep it that way."

"Thank you, then."

"You are most welcomed. And when you go to bed tonight, say a prayer for my immortal soul, will you?"

Angelique thought it a strange request, but then, she considered the circumstances and simply whispered, "of course."

She returned home, hoping that her family was otherwise occupied. It would be difficult to explain why she was out at night, certainly, but even more pressing was the secret she held.

Andrew was in his office, writing. Aimee and Franklin had both gone to bed early, worn out, no doubt, from the combination of work and anxiety. She tiptoed up the stairs into her room.

As she sat at her dressing table, brushing her hair, she thought of the poison in her purse. More importantly, she considered what she intended to do.

Had she lost all reason, she wondered? Was she truly capable of murder?

"There you are," Andrew said, moving to kiss her on the neck. "I didn't hear you come in. And I missed you. Dinner alone isn't nearly as nice."

"I'm sorry, darling. I had a few pressing things to do at the orphanage, orders to place and such. And I see that you managed to find something to eat."

"You work so hard, Angelique. I know that you love those children, but you are positively driven, much like when you took over Chauvin. I hope someday that you are able to understand the meaning of balance."

She laughed. "I will try. I know I have neglected you lately. I am sorry for that. In a day or two, I will turn over more of the responsibilities to Miss Martin. I needed to make certain that things were running smoothly before I did so."

"And Franklin's clinic? Looks like you have a small hospital in your backyard. I need to come and see it. He is incredibly enthusiastic about his work. He and Aimee both."

Angelique simply nodded. She couldn't talk about the clinic, not tonight. Tomorrow, she assured herself it would be over and perhaps then, she could begin to truly live. It had been so long, she hoped that she remembered how.

Chapter Seventy-nine

Sleep escaped her. She was not surprised that her spirit was so restless only a few hours before she was to take Jean Paul's life. When the sun finally rose, she breathed a sigh of relief. Dressing quickly, she summoned the carriage to take her to the orphanage. If all went according to plan, she could have the tea made, the hemlock buried, and the deed done before breakfast with the children.

Angelique could hear the beating of her own heart as she donned the gloves and removed the toxic leaves from her bag. She had managed to eliminate any suspicion from cook when she offered to make the tea for the clinic. "I'd like to help Franklin in some small way," she said, which seemed not only plausible, but noble as well.

She placed the spent leaves in one of the gloves, which she returned to her bag and carried it, along with the cup, into the clinic.

"Good morning," she whispered to the volunteer on duty. It was nobody she knew, which was even better. "I have some tea for Monsieur Gaston."

The young man nodded before returning to his book.

Her hands were shaking, and she willed the deadly potion to stay in the cup. She placed it on the nightstand and moved a chair close to the bed. He was asleep.

"Jean Paul," she whispered. There was no response.

"Jean Paul," she repeated.

He opened his eyes and looked at her. She felt a rumbling deep inside her stomach, and for a moment, she feared she would be sick. Taking a deep breath, she tried to calm her frazzled nerves.

For a long while, she sat there as he stared at her face, his gaze ho
llow and distant. He reminded her of a wounded animal, helpless and pathetic, suffering in silence because of its inability to speak. She swallowed hard as she looked at the cup. It could wait.

"Angelique?" he said, his voice barely audible.

Her eyes grew wide. Had he recognized her or was he perhaps hallucinating?

"Is it really you or are you an angel come to take me to heaven?"

She thought it odd that he spoke of reaching the pearly gates, given his choices in life.

"Jean Paul," she said. "I have brought you some tea."

He smiled. "You extend to me a kindness that I don't deserve."

She reached for the cup. "Angelique," he whispered. "Please forgive me for all I have done to you. I was wrong, terribly wrong. I have prayed for the forgiveness of our Lord above, and tried to make amends. Now, I humbly beg for your mercy."

His words were unsettling, and she wondered about his sincerity. Could he actually feel remorse? Had he changed? She remembered those days on Last Island after the storm when so many had perished in her presence. Their last words were often meaningful. There had been moments of great clarity, genuine enlightenment among them. And she wondered if that was God's gift to us in our final hours. Perhaps then, we are truly able to understand the meaning of life, embracing the glory that comes with passing from one existence into the next.

"Tea," he said.

Bringing the cup to his lips, she paused to consider what he had asked. Is to grant forgiveness admitting defeat or is it an even greater victory? Could she open a door and clear a path to ultimately set herself free from that which was hurting her heart and soul?

She sat quietly considering the answers before she finally rose to throw the tea out of the open window. Ultimately, she thought, only God Almighty had the power to determine who lives or dies. And when.

Angelique exhaled. She had once loved him, once dreamed of a future together. It seemed so long ago, another lifetime. And even though he had broken her heart, hurt her in ways she never thought possible, he would have to answer for his sins, just as she would have to answer for her own. Aren't we all worthy of redemption?

Everyone we have ever loved has a place in the garden of our hearts, she thought. Some are lovely flowers and others, noxious weeds. Their history becomes tangled in our roots, impossible to sever. This seemed true.

And then, it came to her with a reasonable certainty. Time passes. The years go by as one day flows into the next. And therein lies the cure, the healing power of simply letting it be. There was great power in that knowledge.

As morning became afternoon, she remained at his bedside. His breathing became shallower, and he winced in pain. She wet a cloth in the nearby bowl and placed it on his forehead. His eyelids fluttered.

"Angelique," he whispered.

"Quiet now," she said. "Reserve your strength."

He took another breath, slowly exhaling. And then, there was no more.

"I forgive you, Jean Paul. Rest in peace. Perhaps now, I can find mine as well."

Our long standing argument with life, she thought, is that it is unfair, that people we love hurt us and circumstances are often difficult. We work to reconcile it, accept it, understand it, but this is the big dilemma we must each face on our journey. All of us are searching for peace. It often feels elusive, impossible to achieve. And to find it, we must learn to forgive.

Jean Paul's death somehow brought Angelique into the fullness of life, drew her deeper into her own soul, and changed her into something new. For someone who had robbed her of so much, he had delivered a mighty fine parting gift

Andrew, Aimee, and Franklin were standing on the other side of the partition when she emerged.

"Is it really him?" Andrew asked, placing his arms around her.

She nodded. "He's gone now, along with so many of the secrets his life represented."

Wordlessly, they walked to the courtyard where they sat under the shade of the tree where James and Stephen had bathed Jean Paul a day earlier.

"I might have killed him had I known," Andrew said.

"I thought of it," she said. "Actually, I came close. But strangely enough, I remembered a legend that Hannah used to tell me when I was a girl."

"Do share it with us," Aimee said.

"Is this the right time for that?"

"It is the perfect time, Momma."

Angelique leaned against the tree. "There was a multitude of bees in the garden of Eden, buzzing among the flowers, gathering nectar for the finest honey. When they had produced the sweetest and most special batch, they offered some to the Lord to taste. He was delighted, and offered to grant them one wish. They conferred among the hive and decided that in order to protect their precious honey they would ask for the power to injure anyone who came too close. The Lord agreed, but added this warning. 'When you sting, it will remain in the wound you make, and you will die from it. '"

"I never understood the meaning of the tale, although I had heard it many times, until I sat with Jean Paul. When we let the bottom of our hurt define the world and who we are, the law of spite will plague us and a part of us dies to life. I have carried this hatred and resentment with me for far too long. I prayed for the courage to put my stinger away, to see that in killing him, I would kill a part of myself. It was time to let go of the anger and forgive him. And you know what? Something miraculous happened along the way. I found peace, precious, beautiful peace."

"I'm afraid that I am confused, Momma," Aimee said. "Who is Jean Paul?"

Angelique took a deep breath as she reached for her daughter's hand, "Come. Let's go home, and I will tell you the story about how a young woman was hurt and betrayed, how she struggled to remain strong, ultimately learning who she was as each chapter of her life unfolded. It is quite the tale, my precious girl."

Chapter Eighty

The next day, they laid Jean Paul's body in the tomb that had already been inscribed with his name, next to sweet Josephina, who had gone to live with the angels so long ago. There was no ceremony, no words of tribute, just a quiet moment as Franklin, Aimee, Andrew, and Angelique stood nearby, each lost in their own thoughts.

As for Angelique, she had come to fully realize that being human, by definition, is to exist with limits, to experience heartache that tempers the moments of joy. We all must trudge through the muck of existence, step over boulders and climb the steepest mountains, while avoiding the quicksand. Ultimately, we must reconcile ourselves to the fact that we are sometimes weak and sometimes strong, often greatly challenged, but always, we are connected to all that lies within the universe, including each other. Life will teach us lessons, and we must learn them, even the difficult ones, those that test us to the very depths of our souls. But we are also entitled to every blessing, every moment of joy. It is a birthright we must claim. Angelique firmly resolved to live happily ever after. And so, she did.

Author's Notes

Penning the last few words of *Angelique's Peace* was a bittersweet moment. On the one hand, it was the culmination of a two year project, a time of celebration, but it also meant saying goodbye to Angelique and Andrew. It is funny how each day as I sat down to write, I would find myself transported to the Victorian South and the world where my characters lived. They showed me how they wanted me to tell their story. Honestly, I just typed the words. So few people are allowed to go on an incredible journey such as this. How fortunate am I?

I managed to finish *Angelique's Peace* in two months. I had no idea where my motivation to write daily came from, except that perhaps my muse was in work mode. I took full advantage of the creative energy that surrounded me. But it is interesting how the universe works. I didn't know that my time would be finite and that finishing the book was an amazing gift. There were days when I felt less than ideal, an inconvenience at best. I have always been healthy. Finally, I went to see the doctor. The diagnosis came quickly: I have stage four ovarian cancer. And so, while the book is not perfect, while I had hoped for another round or two of editing, releasing it in a timely manner was important. I certainly didn't want to leave my readers without a satisfying conclusion to the series.

The irony is not lost on me. I wonder if saying goodbye to Angelique and Andrew will be a metaphor for bidding my own farewells to all that I have come to know on this earth. It is strange how your mind works when your days are not guaranteed. And for a moment, I even visualized the Countess, waiting for me at the pearly gates, anxious to tell me about the social hierarchy in heaven. My imagination seems to have slipped into overdrive.

You know, during the middle ages, Alchemists were intent on discovering the philosopher's stone, a legendary substance that could turn iron into gold. And I am reminded of writers, who hold fast to the dream of turning ideas into a story, something ultimately worth reading. We grasp the pen tightly in our hands as we shift through plot devices and give life to the characters, hoping to find bits of gold dust among the words. And when it happens, we feel the rush of exhilaration, deep joy and satisfaction from the treasure. My short-lived writing career has been so gratifying, bringing me such pleasure. And I try not to mourn for the unwritten stories, the ever-present parade of tales that runs through my mind, begging to be brought to life. Miracles happen every day, and I will focus on my own happy ending.

I have always thought that part of a writer's job is to find their readers, people with whom the story resonates in some way. A connection between us, a bond of sorts, occurs for a brief moment in time. And that is the magic. I thank you for being a part of my life, for reading my books, and for helping make my dream a reality. May God bless.

Please feel free to follow along as I blog about my next great challenge, which ultimately, I hope to turn into a book. I am trying to think of it as an adventure, but somehow that seems like a pipe dream. But I am a fighter, much like Angelique. My website is www.paulamillet.com. And I still maintain my Facebook page, Paula W. Millet, Author.

Made in the USA
Middletown, DE
28 July 2017